For my mother and father

'Conrad Williams's new novel examines in devastating detail the inner life of a concert pianist undergoing an existential crisis . . . This thoughtful novel hits few false notes in its presentation of the classical music business. Unlike many fictional treatments of this world, it manages to eschew melodrama, despite its dramatically heightened plot. Intellectually engaged with the aesthetics of music and humanly engaged in its protagonist's story, it transforms its material into a remarkably well-made narrative'

Lucasta Miller, *Guardian*

'Williams takes us to the heart of the creative condition . . . [He] writes intelligently and sensitively about music and the musical world . . . [His] rich cast of characters – pushy but priceless patrons, charming but tricky agents, critics and mentors – explore the place of the high arts in contemporary culture . . . [and] the restless and often excruciating journey undertaken by all who attempt truth-fully to create or interpret works of genius'   *Sunday Telegraph*

'A savagely acute novel . . . No critic, agent, entrepreneur or fawning amateur is safe from Williams's glittering, scabrous and rhetorical assault, and there are enough disturbing psychological resonances to make even the most hardened careerist retreat from the field of battle . . . Would-be concert pianists should steel themselves before reading this novel. The ring of truth . . . is brilliant and enlivening and will stop even the most blasé reader in his tracks'   Bryce Morrison, *The Gramophone*

'Flying colours . . . Williams writes with easy grace and an evocative turn of phrase . . . He follows his character's emotional trajectory like the best kind of psychoanalyst, and makes us care what happens to him . . . The book's gradually revealed truths come as a shock, which is testament to Williams's narrative skill. He achieves a series of stylistic tours de force, some involving Philip's re-encounters with the landscapes of his childhood, others moving into the world of dreams. The book ends with a starburst, in which the music of Chopin becomes the vehicle for Philip's salvation'

Independent

BY THE SAME AUTHOR

SEX AND GENIUS

The Concert Pianist

CONRAD WILLIAMS

BLOOMSBURY

First published 2006
This paperback published 2007

Bloomsbury Publishing Plc,
36 Soho Square,
London WID 3QY

Bloomsbury Publishing, London, New York and Berlin

A CIP catalogue record for this book
is available from the British Library

ISBN 9780747586005

10 9 8 7 6 5 4 3 2 1

Typeset by Hewer Text UK Ltd, Edinburgh
Printed by Clays Ltd, St Ives plc

All papers used by Bloomsbury Publishing are natural,
recyclable products made from wood grown in well-managed
forests. The manufacturing processes conform to the
environmental regulations of the country of origin.

www.bloomsbury.com

Chapter One

HE SAW A LAWN freshly striped by mowing, steps rising to the old
terrace, clumps of aubretia and lavender greening up. The house
was bearded with clematis. A pair of deckchairs faced the glorious
open countryside. He knew at a glance that it had been a waste, or
at least a dumb oversight, to spend his middle years living in
London.

His heart was beating away. Children's voices were audible.
Beyond the walled garden was an orchard. One could distinguish
the upper bars of a climbing frame.

He pushed through the gate and strode on to the lawn, shadow
going before him. The perfect grass drew attention to his shoes –
unpolished. He saw a watering can by a flower bed, and suddenly
there she was. She wore a light-blue summer frock. The skirt twisted
as she came through an archway, wrapping around her thigh and
then blowing free, trailing in the passage of air as she walked
towards the wheelbarrow.

He expected to be seen, but she was picking at her gardening
gloves and for a second he was frozen by the spectacle of her lost in
thought, unaware of him. And then she turned. 'Philip!' she
shrieked.

He could feel the lightness of her body even before she rushed
into his arms, and because she greeted him with such delight, he
swept her clean off the ground and nearly tottered over. The kiss
was warm, straight on the mouth. She looked up at him with as
much glee as a happily married woman can bestow on an old
boyfriend.

'What are you doing here?' She was joyous.

He shrugged and smiled.

'I can hardly believe I'm looking at you!'

'Been ages.'

'Certainly has! Who's that?'

'Ilya, my driver.'

Vadim stood by the wicket gate, gazing at the countryside.

'Your driver!'

He wore a black suit and a black polo-necked shirt and looked rather filmic between the cherry trees.

'Gosh! Would you like some tea?'

'I'd love some tea.'

They drifted towards the house, Camilla still amazed and not knowing quite what to say or where to start – everything to catch up on.

'I keep seeing your name,' she said. 'You were all over the *Sunday Telegraph* a couple of weeks ago.' She turned, smiling. ' "The Renaissance Man of British Pianism!" '

'Yup. I've got a run of concerts on the South Bank so the publicists are in action.'

She was impressed. 'Shouldn't you be practising, Philip!'

'I should always be practising.'

'I'm glad you're not.'

'Children?' He nodded in the direction of the orchard.

'Two.' She smiled with lovely pride.

He was fascinated by the sensation of physical closeness to a woman he had made love to fifteen years ago. He felt the original attraction as a tingle, inadmissible now.

'I think Ilya would like some tea.'

Vadim had progressed to the lawn, and was considering the view, cigarette tipped between knuckles.

'Don't worry about him. Where are your children?'

'In the orchard. Lulu!' she called. 'Fernanda!'

There were photographs of the two girls in clip frames on the kitchen wall. They were pretty; the kitchen was pretty; the mullion windows framed pretty views. As the kettle came to the boil he strolled around, admiring the homely touches and farmhouse feel. He found what he was trying to avoid on the fridge door: a photograph of her husband. It showed the face of a man beaming with pride. Weak features were enlivened by love and purpose and a kind of recovered innocence, as if the possession of farm and family gave him all the future he needed.

Philip glanced at Camilla, busy in the kitchen: a frown of things to do, a ship to run. Her hair was fine and lustrous. It swept away from her forehead with all its original glamour.

'Husband on the farm?'

'He's in Salisbury buying a bed.'

'I like your home,' he nodded.

'Lots of hard work. Don't go into farming, whatever you do.'

'Beautiful girls, Camilla.'

She smiled. 'It's so amazing to see you. Mr Famous Concert Pianist! Is Ilya taking you on a royal spin round the countryside?'

'Tour of old girlfriends.'

She laughed.

He gazed at her with unguarded nostalgia. 'I just wanted to see you.'

'How flattering!'

'Don't be flattered. It's the same old me.'

'You're looking extremely well, Philip Morahan.'

She was so appreciative, and this he always liked. She had loved him absolutely for himself.

'I had an interesting quiz question for you, actually.'

'Oh yes!'

He looked just the same, she thought, distinguished now, with that high, donnish brow and the glittering spectacles and sharp, nervous eyes that looked at you intimately. His face was sensitively creased, frayed with lines of worry and doubt, as though real life were a constant riddle for the concert pianist; and yet how warming was his smile, that heaven-sent smile, that made you want to amuse him and see his face light up. He had put on a little weight, she noticed, mainly in the right places.

'What quiz question?' She gathered the kettle.

'For a maximum score of ten.'

She looked ready and willing.

He drew back a little, hesitating. 'Why did you leave me?'

She was startled. 'Leave you?'

'I know it sounds a bit left field after all these years.'

She shot a glance at the door, suspecting children. 'It does sound a bit left field.'

He smiled encouragingly.

'I hope you're not serious.'

'I'm always serious, Camilla. I play Beethoven for a living.'

She was amused and slightly appalled. 'That's water under the bridge, isn't it?'

'Not my bridge.'

'We left each other.'

'You dumped me like a sack of rotten potatoes!'

'I didn't!' She laughed in protest.

'I'm not saying you didn't have excellent reasons.'

'Philip, shush! Now! Earl Grey or PG Tips?'

'Glass of red would be nice.'

She took the cork off a half-empty bottle at the back of the counter, and splashed some into a mug. 'There. Change the subject, please.'

She had the measure of him, and this he always liked. Camilla's sense of humour fostered his eccentricity, his awkward directness.

'Fine. You're looking more gorgeous than ever.'

She could not help laughing. 'You are hilarious. You haven't changed a bit. I don't hear from you in ages and then you sail in out of the blue asking ridiculous questions. I honestly don't think we were meant for each other. It was a lovely stretched-out fling. And anyway, you were married to the piano well before I came on to the scene.' She smiled.

Philip looked over his shoulder, a door banging. 'Oh fuck.'

Vadim strode into the kitchen like a foreign emissary assured of a gracious welcome.

Philip frowned, looking away in frustration.

'Hello!'

He quickly pulled himself together. 'Um, Ilya. Meet Camilla.'

'Ilya?' said Vadim, as he crossed to Camilla, taking her hand and kissing it like a court noble.

'You're Russian?' She was amused.

'*Ty ochen' krasivaya.*' He bowed, clicking his heels. '*Ya hochu chtoby ty byla moyei seichas.*'

'A Russian chauffeur?'

'Chauffeur?' Vadim glanced at Philip in double admiration.

She beheld him with outright amusement.

Vadim had a sort of grand sweep to his tread, and yet a young man's mock knowingness, too. Despite being the foreigner in these parts, he seemed very at home in English country kitchens amidst Agas and women of a certain class. Dark hair scrolled off a high, photogenic brow, full of noble intentions. His mouth was a rosebud, his nose rather small, his cheeks rather preciously delineated. He had the face of a ballet dancer and the physique of a bear.

'You're not a chauffeur! Philip, you devil!'

Philip shrugged at his diablerie.

'Are you a musician?'

'The Russian Mafia sacked him for incompetence.'

'Professional gambler,' nodded Vadim.

She laughed brightly. 'The pair of you! Shut up!'

Vadim theatrically indicated certain needs.

'Through that door on the left.' She returned Philip a glance filled with delight. 'Who the hell . . .?'

'Friend.' He waved it away. 'Tickles the ivories.'

'A pianist?'

Philip glanced at the door to the loo. He had maybe three minutes to come to the point. 'He's got a concert this evening.'

'This evening?'

'I'm driving him down to Southampton to make sure he plays what's on the programme instead of switching it around or bunking off altogether.'

'So you're *his* chauffeur?'

'His moral and professional minder,' he nodded.

She gazed at him radiantly, as though it had only just sunk in he was here. 'Why didn't you let me know you were coming, you monster?'

'Advantage of surprise.'

She grabbed him by the arm in affectionate remonstration.

He smiled suddenly, brilliantly. He had really adored Camilla.

'So nice to see you, Pip,' she said, squeezing his arm and smiling back. 'Rascal.'

He raised his mug in salutation. It had been such a boon to fall for this sexy field marshal's daughter, a flower of the British upper classes, so utterly different to him and so gloriously unbothered by classical music. She found him, for some reason, funny, lovable, and was quite joyously uncomplicated and vivaciously sexual herself. Yes, sure, he had been married to the piano. The instrument dogged his moods, his conversation, his diary, and trying to plan a relationship around the tours was hopeless, but despite all that she had rescued him from the excruciating earnestness of it all. Philip's nervy demeanour seemed to amuse her. Through Camilla he caught a sense of his appeal to women: a sort of comic helplessness.

'What's going on?' she said. 'What've you been up to?'

'Oh God! I'm doing these three concerts.' He exhaled.

'At the Festival Hall?' she asked.

'QEH. The Great Piano Sonatas.'

'Fantastic! That's coming soon?'

'Next week.'

'How exciting!'

He smiled awkwardly. Now was the moment. Now or never. He had to ask.

The Russian sailed back into the room, hands in jacket pockets. Philip groaned.

'Red wine for health,' said the younger man.

'Steady on, Vadim.'

'Is it Vadim, now?' she said.

'Many identities.'

Camilla was enjoying herself. She poured wine into a glass. 'Are you guys old friends?'

She passed the wine to Vadim, who swept it back like a vodka shot.

Philip rubbed his eye. He was not being fair on his protégé. This detour was completely impulsive and unannounced, and although Vadim was swaggering around nonchalantly, the nerves would be picking away at him. All Philip needed was a couple of moments with Camilla, and then they could go.

He adjusted his spectacles and tried a different tack. 'Vadim, I loved Camilla more than anyone before or since. I realised two days ago in the bubble bath.'

'Oh, here we go!'

'Crabtree and Evelyn, to be precise.'

'Left by one of your numerous lady friends,' she smiled.

'If only.'

Vadim nodded understandingly. Love, romance, grand passion: these were his stock in trade. 'Now I realise why you drive me to Southampton of all places in God's earth. I thought you want to hear Brahms. But always Philip has ulterior motive.'

She smiled expectantly.

'To introduce one of great beauties of Hampshire.'

She burst out laughing and watched in bright-eyed wariness as Vadim executed another knuckle kiss on her left hand.

'I understand "English Rose",' he said, 'only for first time today.'

'Not for you, my friend,' said Philip.

She removed her hand with a twist. 'Are all Russian men this gallant, Vadim?'

'To begin with, yes.'

'Changing the subject,' said Philip, 'if your husband dropped dead tomorrow, would I have a chance?'

'You're appalling. Shut up!'

'Give me hope.'

'Are you another famous pianist?' she said, turning to Vadim.

'I will be world famous in about two years. Five minutes, please, Philip.'

Philip grimaced. Vadim would need time to settle in, try the piano, get changed, eat something. They had to get moving.

Vadim sloped off along the corridor to allow them a moment.

'How's Peter?' she asked. 'Didn't he get married? I haven't seen him for ages.'

He swallowed. He was feeling strange. 'They all got married. Except me.'

'You two were such a laugh.'

He tried to smile.

He owed Peter for so much, including Camilla. This thought had not crossed his mind in a while, and now it filled him with sorrow.

'You may as well see this,' he said with effort, pulling a wallet from his jacket.

He drew out the photograph and handed it to Camilla.

'What a sweet little thing. Not yours?'

'No, no. My god-daughter.'

She beamed maternally. 'Peter's?'

'Yup. Little Katie. Three.'

'Where do they live?'

He averted his eyes.

Vadim stuck his head into the room. 'Philip, I see you in the car in two minutes, or I hot-wire it and drive myself there. Thank you, Camilla.'

'Bye, Vadim!' She smiled.

Philip looked around to steady himself. He was swarming inside.

There was children's stuff all over the kitchen: zippy plastic files with homework reading, Lego bricks on the sill, small shoes on the doormat. This was the primary-colour world that bacherlorhood had denied him. Suddenly, you saw yourself staring longingly into other people's lives, and realising the outcome of decisions made long ago was quite irreversible.

'I'm so pleased you stopped by.'

He managed a convincing smile and turned to look through the French windows.

'Have the last drop,' she said, bringing over the wine bottle.

'I heard about the abortion.' He turned.

'What abortion?'

'You were pregnant.'

She lost colour.

'I got you pregnant.'

Camilla gazed at him in a kind of disbelief. He was already sorry for her.

'Is it true?'

She hesitated.

He could tell from her expression. His chest tightened. He had so wanted this not to be true.

She was startled, but rallied quickly, finding the presence of mind to look him in the eye. 'We were finished for reasons you understood at the time.'

He touched his spectacles.

She frowned.

'Sorry, I . . .'

'Don't rake it up, Philip!'

'I only heard the other day.'

'Who?'

He shook his head.

She was flushed with dismay and embarrassment.

'I needed to know, Camilla.'

'Oh God. This is fifteen years old!'

'It was a very long time ago and I'm trying to . . . work out why, you know, why it's so . . .'

She moved a coffee mug from the dish-rack to the shelf. The

memory of a certain impatience crept into her expression, as though there were things that Philip had never accepted. She looked at him starkly.

'It was awful.'

The words seemed to comfort him.

She gazed at him with candid regret.

'Was it?'

'Of course.'

'You didn't want to tell me?'

The suggestion seemed to weary her.

'I might have . . .'

'Oh, please.' She was distraught now. 'You were completely unviable as a husband or father. On tour, rehearsing . . .'

'I know . . .'

'You were a brilliant pianist. From another planet. There was never any question of us . . .' She shook her head.

He nodded, almost trying to appease her. She had made an executive decision, very definite, very sensible. She knew what was best for herself, what kind of life she wanted, what sort of husband. Not him. He was no good for such a purpose, not appropriate.

He moved away, buffing the palm of his hand on the kitchen counter. He was steeped in unfamiliar feelings. After a long moment he said, 'I've let music dictate my life.'

'Music was always going to dictate your life. You're a wonderful musician.'

He looked up. 'But I should have had a family. I should have found a way. In the end, love is the only thing that can make you happy.'

She could hardly argue with this.

There were children's voices in the yard outside.

The feeling was stronger now, a mixture of suffocating stress and anguish. The woman he loved had destroyed their child because he was a concert pianist. It came to him simply, dangerous to admit, but clear in his mind. 'It's not a sacrifice I want to make any more.'

'Philip . . .'

'I've lost the will to play!'

She wilted. She was so unprepared for this.

Emotion was like a blast of jet lag, or sudden fever. Once expressed it left you ruined, slightly poisoned. He was stooped.

9

Camilla regarded him tensely. She wanted him to go quickly now, because there was nothing she could say to make him feel better, and she was afraid the children would come in. She had loved Philip as a friend before they split up, but he was never the final choice, and if she knew it, in his heart he knew it, too.

'I suppose it's never too late for a man to have a child.'

He looked at her in quiet devastation. The remark relegated him, pushed him off into the average happenstance of human experience.

She looked away, unable to bear his gaze.

'It's not some hypothetical child I want!'

Vadim entered the room and came over to the kitchen counter, placing his palm on the edge of the work surface. He acknowledged the intrusion with a simple nod.

'Philip, we must go.'

'It's *that* child.'

She stared at him bleakly.

As they stepped into the car, she managed a repairing smile. Philip belted himself in and rolled down the window to say goodbye.

'Lovely set-up you've got here.'

He could see in her expression the thought that after this he would probably never want to see her again, and that this was a final leave-taking.

'Give my love to Peter,' she said.

'Wish I could.'

She wasn't sure what to make of this, and nodded as though she understood something she didn't.

He put his key in the ignition.

'Are you and he no longer buddies?'

'Buddies?' It made him smile.

The car came on powerfully. He released the handbrake and revved the engine a little.

She stood there, arms crossed. Behind her he saw the two girls advancing across the lawn. Their two heads of blonde hair glimmered in the afternoon sunshine.

'He's dead.'

She started.

'Why is it always me that has to tell people?'

'Can we go?' said Vadim.

'We're going. We're going!'

She was frozen with horror, and he could see the two girls coming closer, so he flicked it out quickly.

'House burnt down. They all died.'

'No!'

He let the clutch up.

'Sorry, Camilla.'

The BMW circled around the gravel before pulling away down the drive. He saw her half-raised hand through the rear-view mirror and Lulu and Fernanda approaching through the garden gate.

Chapter Two

IN THE DRESSING ROOM it was cold. Brown water came from the washbasin tap. Vadim hunted around for a mirror. Nothing in the WC, nothing on the inside cupboard door. He stood in shirt and underpants holding a cigarette.

Driving into Southampton he had been fine. They had talked about Chopin and Szymanowski. Now in the dressing room he was panicky. His hand shook as he lit a cigarette. He stared at the hand with an almost clinical interest. A grandly confident person in general, he was palsied with fear right now.

Philip eased him into his tailcoat like a gentleman's gentleman; quite an operation because the younger man was heavy and getting heavier. He had a tussle with the trouser clip, problems with his belt, which notched too tight or too loose; and when the outfit was on he stood in the middle of the room looking desperate.

'I'm indisposed.'

'What! The Russian Lion indisposed?'

They had parked behind the building on a meter. Philip went off in search of cigarettes and change, and Vadim checked in at the box office. A dilapidated elderly gent in a tweed jacket with a spotted hanky took him through the hall to the artists' changing room. It was a 1950s civic building, used for lectures and theatricals, with long curtains hanging from high windows. Vadim tossed his bag into the dressing room and returned to the piano for a play. The instrument sounded like cotton wool in the dull acoustic.

'I've got you down for a salami sandwich,' said the old boy. 'Will it be lapsang souchong, or British worker's tea?'

Vadim looked up. 'Working-class tea, please.'

'Right you are.'

He needed a bath, but there was no bath or shower. In the dressing room he became distressed by a patch of rising damp that had corrupted the plaster behind the coat hook. Philip found him rubbing his hands and shaking his head.

'This is not good.'

'You'll be fine. Think biriani. There's an Indian round the corner.'

'I think cancellation.'

'Come on, Vadim!'

'The hall is terrible! I can't have shower. There's nobody here. Why must I play?'

'Just hack through it. You can't play the Brahms in London for the first time.'

'That piece is too long.'

'Play from the score.'

'I haven't French polished it!'

'French polish it out there in front of the locals.'

Vadim looked desperate.

Philip patted him on the shoulder. 'Tie on. Comb hair.'

He would get Vadim through the concert, and then tackle him over dinner – for fucking around. Nervous disarray lurked behind even the most autocratic talents. Beneath nervous disarray simmered infantile egotism and unhappiness. Compressing the ragged human being into an artist was his mission tonight. Urgent, because Vadim's malaise was beginning to harm his career. Promoters and sponsors were already wary of his cancellations and even John Sampson, their mutual agent, was wearying.

'OK. So warm up while I stretch my legs.'

'Stay!'

'Vadim!'

'I won't play.'

'You must! As a favour to your chauffeur.'

'Piano-playing is no favour.'

'Listen! If John hears you've cried off again, you'll get the red card.'

Vadim sucked on his cigarette, thumbed his forehead.

'Pianists come cheaper than agents. Especially first-rate agents like John.'

'Not this pianist.'

Philip stared at him. He felt responsible and yet powerless. The brilliant protégé was turning into a twenty-five-year-old problem child. For weeks Vadim had been stupidly unable to focus. There were marital issues, of course, but the real reason was an adolescent refusal to accept the pressure of his calling, a doomed bid for free will in an industry of fearsome competitiveness and declining audiences. It was as though he had not accepted that, because of his gifts, he had no choice but to play the piano and to try dutifully to be a great pianist, because anyone born with such gifts was too precious to be allowed any other course, and suddenly agents, mentors, and critics were joined in a conspiracy to exert pressure and raise bars. The Moscow years were driven and unhappy (both his parents died in a Soviet air disaster). Vadim was taken over by a grim uncle and the head of the Conservatoire piano faculty, who jointly saw to it that he was grown like the hottest of hothouse flowers, and only rewarded for the death of his parents with early fame. Since moving to London, freedom and choice had engendered a kind of rebellion. No sooner were the foundations of a fabulous career laid than his appetite for experience beyond the piano stool overwhelmed him. He wanted suddenly to do everything, try everything. Vertiginously he needed football matches, water-skiing, nightclubs, sexual spice. Casually he got married, as though marriage were a drug that could be trialled and dismissed. The breaking-free was of course vital, because artists need to live like everyone else, but Vadim's tour of instant gratification became a willed exercise in cultural superficiality, impairing the nuclear-fission programme that virtuosos need to contain safely by focused practice and rigorous self-discipline if they are to erupt brilliantly in concert and not destructively elsewhere. He now had a wife, baby, and mortgage, but his attitude was in tatters and his artistry distempered. This maddened Philip.

'Have you called Marguerite?'

Vadim leaned against the wall, eyes downcast.

'She's left two messages on my mobile. I don't know what's wrong with yours.'

The non-reaction amazed him.

There was a knock on the door. The stage manager leaned in, a young fellow with a neck tattoo, pierced eyebrow and number-one haircut. 'Everythin' OK, sir?'

Philip sighed. 'Everything's fine.'

'A'right, guv. I'll pop by when it's five to go.'

They heard the door click shut.

'Why green paint!' Vadim was incredulous. 'I don't like this colour.'

'Please call her after the concert.'

Vadim looked down, his face overcast by untranslatable feelings.

'I've spoilt your preparation, I'm sorry.'

Vadim pulled away, slumping down on to a chair. 'Cigarettes,' he said.

'Have the pack. I'm going to take my seat.'

There were things he must say, but not now.

On the street Philip gazed at the evening sky and inhaled the bad air. A one-way system brought the traffic in rush-hour surges around the square, wafting fumes across the concourse. He tapped out a cigarette, desperate to inhale. There were so many things he could not bear about the day, the debacle of his meeting with Camilla, the coming struggle with Vadim: an Oedipal vying with an 'adopted' son if ever there was one. And now Vadim's crisis reprised his own. His playing was dreadful at the moment. For days he had been out of sorts and utterly terrified by the thought of his concert and the standard expected of him. He had forced a practice session at the weekend with grim results. Sleepless nights and bad feelings had stripped his playing of its confident strength and control. There were memory lapses, fluffs everywhere, lagging reflexes. The whole mechanism was in turmoil. His sense of crisis was held in check only by a disbelief that this could be happening to him.

The auditorium was large and dull. Curtains had been pulled across the back of the hall, a lectern set to one side. Up on the stage – like an ocean liner in profile – the piano. Two youths at the door handed programmes to the incoming public.

Philip sat in the stalls and gazed at the motley array of humans who, on a Tuesday evening, were attending a piano recital in Southampton of all places. Most were music-society oldies sinking stiffly to their seats, or shakily standing in the aisle – genteel listeners from a bygone age when every parlour had an upright. Two plump grannies sat at the front, cramming flapjacks from tissue paper into their mouths whilst fluttering programmes like fans. There were sundry Plain Jane music maids with lank hair and bony knuckles, a pair of schoolmaster types fruitily murmuring. The rest were odds and sods scattered here and there, laxly curious, vaguely aware that despite all appearances this was an 'event', but the sort of event that drew few people these days, no one funky or hip, or God forbid glamorous or socially exciting, no opinion-formers from the vanguard of contemporary culture whose enthusiasm would make word of the concert ripple through media pages galvanising young readers to see this young pianist, to collar an experience as exciting as anything modern life could offer. It was a pianist's fate to play to this loyal straggle of oddballs, the remnants of an elapsed century's fading mental culture, and despite the drab eclecticism of the folk here tonight, he felt deep gratitude for anybody who could be bothered to turn up these days to a piano recital. For such loyal, rare souls the pianist's anguished craft was still worthwhile.

He pulled a tube of mints from his pocket. He was in a mess, complexly anxious. Fringe issues were irking him: another doctor's appointment for the test results; the unsettling prospect of a new agent John Sampson wanted to foist on him, some gorgeous young woman – the last thing he needed! In a professional adviser Philip required a man of his own age and prejudices who remembered his triumphs and forgave his weaknesses. He was in no mood for anyone modern, attractive, or challenging.

His child would have been fourteen by now. A girl, he was certain. He blinked concertedly, as though on the edge of tears. Sorrow was almost tidal in its surges and abeyances.

When Laura first told him, he managed to ignore the news in the way one would kick aside a rumour too old to bother with. His reaction was a defence against the need to suffer the consequences of unwelcome knowledge. It happened so long ago, but something from those long-gone days was still palpitating, live enough to wriggle into the present so that suddenly he felt the news like a young husband, the marvellous surprise of conception, the heady novelty of creating a child with someone you loved, the warm wash of broody feeling triggered by a pregnancy – all these things he felt, out of nowhere, violently. As if he and Camilla were still lovers, he experienced a disabling love for this glimmer of a child, as though a river of feeling existed within him designed for the purpose that he had never known before. It all welled up, together with a swamping sense of loss and waste that made it impossible to concentrate on the piano, on anything. He grimaced, guarding the edge of his face with his hand.

A man appeared from the wings. He raised an arm to hush the audience. Philip held his breath, fearing the worst.

Holding a scrap of paper the man read out a last-minute change to the programme. Vadim had ducked Brahms's Handel Variations and would play a Rachmaninov selection instead.

Philip looked at the ceiling, struggling to control his vexation. He was acutely concerned for Vadim. Almost for the sake of his nerves he determined to think about something else. He was actually dreading the performance.

It came back to him now, something Vadim had mentioned in the car. Konstantine Serebriakov had been heard by someone or other playing in Reigate. The great Russian was absolutely ancient but he still managed, fifty years after his coronation as the world's greatest pianist, to make music where he could, small venues, private gatherings, nothing grand or pretentious. Philip had been thinking of him recently because a producer friend, Derek Woodruff, was nobly hoping to make a documentary for BBC 2 about pianists. Philip had given him the principal figures, a few basic pointers. Derek was fired up by the whole idea of the artist hero/virtuoso, a priestly figure on the one hand mediating between God (the composer) and his audience (the flock), and a proto rock star on the other. His enquiries were like mirrors reflecting unfamiliar angles and aspects of one's life. He rather rashly decided that Philip should be the subject, and although a TV programme held no allure, Philip was happy to answer his questions. Derek's courteous detachment licensed a kind of intimacy.

'Did you make some kind of executive decision not to get married?' 'I was always a hard worker, a perfectionist. And in the old days I travelled all over the world.' 'You liked the freedom?' 'Well, you can't do it without the freedom.' 'Are you afraid of commitment?' 'You see, for me, playing the piano is the most intense way of being alive. How d'you reconcile the give and take of a good relationship with that kind of consuming passion? I never

17

wanted to take more than I gave, but it seemed I was bound to if I got married.' 'So you have no regrets?' 'I have only regrets.'

Vadim was on stage almost before anyone had noticed. He arrived beside the piano and bowed to a weak burst of applause in which the splatting sound of individual pairs of hands could be heard. He acknowledged the sparse audience with an opaque dignity.

He looked even larger on the platform. His trunk was burly, his head somehow grand in profile. Philip found it almost comforting to see him solidly ensconced at the head of the instrument.

Philip averted his eyes, heart beating hard. He could barely endure the indecent knowingness of being a fellow pianist.

Vadim gazed at an upward angle, slowly raising his hands.

There were blustery coughs and sniffs, chair-creaking adjustments.

The early bars of Rachmaninov's Étude Tableau in C minor were like sounds from a faraway world. Vadim sat at the keyboard as if hearing a call to arms, or the rumour of something heroic. A tethered power lurked in the first gruff phrases. The player was alert, his torso and broad shoulders crowding close to the lower keyboard as if to protect a secret, or the making of a spell, hands moving stealthily, depressing keys with soft creepiness or Stakhanovite force. Vadim's narrowed eyes were trained on the innate sense of sounds, the meaning in certain clashes, the potency of harmonic shifts. He would look down and then upwards, seeking the destination of a phrase, and then to the side, the frequency of dark sound catching his attention for the first time; and slowly the audience settled and became still, subdued by an equivalent concern with the progress of this ominous elegy, which spoke to them of things they knew nothing about. The initial statements were rounded off and now movement began, footsteps, an eerie procession, lit here and there by torches, and still his face was full of pilgrim enquiry, as though he too were following the crowd that seemed to file under the vaults of some massive structure, with baleful octaves deep in the bass of the instrument and great framing pillars of sound rising above tiny humans, until the processional was under the highest point and giant church bells exploded, and Vadim's teeth were set with the effort of massive directed force and the exultant sense of Russian grandeur peeling from the piano.

Philip was fixed dead still with the deepest concentration. After the ringing climax there was a dying away, and tension went out of his body, a gasp of relief almost. Vadim had wrested iron control from utter disarray. Two further études followed, the first a tornado of double notes, blisteringly executed; the second martial, chunky, hectoringly percussive, the crashing last bars of which shook a spastic clatter of geriatric commendation from the floor.

He listened to the second group of pieces with something approaching astonishment. Vadim unfolded a selection of Rachmaninov preludes with extra-terrestrial lucidity. He engaged the swirling semiquavers of the C minor Prelude with the command of an elemental force, propelling notes as the wind drives leaves, a crystalline dispatch evoking huge currents of energy, liquid or electrical, backed up and ready to smite drenching storms of sound, as if music were a kind of exciting weather, something released from on high. Just as his technical aplomb seemed to derive from an almost inhuman configuration of hearing and reflexes, so his playing transcended the little life of man. Epic landscapes were conjured, the chromatic winds of the Steppe, vast skies. Sound had energies and tensions like particles in physics that composers harnessed and pianists released. Listening to him play was hearing nature itself, the force and fabric of Creation.

Philip remained in his seat during the interval, forehead cupped in his hand. As always when Vadim was 'on' he felt the same sequence of emotions: alarm (the talent was so overpowering); defeat (one could never catch up); gratitude (for the existence of such talent); and love (for the regenerative turmoil it caused). Such playing was a gift from the purest, the noblest part of a person; it rescued Philip from the loneliness of a personal quest. In a peculiar way the acute listener was closer than a lover to the being of a musician; and what could one feel for the person who played like that but love?

This he had often thought, and during the interval he was grateful to his friend for reminding him of the point. One owed an almost blind loyalty to such gifted colleagues. Alas, in the second half Vadim's playing deteriorated so abruptly (it was almost pugnaciously brash and insensitive) that Philip's softer thoughts vanished. The Chopin was cavalier, the Liszt exhausting. There was muscular brilliance and power, but no sense of discovery, no care for suggestion. He listened with disbelief, and then boredom. The last blasting cavalcade of Liszt's Mephisto Waltz yanked the audience to their feet, while Philip sat in dismay, wondering what he was going to say afterwards. He had a sick sense that confrontation was inevitable. What, otherwise, did he stand for as a friend, as a mentor?

After the encore he stood up wearily, and made his way past outgoing members of the audience towards the stage door. An idea came to him like the filter on a camera lens, darkening the sky. The unborn child, he realised, was the ghost of the life not lived, something which, by its very nature, would remain unknowable. For days he had been haunted by the sense of that parallel life, the life sacrificed to art, the life irretrievably lost.

He hesitated by the stage door and glanced once more at the emptying hall.

Chapter Three

'EVERYONE CANCELS CONCERTS,' SAID Vadim. 'If you can't play best, you have moral duty to cancel.'

'There's nothing moral about you, Vadim.'

They were seated in a latticed alcove of the Taste of India restaurant. A photograph of the Taj Mahal hung behind Vadim. Two pints of Kingfisher sat on the table, a tray of poppadoms. Both men were suffused in orange light from a nearby lantern, which made them look ill. Bulky local diners sat near by, chatting softly over steamy platefuls of rice and glossy dollops of brinjal. Vadim had ordered to excess, and now leaned back on his chair. He looked a bit gassy after the first slug of lager.

'Michelangeli' – he lifted his head morosely – 'would cancel if one note was not right. One note! What incredible perfectionism!'

'And Dinu Lipatti played when he was dying of leukaemia! I'll take selfless dedication over neurotic perfectionism every time.'

'We are all different.'

'You can do better.'

'I did not cancel!'

'As a favour to me! I can hardly follow you around the country begging you to play.'

For a second the Russian looked almost submissive. He sensed that Philip was annoyed with him, which was tiring, particularly after a concert. Normally he could avoid Philip's seriousness, his holy solutions to the problems of life, based on different weaknesses that were irrelevant to him. Nobody had these same musical thunderbolts living in his sleeve. Olympians could not be advised by anybody, however well meaning.

'Do you play for yourself, or for your audience?'

21

'I play for every beautiful girl in Hampshire.'

Philip sagged. He had so little energy for a showdown. 'Shame none of them turned up tonight.'

'Which is mistake because classical music is sexy. It should attract very sexy women who you want to fuck for the rest of your life.'

'It did! Marguerite. Your sexy wife. Whom you still haven't called.'

Vadim wiped his eye. 'So I'm married, which is unfortunate. And you're depressed, which is tragedy. Because you are bachelor and should be over the moon.'

'Listening to you I feel quite depressed, actually.'

Vadim looked at him directly. Philip's carpings were aimed at the thickest part of his hide. He could understand, but not really feel these criticisms.

'In Spearmint Rhino,' he began, pausing for effect, 'it's hard to be depressed.'

Philip regarded him coolly. 'Unless you work there.'

'The arses are fantastic. For depression I prescribe two visits a week.'

'Can I have a glass of red?' he said to a passing waiter. 'I'm not depressed. Just desperate.'

'Even better, "Ivan the Absolutely Terrible". Girls from Slovenia, lap dancing, American cigarettes, everybody in kind of fantasy. Let me take you there. You have some therapy for your desperation.'

'Only you would call lap dancing therapy.'

'Cheaper than psychoanalyst.'

'But more expensive for your marriage!'

Vadim was not so sure about that. 'Marriage is maybe another kind of Russian roulette.'

'Getting married to you would be. With all the chambers loaded.'

He liked this and smiled appreciatively. 'Philip, you must try to have more pumpy rumpy.'

Philip grimaced and shook his head. 'You're a bad boy.'

The trolley rolled up to the table. Hot plates were distributed, space organised. Vadim followed the arriving trays with interest: chicken tikka masala, sag aloo, a team of onion bhajis in case there was a hole in his total satisfaction after the set-pieces had been obliterated. He took a long draught from his lager. Both pints were his.

Philip lit up a cigarette, exhaled away from the table. He regarded the food neutrally as it mounted higher on Vadim's plate.

They had met years ago when Philip was touring the Ukraine, and Vadim was a remarkable eighteen-year-old with two international piano competitions behind him. Like most young pianists he idolised Philip, was honoured to meet him. Philip reciprocated with the older pianist's judicious reserve. In fact, both saw elements in the other's playing beyond his own capabilities without realising the envy was symmetrical. If Vadim regarded Philip as a role model, Philip might consider Vadim a successor of sorts. A latent rivalry was thus relaxed. Later, in England, after Vadim had won the Leeds, Philip helped him find a flat, contacts, and representation. Vadim joined a growing band of world-class pianists who had made London their home. For a while, they lived around the corner from each other, went to concerts together, and sometimes shared a platform.

For Vadim, London was a relief. He was liberated from his uncle and the madness of Moscow, and took in the galleries and parks with elation. If nowadays there was no aristocracy to greet and pamper musical genius, Vadim would flaunt the peacock fan of his talent by insisting on freedom. He did what he liked, when he liked, odd things, good things, reckless things, and made it clear to everybody involved in his life that this was the way it had to be because he could not suffer boredom, and only worked hard when the cross-hairs of a growing obsessive-compulsiveness were aimed at the keyboard, frequently, but not often enough for a pianist who wants to conquer the world. Having been tied to the piano through his teens, he would no longer be tied to anything. He needed to displace the energy focused to an unbearable degree by his training and talent. This Philip expected. What bothered him was Vadim's new tendency to use dissipation almost as a means to electrical pianism. His unruly lifestyle generated mood-swings that infected his playing, sometimes dazzlingly. Every concert became a kind of crisis, with higher stakes, and mixed results. Brutality had crept into his touch, for sure, mirroring the conduct of his marriage. Already, alas, there had been infidelities, casual cruelties. Marguerite was possessive, but Vadim was impossible to own, and already the pact was in train whereby heady acclaim set the seal on an independence no valuable relationship could survive. These days he was a good companion only to those who made no demands and were tolerantly dazzled by his company. More responsible relations he found suffocating or tedious. Philip feared both a moral decline and an emotional depletion. He feared that Vadim would evade the maturing bonds he needed most. How to say this was another matter.

After an interlude, Vadim wiped his mouth. He was not unthoughtful.

'It's easy for you to be good boy,' he said. 'You are alone. Nobody cares if you do Internet porn or get drunk.'

'D'you really want to know what I thought of your concert?'

Vadim swigged at his beer.

'Nobody else will say this to you.'

The Russian suddenly lunged forward and grabbed Philip tightly by the hand. 'You're so marvellous, so happy, such wonderful pianist. Tell me the secret of how to live my life.' He squeezed harder.

Philip stared at him, his hand trapped.

'You were a god in the first half, and a charlatan in the second.'

Vadim released the hand and flung himself back in his chair. He glowered for a moment.

'Good, I have range at least.'

'You're ruining a great career.'

'I'm bored.'

'If that's boring, you're in deeper shit than I thought.'

Vadim cracked a poppadom and flicked on some lime pickle. 'Deep shit is quite interesting. You should try it. Because, Philip, you have to live. Even if it's a mess. Monks do not make virtuosi.'

'You're brilliant, but not great, Vadim. Greatness has to be earned the hard way.'

'Greatness is given by God. Not earned by sad workaholics.'

'Practice, reflection, dedication.'

'I'm not a priest!' He was suddenly outraged. 'I've been to hundred boring concerts by good-boy pianists who respect their teachers and think composers are gods. They get on and off planes. Check into hotel, play Chopin Ballade for millionth time, same boring interpretation, same reverence for music.' He raised his voice. 'Music does not come from this treadmill. Music comes from excitement, madness, energy. Not how much hours you practise. Not how humble and well behaved you are. Don't believe this German bullshit propaganda!'

'You complain about boring concerts. You've just given one!'

He waved it off. 'If I want to, I play better. I don't want to, but for your relationship with John Sampson I do a big favour.'

Philip was offended. 'What about poor old Chopin? You didn't do him a big favour.'

'I sacrificed my childhood for dead men like Chopin. I don't owe him anything.'

'Emotional negativity is affecting your playing. You've stopped feeling tenderness, love, happiness. It shows.'

'I'm bored. You are boring now. You are giving boring conversation.'

'Your lack of empathy for people is reflected by a lack of empathy for music outside the Russian tradition.'

'I take the train back.' Vadim made to rise.

'What!'

'I am not your student.'

Philip was startled. 'Don't be ridiculous! We're having a conversation.' He reached over to grab his forearm but Vadim pulled back. 'You're going to end up like me if you're not careful. Solitary and middle-aged and . . . Sit down!'

'You're jealous.'

'What!'

'Always I have jealous friends. They want me to do this, that, how best I should live, play the piano, what to do with my talent. Nobody plays these pieces like me. Maybe two other pianists in the world.'

Philip stared at him in disbelief.

'Nobody can tell me where to go. How to live my life. I don't have to obey the rules for depressed English pianist.'

Philip's heart pounded. He felt the hostile force of Vadim's self-confidence.

'To hell with your morals and your advice.'

'Listen to me . . .'

'I'm not listening to you.'

Vadim pulled away, tossing the napkin down. 'Philip, stop telling other people how to live. Get a life yourself.'

He pulled some banknotes from his pocket and left them on the table.

'Where are you going?'

'Taxi.'

'Oh, for God's sake!'

He patted his jacket, returned the pack of cigarettes. He picked up his bag and made his way out from behind the table.

Philip looked on in astonishment as the Russian strode towards the door.

For a moment he was almost paralysed; then he got up and followed him out of the restaurant. By the time he was outside, Vadim was walking towards the traffic lights.

He stood there, hoping that Vadim would about-turn, but off he went, forcefully subtracting himself from Philip's life, taking his brilliance to where it was better appreciated, and as Philip watched him bobbing into the distance he felt a stab of despair.

He went back into the restaurant, passing slowly to his chair, where he sat for a moment. He looked at the bill and picked at Vadim's banknotes, unable to concentrate.

He glanced around, as if looking for help. He could not believe what had happened.

Chapter Four

THEY SAT ON THE pavement tables outside Chez Gerard, steel decking underfoot, bay shrubs in boxes framing the scene, check tablecloths under their forearms. The Charlotte Street Union Jack rippled across the street. Office workers and law students straggled on the kerb. Young women walked the pavement like flowers responding to sudden sunshine. There were taut navels and lacy cleavages on offer today, and eyes everywhere raking it in, the comings and goings, the rushing waitresses, the striped awnings and glancing sunlight.

Derek was poised. He managed the wine list like a veteran producer. Once again the BBC had leveraged him into the company of a very distinguished man. They had met at Laura's, of course, but this was a different order of exchange. He had to be alert and agreeable, respectful and precise. He paid close attention to what was being said, nailing the logic to secure his understanding, and then made intuitive jumps. Despite his modesty of manner, and mildly tense ignorance of everything to do with classical music, he had the short man's tenacity. Now he steered conversation gently whilst sectioning his steak and hailing the waiter for cruets and mustard.

Philip had ordered on no appetite at all. This was the fifth day in a row he had been unable to practise. Various catastrophes lay on the horizon, but for Derek's benefit he tried to be bright. That morning he had fiddled around with the cistern ballcock in his upstairs loo to stop the overflow pipe from spattering into the side return. Coming in for lunch he had done a little shopping: books and fresh coffee, anything to make himself feel normal. Derek's plan to get him on television no longer seemed real. Although in a corner of his mind Philip knew that he was a distinguished pianist, his current aversion to the instrument made the idea of a documentary seem absurd. If he could not play, he could hardly talk about playing. And yet Derek's interest was addictive. The very simplicity of his questions let Philip see his life from outside, almost from the point of view of someone who had lived a different life. For the programme pitch Derek positioned him as an 'ordinary man in extraordinary circumstances'. It was good to be ordinary for a change, to see one's obsessions and sacrifices for what they were.

'What d'you have to go through to make the big time?'

'Oh, God!' He pulled his shades off and grimaced. Merely to contemplate the question was somehow draining.

'It's never enough to play the notes, but playing the notes is no easy matter. Entrenching technical security is a priority that steals your youth. Because, you see, this incredible repertoire that we play is so difficult.'

Derek was ready with notepad and biro.

He paused to consider the issue more carefully. 'Difficulty is a metaphor for emotional adversity, for psychological terrors and demons. The greater the difficulty, the greater the triumph. In mastering difficulty the pianist purges the audience's suffering and fear. He's a kind of gladiator. His adversary is the emotional extremity of life transformed into the symbolic language of music expressed through technical difficulty. You see,' he was warming to his theme, 'the composer pianists of the nineteenth century wanted to burst open the expressive potential of the piano. In the course of fifty years Mozart's domestic pet of a piano gets turned into a thrashing Moby Dick.'

'That's good.'

'Court pianists become artist heroes. The result is a repertoire of impregnable difficulty for laymen and epic challenge for professionals. To have a prayer in this extraordinary arena, your aspiring pianist needs to practise fanatically the length and breadth of his childhood.'

Derek was feeding in steak morsels with one hand and burning down notes with the other.

'So you don't develop like ordinary kids. You lose the timelessness of childhood, the mental space for fantasy, the first innocent impression of the world being carefree – those halcyon years are colonised by Czerny études, Mozart piano concerti, the ladder of technical hazard from Bach to Godowsky, with a few million contrary motion scales thrown in. And your character suffers in ways that are later damaging. Because you are made such a fuss of, you don't work hard to win friends or relate to people who aren't consumed with the same interest. You're inclined to be narrow, precocious, wretchedly competitive. The gifted child's preened self-esteem is a two-edged sword. If everything hangs on one's musical brilliance, it comes as a mortal blow to discover one's talents are relative when some little shit superstar blasts past at the speed of light, turning you to stone. It's always a gamble that you've got what it takes.'

Philip glanced up at the waiter – showing someone to a table. Everyone on Charlotte Street seemed so young, so innocent of the twentieth century, so entitled to success and happiness. Had people suddenly got younger-looking for their age? Or was he just feeling older than he was?

'Technique's not enough, of course. You have to understand the purpose and placing of every single note. Where does it come from? Where does it lead? Why this note and not another one? You need to shape line and dynamics, make phrases logical and movements inevitable. Instinct and intelligence working in tandem. Talent, as much as you like, curbed by humility. A good student needs a healthy respect for the greatness of music.'

He scratched his head. His lamb cutlets lay before him, un-touched. 'But that's not enough. The repertoire engages an incred-ible range of experience: mystical, romantic, erotic, poetic, religious, which you need to discover emotionally and then convey, and that's a harder challenge because our modern lives are so comfortable and godless and insulated. Feelings run at a lower level these days, so it's sometimes hard for a young person who has never known unrequited love, because sex is so available, to understand yearning in the way Schumann felt it. Music reifies so many dimensions of feeling. It's only through a student's sentimental education that he makes the link between his inner life and the psychological truth of music – the truth of the way music structures emotion – which is why you never stop suddenly grasping what a familiar piece really means. Without emotional intelligence the biggest technician is just a bore. Of course . . .' He was happy to natter on, letting it all flow out, as if from some mechanically competent part of his brain, though the tiredness was gathering. One sip of wine brought it on. 'The emotionally vibrant player has his own problems.'

'Why?'

'Because emotions can't be restricted to one application. An intensely feeling musician will feel rather too intensely about everything.'

'The so-called artistic temperament.'

'Yes, but living with that particular cliché takes self-knowledge, or you go off the rails. I'm sure it's just as hard for accountants.'

'So what are the obstacles, the make-or-break moments?'

He looked at his cutlets. He felt odd for a moment. The world seemed to edge to the side by a couple of degrees, as though vision were sliding off. He blinked and stared at the street, fixing buildings and cars in their place. The day's colours and shadows were steady at the centre but fuzzy at the edges. He had not slept well for nights and was aware of an ocular compression effect, as though sight were screwed too tight for its own good. He was suffering the physical symptoms of stress, no doubt. When he should have been practising he was sitting in a restaurant pretending this emergency did not exist. It came to him suddenly that he should cancel. Anybody else would have by now. But cancellation seemed as unthinkable as the concerts themselves. This was an important series, his first in some time at the South Bank. The publicity was behind him for once. John had a record deal lining up. Derek was making headway with the documentary. His reputation was rising up to haunt him on all sides and it just seemed impossible to turn his back on all the timing and opportunity, and on the million man-hours of practice he had invested.

'Sorry, what was that?'

Derek had described the difficulty of selling arts programmes to BBC 2, where so many of the decision-makers saw classical music as off-limits, old-fashioned, elitist, too plummy for words. To bypass prejudice one needed to crank up the pitch, max the stakes, rack up the spin, and generally think of any conceivable reason why a classical-pianist documentary might perforate the audience's apathy and indifference. There was talk of the pendulum swinging back, but Derek figured the pendulum had been snapped off or got stuck. He assured Philip that there was 'interest', if only because Derek's last film had ticked boxes, rated well, bought kudos. BBC 4 was a fallback, but the budgets were minuscule, and Derek wanted Two, or 'Toe', as it was now pronounced. 'Bay Bay Say Toe'.

'I want the crisis points,' he said, chewing meat. 'The "Oh shit" moments. The story structure of triumph and failure.'

Philip frowned, trying desperately to concentrate. He was feeling hot around the collar. 'A major competition victory is virtually essential. A record deal. You need to find patronage, benevolent promoters, an agent. You need to hit the ground running because there's so much competition. So technique, musicianship . . . But they're not enough. The X-factor,' he grimaced, 'is . . .'

'You have to look promotable?'

He was suddenly overwrought. 'Great pianists are extraordinary human beings. They hold an intense vision of music and communicate it hypnotically. The ability to master the instrument, perform under pressure, maintain artistic purity – that takes real heroism! Not just talent. Great moral strength.'

'Which some people don't have?'

'The loneliness, the solitude, the esotericism, the competition. You have to survive all that! You have the task of constant regeneration. The conflict between what the business asks of you and what your inner world requires. You endure terrible crises of faith. Are you living your whole life in the past, playing old music to shrinking audiences, or are you recapitulating the very development of the human soul? Are you the guardian of sacred fire, or a cultural anachronism?' Philip stared at him. 'You have to commit everything. Not everyone has the resilience.' He wiped his forehead. He was feeling so bad.

Derek nodded. 'So you win a competition, earn a few engagements. What happens then?'

'A ten-year struggle for consolidation. You tour and record and suddenly, somehow, you become necessary.'

Derek was chewing hard. 'Necessary?'

'The people of your age must hear you play.'

'Meaning what?'

'Great music is so because it is necessary. Interpreters must be necessary, too.'

Derek looked at him strangely.

31

Philip had to leave. His mind was boiling over. He felt absolutely restless and drained at the same time.

'You'd be in the top twenty or thirty in the world?'

'I don't know. I don't care.'

'How d'you make top ten?'

Philip gave him a strained look.

'Like, who are top ten?'

He sighed profoundly. 'Amongst the dead, some stand above the rest.'

'Death's the final career move?'

'Death is a test of the eternal spirit of the artist.' He wanted to cry. His tear ducts were swelling. 'Great recordings collapse time.'

'It takes thirty years of posterity to know whether you've made the pantheon?'

'Excuse me.' He put his napkin on the table. 'I've got to go.'

'Are you a great pianist?'

Chapter Five

IT BEGAN WITH A dot on the carpet, a circle of carbonised fibre that dilated gradually and darkened like blotted ink, joining with other dots, travelling outwards, merging and then racing to the edge of the carpet, and running at its curved periphery a blue flame that seemed almost too frail to ignite a magazine or the hem of a sofa, until both objects were smoking, and the wood basket was burning nicely, its wickerwork snapping and crackling, and the footstool rug was glowing orange, shedding sparks, and smoke was winding between beams, and drifting under doors, and sneaking in wraiths between floorboards, while the sound of burning developed from hisses and pops to the wind noise of incineration, the violent crackle and whir of intense heat engulfing everything, using everything to create more heat, curtains, furniture, dried flowers whisked into flame swirling up the walls. Peter was outside now, smashing through the window, and then the stairwell erupted to the sound of screams as Jamie and Clarissa were trapped in the upburst, hair twisting into smoke and pyjamas curling and browning like leaves on a bonfire whilst Peter lay under a post on the living-room floor, head stoved in like a plastic doll's. And now more smoke billowed from the cottage as the living-room ceiling collapsed and the roof caught fire and flame twined through every attic gap and cupboard space as rafters went down, crashing, and thick clouds were emitted in pulses from the roof into the night sky, hellishly underlit by an orange glow, which seemed to catch his sleeve and wake him with a jolt.

He drew himself up in bed, heart beating hard. He felt frightened and alone and remained propped up on his pillow for an hour as dark faded in the early daylight hours and the grey lines of the bedroom cupboard became visible.

Philip stood in the hall trying to remember what he was looking for. Sleep-loss had engendered a sort of hangover. He was in a daze and kept forgetting what he was doing or which room he was supposed to be in, and as the morning progressed he kept hoping that a cup of tea, or a shower, would clear his head and let him get going. But with each passing hour his mind seemed foggier, his will weaker, and now at midday, sun pouring in the bay window and casting spots of colour on the tessellated floor of the hall through lozenges of stained glass, his motivation expired completely. He held a credit-card bill and appeared to be taking it either to the kitchen, where the kettle had boiled, or to his study upstairs, where it could be neatly lost on a desk. But there was something else as well. John's assistant, Serena, had posted a packetful of flyers for his concert and these were around somewhere, and, although he had no intention of mailing them to friends, he wanted to look at them for a reason he couldn't remember, in which case he should go to the piano room and have a root around there.

Today he would practise. That was the plan, an iron resolve made the night before. He would force himself back to the piano. He would hack through the Waldstein, the Funeral March Sonata, the Samuel Barber, the Rachmaninov. Somewhere inside the shuffling shipwrecked figure he saw reflected in the hall mirror was a virtuoso pianist, and he had to become that person quickly. The day was zipping along, unfortunately, and Philip had accomplished only basic tasks (with strain), and was limiting himself now to a vegetative shuffle round the house.

His cleaning lady had been the previous day, passing a duster along dado rails and picture frames, returning the shirts that she ironed to shelves in his bedroom. The house was spick and span, in its usual state of fading readiness for guests who never stayed. Light blazed in bedroom windows warming carpets and stirring dry dust, bedspreads were neat and taut in spare rooms, chairs squared against the wall. It was like a family home that had been at the ready for years, never filled, never disrupted, and now the wallpaper colours were softening and fabrics were fading. The second-floor bedrooms were almost empty. He lived mainly on the ground floor and had grown oblivious to the covetable Edwardian features that a young couple buying their first house would have prized: ceiling mouldings, art nouveau fireplaces. His ex-girlfriend Laura had made certain changes in her own bohemian taste. The piano room had become something of a salon: swags on the garden window, pelmets around the bay. A pillar from an overpriced garden centre had been found to support his bust of Beethoven. She spent his money on floor rugs, on an easy chair to complement the recamier, which together with the Steinway rather half-heartedly suggested nineteenth-century paintings of Liszt playing to divas and grandees in damask-draped Parisian apartments; and yet despite these add-ons, the room in daylight hours looked like a musician's den with its alcoves crushed full of sheet music, and its tottering CD stacks, and slumped yards of LPs against the wall. A life's worth of accumulated orchestral scores was shelved in the room beyond the arch, along with his library of composer biographies and reference tomes. Laura's touch had made more sense in the kitchen, overhauled at remarkable cost, and now a shrine to Italian elegance and German efficiency. Floor tiles and ceiling spots set off marble work surfaces with integrated hobs and concealed white goods. The kitchen cried out for dinner parties, or cappuccino breakfasts, or candlelit à deux. Her vision of their mutual future was not to be, alas, and so he had a woman's taste everywhere and no woman to share it with.

He sat on the stool by the counter sipping coffee. He would finish the coffee and then practise. He could feel the lines in his face this morning, the weight of his eyelids, the prickly surface of his skin. The prospect of his concert was solidly in view and, as he gazed through the mesh of his decrepitude towards that prospect, it seemed like someone else's bad dream. How could a man in his state deliver those titanic pieces to a paying audience? He should cancel, of course; but cancellation seemed almost as absurd as the concerts themselves. Cancellation was an obverse disaster no less forbidding than the thought of the first recital next Wednesday evening at seven-thirty, when a thousand listeners would pack the Queen Elizabeth Hall in complacent expectation of absolute brilliance.

A few minutes later he passed from the kitchen into the hallway, and from the hall to the music room. He went steadily across to the piano and sat down on the stool. The lid was raised and ready. The stand he set flat. He arranged his feet on the pedals and glanced down the long length of the instrument, allowing his shoulders to relax and waiting for the impulse to gather, to rise up as a tactile need for the keys. He placed his hands on his lap, holding back a little, marshalling himself. He regarded his hands, conjuror's hands, unusually lined and walnut-creased at the finger joints, cross-hatched on the palms. The skin was weathered and elastic around the knuckles and smooth near the cuticles. He had large, well-architected hands, good hands for a pianist. He looked at them now with a kind of compassion for their hard-won suppleness and strength. The open piano was a sorcerer's brazier from which these dextrous hands had conjured the most marvellous sounds, gossamer traceries, exquisite cantabiles, thunderous fortissimos, prismatic washes, aqueous translucencies. These hands had worked hard to transport and enthral. They had served music well.

Slowly he shut the lid of the keyboard and sat motionlessly on the stool.

He found the packet on the shelf and opened it carefully. He sat down with the contents spilling into his palms, leaflets, copies of the concert programme, Xeroxed ads from *Piano Gazette* and *Music Magazine*. John's assistant Serena had photocopied all four pages of the *Sunday Telegraph* article and folded them in. The flyers were gloss-finished and showed a profile of Philip at the keyboard in his usual convulsed state. He flipped the programme, saw the heading 'Sonata Series', the works listed in each recital, and a commentary by someone called Geraldine Mercier. 'An epic journey of Himalayan purview,' she wrote. 'A traversal of the repertoire's most spiritually demanding summits, culminating in Beethoven's Hammerklavier Sonata. Morahan's sequencing demonstrates the aesthetic and emotional range of sonata form, its narrative properties and metamorphic imperatives. From Haydn to Scriabin, Mozart to Medtner, Chopin to Samuel Barber, his selection encompasses phenomenal diversity and the coherence of a remarkable tradition.'

He passed a hand across his face, dragging at the sallow skin under his eyes. Was sonata form itself to blame, he wondered? The element of quest, the struggle for transformation, the harnessing of extremes and the reconciling of opposites: was it too much to ask that one played these highly wrought works in sequence? In the first recital he would play Beethoven's Waldstein and Chopin's Funeral March Sonatas before the interval, and pieces by Scarlatti, Barber and Rachmaninov in the second half. Setting aside the epic concentration required to play these works, he wondered now whether it was really the concert's underlying theme of death and regeneration that was sapping him. How could he approach the Funeral March Sonata in this frame of mind? The whole piece screamed out a negative transference of its composer's terror of death.

His hands were shaky now: the coffee and insomnia, the hive of nerves in his belly. Hopelessly he unfolded the *Sunday Telegraph* article, eyes skating over the column inches and the full-page photograph that meticulously investigated the lines in his forehead, and captured the defenceless light of his blue eyes behind specs. He looked like some sort of intelligent life form from outer space, caught on a brief visit to Planet Earth, his craggy face strangely innocent of the ways of the world whilst looking fraught with otherworldly concerns: a face that had lived life from the brain out.

Philip could not believe this was him. The man he read about seemed like a stranger. The article was penned by a well-known music journalist whom he had met once or twice and who asserted that Philip was a national treasure, a world-class artist of remarkable pedigree, whose musical lineage hailed from Solomon and Hess. His blood pressure rose as he read the florid tribute:

Morahan's art is mysterious. He has technique in spades, a rich tonal palette, rhythmic suppleness and strength, all of which you forget when you hear him play because he tells the story of each piece so spellbindingly that heart and mind are in thrall. He is the music, and whether it comes from long study or some God-given instinct, time after time he gets it right. Familiar repertoire is reborn under his touch. One is allowed privileged communion with the first poetic impulse, the composer's first rush of feeling into music. This sense of a re-incarnation is the kernel of Morahan's art. Compositions cease to be musical artefacts, susceptible to this or that approach, but living organisms of startling immediacy.

He stared like a dead man at the shelves of sheet music rising above his head. The papers and flyers slid off his lap on to the floor. He did not understand his past any longer. It seemed as though everything that had happened to him belonged to another man's life. It was a life that until recently he seemed to enjoy. In the last two years he had become busy as Guest Professor at the Academy. A new generation of students disarmingly looked up to him and he straddled the steed of reputation as best he could. Life's long central plateau had become endurable at last. He was reconciled to the consoling habits of a working life and enjoyed teaching. Classical virtues he now preferred to romantic extremes. Sex and love were pleasures, not necessities. At fifty-two he was doubtful whether any truly new emotion or experience might be in store for him. Pleasurable repetition, he suspected, was the game from now on. Without dwelling on it, he guessed the relativity of his achievement as a pianist. He had heard so many wonderful players in his time. The effort of topping previous achievements seemed daunting, anyway. Talent was perhaps a kind of fate, driving you or leading you, but always in charge, setting the tempo for your life.

Philip knew that he had entered a settled managing phase harnessed by routine, and the sense of having fewer nerve endings but more knowledge than before, more depth and experience to call on, except that depth was calling on him now, surging up, a retributive bonanza of suffering and anxiety that pained him more than he could bear. He did not like, could not endure, what he thought of his life. When he learned of the abortion it threw a switch, as if only now were he fated to suffer what he should have been rueing for years: loneliness, childlessness, a life without love.

Marguerite had phoned him the day before. A pitiful call. He could hear her baby screaming. Vadim had deserted her, it seemed, walked out as if she did not exist and did not matter. She copiously wept, lapsing into French. Did Vadim no longer find her attractive or interesting? Was he bored with the mother of his baby boy? How could he leave her on her own like this? He was inhuman, a bastard. She should never have got involved with him. Poor Vadim, if only he knew how much she cared for him. She had left three messages on his mobile declaring her love but now regretted this sign of weakness because he deserved not love but a decanter over the head, or a dinner plate, or a knife in the 'eart, the imbecile, the blackguard.

He listened with terrible pity and a kind of moral paralysis, as if it were too late and futile anyway to hope for reconciliation. He begged her to be calm. Sooner or later Vadim would return to the flat because that was his home, and she was his wife, and in the meantime she must think about her marriage. Vadim, he said, was not an ordinary kind of husband. He was an artist and artists crave freedom. And Vadim was no ordinary artist. He was a phenomenal talent with a complicated, difficult temperament that was not his own fault. He was under immense pressure, and the pressure was causing misbehaviour, stupidity. She had to remember that his parents died when he was fourteen, that his uncle was a nasty piece of work, that everybody in Moscow wanted him to be this or do that, and that Vadim had been locked in rooms to practise the piano and beaten for bunking off lessons, and tasked by his music professors with the most horrendous weekly challenges that he had met head on with all his defiant brilliance as if to say there was nothing he could not do. Philip asked her to forgive him because Vadim was a sweet man despite his misdemeanours. The complex adult harboured an innocent child. If the adult mistreated her, she must tackle the child. She must support and nurture and pacify. She must grant him his freedom and love him for what he was. It sounded, he later realised, like a plea in mitigation for all pianists – for himself in particular and a rotten one at that.

Later that day he attempted to cancel the meeting John had set up with Frank Bulmanion. Bulmanion was a City man turned arts angel with a fledgling record company. He wanted to sign Philip and Philip did not want to be signed. John thought a meeting would help. Philip disagreed. A meeting had nonetheless been arranged for the Saturday, and Philip was determined to get out of it. There was no point John parading him in his current ruined state.

'I want to cancel the meeting,' he said smartly over the phone.

'Don't do that!' said John.

'Not up to it.'

John was resilient. 'I've booked a flight back from Barcelona for this meeting. Ursula's coming up from the country. I don't want to give Frank the wrong signal.'

He needed to confess. He wanted to tell John the truth. 'Bulmanion knows I have a concert.'

'Of course! He'll send a limo to collect us both. You'll be

pampered and flattered for an hour. Then you'll be driven home. Plus you need to meet Ursula. She's dying to be introduced to you.'

'John, listen . . .'

'I'm listening.'

'About Ursula.'

'What about Ursula?'

'Oh God!'

'Oh God anything in particular?'

'I . . .'

'You what?'

He swallowed. 'She's only twenty-six!'

John was baffled. 'I've never heard a man your age complain about a woman being twenty-six.'

'It's . . .'

'You'll love her. I promise. She's a sweetie. And really capable. Listen, Serena's booked us a table at your favourite restaurant for after the concert. Anyone you'd like to bring along?'

'No.'

'Right. Saturday's a date. Be ready for a pickup around 3 p.m.'

He lay on the spare-room bed, looking at flecks of rain on the windowpane. He stared at the ovolo cornice, following it along the edge of the ceiling into an alcove. He looked at the changing hue of the walls, a pale green with a hint of yellow in it. Here in the suburbs it was deadly quiet. He could lie on this bed for years and nobody would know. He allowed his thoughts to drift and ramble, snaring at this and that, Camilla weeding in her garden, the ceiling of the Duke's Hall where he had judged Academy competitions; and gently he pictured Katie's bedroom in that beamy cottage the morning after the fire, her room intact and door shut, a capsule of preservation attached to a blackened skeleton. They had found the three-year-old under the covers, curls on pillow, teddy clutched to her breast. She had died of a heart attack.

He glanced away. It was dangerous to lie down sometimes. Camilla was to blame. She had mentioned Peter, bringing it all back, entwining sorrows. He had managed to forget all that misery, pushing it away, locking it up. Black thoughts were to be struck off the edges of the mind.

He swung his legs off the bed.

An hour later he was standing on the kerb at Oxford Circus, gazing at the grey façades of buildings and at pigeons zooming from their niches across the heads of milling pedestrians. Moments later he was heading for the down escalator inside HMV.

If he couldn't play, at least he could listen. He had recalled Alfred Cortot's version of the Funeral March Sonata – not in his collection. Cortot had a special way with Chopin and to hear him again might be helpful. Philip was thinking positive, and anyway it was good to be out and about.

As ever, they were shrinking the Classical department. Glass partitions were on the move, breaking gaps into the rest of the store so that Classical's meek sound signature was garishly perforated by pop strains from neighbouring sections, colours running between Britney and Vivaldi. Diffident Angus stood behind the service counter, tracking obscure recordings for nerdy customers with his usual dandruffed brio. Everything was on offer. Box-set clearances, twofer discounts, bargain-table giveaways.

Philip strolled along the aisles getting a sense of the layout and absorbing the chocolatey posters of lovely divas whose physical charms eroticised the retail process: Oh, to possess a golden voice and a gorgeous pair. What talents! What pleasures for the world! Cellophane wraps sparkled in halogen light. Hi fi mags glittered on the shelf. He was nearly happy.

The Chopin rack was tightly packed with recordings by old frauds and younger rivals. He flicked through quickly, searching for the Cortot, first under 'Sonatas', then under 'Ballades'. Perhaps any unfamiliar recording would help. He needed to hear the piece as if from outside, agonised into life by some other poor sod.

Then he saw himself.

His own face stared back from the CD cover.

Philip frowned. He plucked the disc from the shelf.

He was puzzled and curious. Two years ago he recorded the Chopin Ballades for Cecilia, who went bust prior to release. Cecilia's catalogue was subsequently assigned to Planetarium, who did nothing. John had told him to let things stand until he had a new contract; so he forgot about these particular recordings.

Philip held the disc in his hand, vaguely disconcerted. Maybe there was a review somewhere. Unlikely, given the label.

He drifted off again, uncertain what to look for now. At the end of the aisle he came to a magazine section in racks on the wall. He hesitated a second before reaching down the new *Gramophone* edition. He flipped the glossy pages. The 'instrumental' review section seemed to have disappeared between a pull-out and 'Opera'. Suddenly, he saw his name in print: 'Chopin Ballades, Logos, £5.99'.

Philip looked over his shoulder in the direction of Angus and then moved behind a pillar. His heart fluttered with a mixture of vanity and dread. This was his first release in years. They had reviewed it all too promptly. He glanced to right and left, ashamed of his sickly excitement. He pulled open the magazine, flattened the spine, folded it over. He gripped the thing in both hands as if trying to control it.

Right from the very first line he sensed something odd. He would not skip ahead but read each sentence closely, hope on hold as he turned the page. There were neutral comments and impartial remarks and patches of lip-service that reflected his stature with preliminary conscientiousness, but the air of reserve grew chillier and chillier, and as he read on down the column unease became horror. The chosen comparisons were delicately destructive, favouring the recordings of Perahia and Zimmerman, and the summing-up was respectfully dismissive. But the last paragraph was awful. His playing, he read, had become 'an anatomy lesson'. He 'exposed everything and said nothing'. In this recording 'spontaneity has been supplanted by intellect, impulse by calculation'. 'On the evidence of this CD,' concluded the reviewer, 'Morahan's playing has wholly lost its former incandescence.'

He sighed, fending off the shock, and then, head swimming, read it again. He drank in every word, savoured every sentence, steeped himself in every phrase, as if to know what other people would be thinking of him.

He replaced the magazine and walked in a daze along the aisle, passing out of Classical into Jazz. He was soon standing between display boxes of Oscar Petersen and Dizzy Gillespie. After a moment's light-headedness, he went to the escalator and ascended to the ground floor.

He halted outside on Oxford Street, registering noise and smell, and then dragged himself back to the underground entrance. One had to get through it. One had to press on, keep going.

Back at home he put the kettle on. While it was boiling he frittered around nervously with sheet music in the living room. An hour later he sat dead still in the armchair, hands clubbed together, staring at the floor.

He was sitting in the same position at 9 p.m., amongst the shadows of a room lit only by lamps in the street outside.

Chapter Six

URSULA CAUGHT HIS EYE as she entered the room.

He sat with John Sampson in the Highgate millionaire's music room, surrounded by abstract paintings on bare brick and art books across coffee tables. Behind him reared a grand piano, white. Before him lay a view of the garden: Monet bridges over lily ponds, cherry blossom and forsythia, glancing light through the still bare limbs of an acacia tree. His hands were tightly clenched, John was handsomely beaming everywhere, and now as she entered in haste, coming through from the hallway (she knew she was late), he could see in a glance why John was so chuffed with her.

Ursula's face was flushed and yet she met him with the togetherness of high female confidence, aware of the effect – impossible to disown – of her looks on first-timers. She possessed a long-limbed figure of line and buoyancy, a radiant smile, twirling black hair. She stood before him like an unexpected gift or tribute, and was almost amused by the look on his face. For a moment she let Philip adjust to the spectacle, the smell of perfume, the gloss of hair, and readily followed whatever anybody else was saying. As John made introductory jokes about their client, she kept returning her eyes to Philip, looking for her chance to be more than a first impression.

They sat down on white chairs and sofas. John was manfully pleased with everything, particularly the Corot over the grand. Philip combated his unease with interlocked hands and did everything to avoid eye contact. John chatted on, drawing Ursula's attention, and Philip stole quick, disbelieving glances at his new agent. She sat forward on her chair, hair trailing in a cloud of curls to the small of her back, which rose from the bulb of her hips and bottom like the stem of an exotic plant. The tapering line of her forearm and wrist followed the long arc of her thigh. Her momentary glances were full of innocent goodwill.

He looked away. This was not what he wanted, not what he could bear. Ursula's beauty impaled his privacy. The very look of her appealed to a vitality he could no longer supply. Just to behold her was to experience, in a flash, generational redundancy. What could a perfect young woman know or care to know about the trials and tribulations of a medieval bachelor? He would have to talk to John about this later. He was desperate to be out of here.

All morning Philip had been trying to tell John he would cancel. He tried on the phone: John was too harassed. He tried in the limo: John was too talkative. He tried in the hallway of Bulmanion's mansion, but John was so urgently positive about this coup of a meeting, so buoyed by the concerts and publicity and the magnificent interior of this splendiferous house that it just seemed impossible. There was no right moment and no reprieve from this headlong charade and Philip knew anyway that John would never recover. Because Philip wasn't ill or dead or injured and John had invested so much time in setting up the concerts, and life was complicated enough without the nervous breakdowns of artists, besides which Philip was British, for Christ's sake: his only sane client! For Philip to cancel in these circumstances would be absolute bollocks.

So Philip had been thwarted and was now boxed into this false meeting, his frame of mind decaying, his social skills on holiday. Bulmanion's spectacular residence made it worse. Every grand room and chandeliered corridor and gilt-framed mirror breathed expectation, privileged opportunity. And Bulmanion had sought him out. 'Ex-City, hedge fund, or some bullshit,' said John. 'Cleaned up merrily, now worth a ton and is crazy about music. He's a veritable Medici, gets whole symphony orchestras to play in his country seat, sponsors the South Bank, lays on grants and scholarships, and now runs his own record label, specialising in guess what? Pianists! He's a great flapping angel for the music biz, and I've been stalking him like a puma.' John rubbed his hands. 'Business warlord turned Renaissance man. Don't be put off by his face.' Bulmanion's first record label was launched in the nineties. Endymion, he would say, was 'a learning curve, not about money – you lose money in classical – but values'. He was gearing up for a new venture, with a clearer philosophy, and seeking new artists. Colossally well informed about pianists in particular, he was keen to meet Philip. He thought Philip outstanding and under-recorded and envisaged a long-term arrangement of the greatest flexibility. Philip had resisted such commitments in the past, somewhat to his detriment, and John was determined that he grab the chance. 'You'll find him civilised and persuasive if you don't look too closely at his face.'

'I don't like business warlords.'

'You'll love Frank. He's your number-one fan.'

John was convinced, if they met, that Frank's knowledgeable enthusiasm would overwhelm Philip. Philip's misgivings had meanwhile turned to rank antipathy.

'Can we cancel the meeting?' he had pleaded on the phone that morning.

'If you cancel the meeting, I'll slit my throat and bleed to death and leave a suicide note blaming you.'

'I'm not signing anything.'

'Just come!'

He sat in his seat, staring hard at the wall. They were waiting for Bulmanion the three of them, waiting for the lord and master to arrive and shower them with the gold dust of patronage. He could get up and go, just scramble, but John's mumblings to Ursula paralysed him somehow.

His agent brimmed with health and dynamism and sheer love of the job. His brilliant blue eyes glittered for Ursula. He listened in animation to some piece of office news and used the thrust of his dimpled jaw to affirm what she said. Because John was always scuttling back and forth – Milan, London, New York – to find him physically incarnated in any one place was almost uncanny. John did not have time to be in one place. John's time was so preciously and infinitely divided between the demands of his clients and the web of his activities that he had virtually ceased to exist in human form. He was ubiquitously absent and dynamically omnipresent. In some ways he was too switched on for ordinary social consumption, rushing through the day like a super-charged tennis pro, stretching, running, smashing hard. He had used cocaine in the past to good effect and would deploy it in the future. Ursula he clearly adored. A fabulous acquisition for the agency. With her full bosom and his dimple jaw what promoter could resist them? What artist could resist them? Young pianists would be smitten at a glance.

Philip gazed at Ursula and wondered what was in it for her. She had been catapulted into a milieu of the super-talented and frequently famous, but was it enough to be mere decorous scene-setting for those after-concert parties, an agency fillip for the brand-name clients? It was hard to believe the hand-holding and neurosis management would interest her for long.

John slipped off to the loo for a moment.

Ursula turned to face him, steering her legs round and flipping her hair back. She smiled uncertainly. She could see he was uneasy and no doubt felt uncomfortable herself.

'I'm so looking forward to the concert.'

Philip inhaled deeply.

'D'you get very nervous?'

He frowned.

She seemed to take this as a 'yes'. 'It's such an honour to meet you. I've always admired your playing so much.'

Philip forced himself to sit up a little.

'Isn't this place incredible?'

He nodded.

She glanced over her shoulder. Her gaze was now very serious. She seemed troubled.

'I do hope this isn't an imposition.'

'Um . . .'

'If you think it doesn't work out with me, please say. I'd love to represent you, but your wishes are paramount. I don't want to come between you and John. I just want to help.'

She looked at him with sweet sincerity. She had taken a risk in saying this and it seemed impossible not to come to her aid.

'I'm sure it'll be fine,' he nodded.

Her smile intensified to a new level. The warmth of her expression he found unsettling. She seemed already to have nurturing feelings in reserve for him. He looked awkwardly around, amazed that he had capitulated so easily. Things were happening that he had no control over. Was she very kind, or was she just handling him? Was he just product now, to be stroked and schmoozed by personable executives, or did she really care, and if so, why? What could she possibly want with a crabby bachelor like him, a bespectacled relic, a man of self-defeating self-knowledge and no horizons beyond the ceaseless toil of his trade? Just to look at her was to feel in a glance the immunity of her sparkling youth to his shelved middle age.

John was back now, rubbing his hands and checking his watch and glancing nervously at Ursula and solidly at Philip. He pointed in the direction of a pair of loudspeakers beyond the piano. 'You want to hear those guys, Pip. Two hundred grand's worth of high fidelity. Amazing.'

He tugged around to look over his shoulder.

'British designed, God bless us. Bloke called Williams, lives in a shack in Suffolk or something. Total nutter.'

He nodded, unable to take anything in. Ursula was now looking at him with some concern and he found himself wondering in retaliation what reckless acts of submission she would perform for her lovers, what picturesque pairings she would instigate with the trendy young males whose lust she inspired.

They heard him first, barking orders in the hall with humorous menace. The grand vestibule took up the sound of his voice, distributing will power to the four corners of the house. Bulmanion entered the room and moved into their midst before anyone had time to stand up.

'Have you had tea?'

John smiled appeasingly.

'God, bloody hell!'

He swished off back to the door and bellowed down the hallway. 'Jeremy! Guests! Tea! Music room!'

He returned quickly, huffing theatrically, his hand already extended in Philip's direction.

'It's a great honour to meet you. I'm so pleased you could come.'

Philip rose and had his hand shaken.

Bulmanion nodded quick hellos at Ursula and John and reversed on to a sofa. He ran a finger around his cheek, as if to clear thoughts, and then launched in quickly. 'I think you are one of the great artists of our time,' he intoned. 'I'm immensely grateful that you've agreed to see me. I'm wealthy but I take no one for granted. I wanted to meet here because this room is a shrine to the sort of magnificent playing one hears on your records. I've sat in that chair and listened more times than I can remember to your Brahms and Liszt and everything else.'

He seemed to halt rhetorically. His eyes were fastened on a point in the air. His mouth ran agape.

Philip looked at him in amazement. Bulmanion was a rotund and emperor-like figure with a sack of a jaw that slumped on his collar and Humpty Dumpty legs that hung weakly from the sofa. He wore a fleece, tracksuit bottoms and open-toed sandals.

'I'm interested in artists,' he announced, 'not record companies. Recordings, not labels. Music heritage, not marketing. My mission will never be corporate. I aim rather higher, or so I like to think.'

John and Ursula came nervously to the edge of their seats, as if in support of their patron's candour.

'I want to make possible things that are not possible for conventional record companies.'

This was his rallying call. This was why they were all here.

'Forget the balance sheet.'

Philip was unblinking.

John nodded wisely.

'You see' – Bulmanion cleared his throat oratorically – 'so many of the great artists have been underserved by the record biz.'

He had the gravelly voice of a boardroom conquistador, the vowels of a football-club owner. His authority in the realm of classical music was utterly incongruous.

'You, for example.' His gaze was unflinching.

Philip was unsettled. 'I haven't been underserved!'

'I would say that you have.'

John leaned forward. 'Frank isn't . . .'

'I've done OK.'

'Yes, of . . .'

'Grand Prix du Disc. Diapason d'Or.'

'Very good.'

'Gramophone Record of the Year.'

'A magnificent recording!'

Bulmanion nodded emphatically.

Philip stared back at him.

'What are you trying to tell me?'

49

'Given your stature, you've been undermarketed, badly positioned, under-released.'

Philip regarded his host irritably. 'I've been bloody difficult!'

'You're entitled to be bloody difficult.'

'Am I, indeed?'

Bulmanion calmly smiled.

John leaned into the conversation. Frank was clearly inexperienced at dealing with artists and somewhat socially abrupt. His own legendary emollience was in order. 'Frank has spotted something key. You hate recording, but whenever you go into the studio the results are marvellous. You're brilliant in spite of yourself. The problem is that without forward-planning those recordings are a series of one-offs. The repertoire is fragmented, the portrait of an artist incomplete. Frank's idea is to provide the most flexible partnership fully responsive to your creative impulses so that, in a completely spontaneous way, you can do yourself justice and your recordings can do you justice.' He smiled definitively.

Philip glanced sharply at Ursula. She reciprocated his glance. Her expression was one of humble complicity with whatever he chose to say.

He stared them both down. 'I have never done myself justice. That is the condition of my life. Make of it what you will.'

'You could record whatever you liked, whenever you liked.'

John was direct. 'How many record companies would offer that?'

Philip could not believe he had to go through this meeting for the sake of a deal he would never sign on the eve of a concert he was determined to cancel. He was annoyed about everything now.

'Very flattering,' he said voicelessly.

'I'm not trying to flatter you.' Bulmanion was level. 'I'm trying to register my commitment.'

'Yes.' He felt like a different person today. 'Probably I'm not ready.'

John laughed uneasily and swapped looks with Frank.

The businessman remained calm. 'The frequency of releases would be dictated by your timetable, your musical agenda.'

'I mightn't be ready for years.'

'Come on, Philip!' John was suddenly exasperated.

'That would be a loss,' said Bulmanion flatly.

'Not in my opinion.'

'Art is long and life is short,' said Frank.

'Art is bloody difficult.'

'You're at a vintage period in your life as a pianist. Maturity, vision . . .'

'I'll be the judge of that.'

Frank nodded, as if in acknowledgement of Philip's adverse temper. He could draw the meeting to a halt if he chose. As a rule, people were more in need of his money than he was of their goodwill.

'I want to be responsible for moving you from the cult fringe to the canonical centre.'

John made no facial response, but did not demur, either. Only Ursula seemed uncomfortable on Philip's behalf. Her posture became more erect, as if in disdain of such terms.

'Cult fringe,' said Philip ominously.

'The reality of your position in posterity.'

This was too much. He had no need of such home truths today. Why was he here? 'Oh, I see. You can do that, can you? De-cult-fringe me?'

'With your help.'

'What Frank means is that you're not a corporate pianist,' said John tensely.

'Well, thank you very much!'

His agent looked darkly into his palms. He had not anticipated this kind of prickliness. He offered Philip an expression of unsmiling seriousness so as to leave him in no doubt of the critical importance of the meeting.

'Listen,' said Bulmanion judicially. He halted for a moment. He knew his mind and wanted others to know it, but as Philip later realised this was not the egotism of power so much as the unvarnished manner of a man who never expected to be liked for himself. He spoke at length, not to proselytise, but to expand an understanding. He did not trouble to 'sell' his ideas because he perceived them as facts.

'You're an artist. Your whole life is music. That's as it should be. What you don't see is the slowly turning wheel of musical fashion. We see it, or think we do, because it's a function of our perspective. Modern marketing. An oscillation between style and substance. Classical-music recording is one of the few areas where you can't fake it. The diametric opposite of pop – where you absolutely must. The listener is so sophisticated, the product so incorruptible that style can never triumph over substance. Even so, audiences crave contemporary talent with something distinctive to offer, and that something is more often than not a kind of technical charisma. Awesome virtuosity has always been a calling card. You don't get in the door unless there's something sensational about the mechanism, some standout quality that tells the listener, "Wow! With this kind of equipment the unprecedented can happen." So every few years there's a Kissin, or an Ivo Pogorelich, or some other whizz-kid. These guys get pulled to the fore and set in the limelight, and suddenly everyone else is made to look kind of "also ran". The biz has to have tentpole newcomers. But they're rarely the best or the most enduring, and what we're now seeing is a thirst for true greatness as opposed to marketable panache. The mass-media culture is so junky and reprocessed there's an upsurge in the need for profundity.' He paused, enjoying this last phrase. 'People want an older kind of pianist. Performances from artists who are miraculously untainted by the emotional shallowness of con-temporary culture. It's a definite trend. And that's where you come in. Because you're in a line with the three great British pianists of the last century: Curzon, Solomon, and Hess. Music history is ready for you to take centre stage.'

Philip looked away in distaste. This was a perspective he found utterly trite.

Bulmanion was thoughtful. 'The public domain has limited reputation-carrying space. It's like a highway, with only so many lanes, which is why in every branch of the arts there are great talents unjustly on the fringe, awaiting their moment of motorway access to the brand-name freeway. Then suddenly the time arrives when a talent can be slipped into the zeitgeist, because the opening is there, and the talent fits the opening.' Bulmanion regarded him with a profound expression. 'Once on the freeway you have irreversible fame, an asset nobody can take from you, and the inherent value of what you do is disseminated to the widest audience. Philip, it's my perception that your time has truly come. I see it as my role to create that access.'

There was a moment of silence in which John waited respectfully and appreciatively, Ursula's melting gaze swung from Frank to

Philip, and Philip sat inertly, hands clamped to the ends of his chair arms.

The comparison with Solomon he found suffocating, unbearable. He looked askance. He was not a pianist any more. That was the problem. He was a distressed fifty-two-year-old man with nothing in his life to cling on to. They might have been talking about someone else.

'Maybe . . .' Ursula was hesitant. Her hands moved gracefully, as if to break in an idea before it was uttered. 'I totally agree with what Frank says, but I think that maybe Philip is worried that we are trying to canonise – to use Frank's word – recordings that haven't earned their reputation yet. Which puts pressure on Philip.' She looked at Philip, collecting her thoughts. 'I mean, Myra Hess didn't worry about ending up in the Great Pianist series every time she recorded a Beethoven piano sonata. If Frank is right, Philip will have a brilliant posterity on the strength of his occasional recordings, rather than absolutely everything he commits to disc under a new label . . .'

He stared at her. She was beautiful. She was articulate. It got worse and worse.

'Correct,' said Bulmanion, adroitly incorporating Ursula at once, and suggesting a dialectical process of evaluation so conscientious that Philip did not need to think for himself. 'My concern is to be on call when Philip is doing his best stuff. Retrospectively every pianist has a golden period. Look at Solomon in the early fifties. Richter in the sixties. Pollini in the seventies.'

'Maybe I've had mine.'

'I think you're there now.'

Philip's face creased up. This was too much. Their words were hurting him.

'Is my view completely irrelevant?'

John tensed.

'Of course not,' said Bulmanion more gently.

'God,' Philip gasped. 'I really admire people like you! You have to deal with hard cases like me.'

'That's because there's more at stake than pretty conversation,' said the financier. 'You have great talent.'

'Philip!' said John breathily. 'Frank wants to record the three concerts as the basis for a CD sequence on the great sonatas. I think it's a fantastic idea, nobody's ever done it before, a themed sonata series, mixed composers, mixed eras, with maybe a biennial concert series and a tour to drive the releases.'

'One small problem,' said Philip, looking away.

'What?'

'I'm going to cancel the concerts.'

John's head turned slowly.

'I don't think I can play next Wednesday.'

There was a silence, a snapshot of nothing.

'We've got to talk.' He covered his face. 'I'm going to have to cancel.'

Ursula's hand slid from her thigh on to the sofa cushion.

'Excuse me, ladies and gentlemen.' Frank rose from his seat. 'I'll be with you in a second.'

He pulled the door shut behind him. They heard him calling someone in the corridor.

John glanced over his shoulder at the door. Then he looked at Philip with an expression of needling incredulity.

Philip remained embedded in the armchair. His expression was frozen.

'What's going on?'

'I'm indisposed.'

'You're not indisposed!'

'Can't play.'

Ursula let out a deep breath, almost a gasp. 'Has something happened?'

He could not answer this. He could hardly speak.

There was a peculiar silence, a stock-taking silence as John tensely figured his options and wondered how to proceed. He looked glassily at Philip, maintaining the pressure of his astonishment. Ursula glanced discreetly back and forth, panic in her eyes. Philip remained stubbornly haunted and fraught.

'What d'you mean, "can't play"?'

'I've been trying to tell you.'

'So tell me now.'

He shook his head. He was suddenly unwilling to explain. He gazed off in the direction of the garden.

John pulled himself to his feet and passed slowly around the coffee table, hands in pockets. His face was distorted by the sense of emergency. He bit his underlip, eyes flickering uncertainly. Suddenly he spun round, almost like a sharp-shooter. His gaze was burning. 'Hah!'

They both looked at him in surprise.

'You're not . . .' He composed himself, tried to slow down, swallowed. 'You're not upset by that silly monkey's arse of a review?'

He flinched.

'Philip!'

He looked away, feeling foolish.

'Is that what this is about! For God's sake, it's a wonderful recording! A magnificent recording! You can't let some idiot reviewer cramp your style.'

Ursula smiled anxiously.

'Water off a duck's back, Pip. Come on!'

Ursula leaned forward, her hands clenched together. 'Were you very upset?'

Philip looked at her, fed on her sympathy in spite of himself.

'If every artist bunked off every time there was a duff review, we'd have no industry.' John hoiked his trousers. 'I'd be flat out of a job. Those boys think they're God, but they're just two-bit hacks scratching a living.'

'I've taken a wrong turn,' he gasped. His voice was thick. 'Something's gone out of my playing.'

'Oh, Phil! Which side of the frigging four-poster did you get out of?'

Philip shook his head.

John laughed nervously. 'You pick your moments. Do us a favour.'

'I . . .'

'Let's say for now you'll play those concerts. As soon as we're out of here, we'll go to a pub, have a drink and a chat. You've got worked up about something that doesn't matter.'

'It matters to him, John.'

'I can't play any more!'

John was super-tense. 'I just need to end the meeting on a constructive note!'

'I just need to end the meeting!'

'Philip, Jesus! D'you really have to piss on his enthusiasm? This

guy is total gold dust. Your fairy godmother disguised as a fat toad.'
He smiled mock-manically.

There were tears in his eyes.

'What's the problem?' said Ursula.

He blinked in her direction.

'D'you need someone to talk to?'

John cottoned on. 'Talk to us.'

'I appreciate . . .'

John nodded intensely. 'Family problems?'

Philip shook his head.

'Oh . . . um . . . is your mother . . . is she . . .?'

'My mother died years ago. I have no family.'

'Oh sorry. Listen, Pip . . .'

'I appreciate your sympathy.'

'Well, yeah . . . just that . . . this is such a great opportunity. You know, the concerts were a bit of a fluke.'

Philip looked up in pain.

'Well, not a fluke, obviously.' John crushed his face with his hands, stress-exhausted. 'You have no idea what goes on behind the scenes.'

There was a pause. Philip wiped his eye. 'What d'you mean fluke?'

John drove the fingers of both hands through his hair. 'Philip, I love you, I admire you, I'd do anything for you, but the business is relentless. You won't let me forward-plan. We've had no record contract in three years. There's a new wave of competition-winners and plastic Chinese wunderkinder and Russian cyborgs who play Islamey with the backs of their hands. The industry's in chronic recession. You have a loyal public, immense critical stature . . .'

'Till yesterday.'

'But your international career is dwindling. And there's a feeling abroad, um, I don't know, that you're . . .'

Philip looked away. 'Go on! What?'

'. . . resting on your laurels.'

He was amazed to hear this from John, of all people.

'It's a fact. Great pianists are immortal but careers come and go!'

'So I owe it to you I've been sponsored for three South Bank recitals which are all sold out?'

There was a moment's silence as John stared flatly at him. 'You owe it to Frank.'

'Frank?'

'Your angel.'

'What?'

'South Bank sponsor with uncustomary leverage.'

'A sponsor!'

'You know this. Promoter, sponsor, record company.'

'I need to be told who my sponsors are!'

'You don't give a flying toss. You like to think venues are allocated according to some system of interpretative merit. But there's a lot of shoving and pushing because the whole game's so competitive and Frank's sway made the difference. Don't ask me how. He wants you on the platform and in the recording studio and can make it happen. Isn't that good enough?'

Philip gazed at his agent in astonishment. Suddenly he owed everything to a rich amateur. 'One minute I'm a so-called "great pianist", the next my career's dangling by a thread!'

'Which you seem keen to snip through.'

'So which is it? Am I a "has-been" all of a sudden?'

John's face darkened at the testiness of his tone.

Philip subsided in his chair, hand against his forehead. John's sense of critical pressure had connected at last. Beyond the enthusiasm, the flattery and courtship was the usual abyss of uncertainty that dogged every pianist's life. The flip side of opportunity was abrupt marginalisation. One had to compete, one had to prevail, or the world moved on. There was nothing he could say. Common sense could not explain what was happening to him.

'Would you play for me?' said Ursula.

He could see the suspense in her eyes.

'I . . .'

'It's to do with the playing, isn't it?'

John glanced carefully at Ursula.

Her lips parted.

Philip was steeply uncomfortable. Even the simplest propositions were impossible to construe.

'Would you play for me? I could come to your home.'

His lips were dry.

'I remember your Amsterdam recital so well. Schubert, Brahms. Ever since then it's been a kind of dream to meet you.' She hesitated, her neck muscles working. 'I think it's terrible that someone who has given so much should feel as you do now.'

Her sympathy was distressing. He could hardly bear to look at her.

Ursula's face was a picture of compassion. Her fraught eyebrows dramatised a deep concern. 'It's difficult for you to know how much your playing means to other people. You communicate everything to us. We can only receive. We can never give back the same thing. Words are useless. But how you play a certain phrase means so much to a listener. What you do goes to the heart and people are so grateful for that.'

John rubbed his cheek and looked at the floor.

'Let me hear you, please! You need to play for somebody who really cares.'

The directness of her appeal was unendurable. He would dissolve in her kindness if he were not careful; and whereas it would be a relief to dissolve, to disintegrate, it was not something to do here.

He nodded tightly, holding on for dear life.

He felt the heat of her gaze on the side of his face.

John was consumed in his own thoughts at the end of the sofa, hands worked together on his lap.

Philip turned towards her and offered a look of tacit appreciation and, for a second, he felt her acceptance of this look as a kind of pull on him, as though she had drawn something into her self. He had no idea what. He experienced, momentarily, the balm of an intense relief.

Bulmanion cleared his throat before opening the door, and then came into the room in such a way as not to notice what was being said, or what he might be interrupting. The housekeeper followed him in with a tray.

'Sorry about that,' he said, resuming his position on the sofa. He gazed airily about him, not wishing to impose. 'Jeremy's a little short-staffed today.'

John glanced carefully at Philip.

'Drop of tea, miss?' said the housekeeper.

Ursula drew herself up, making an arrangement of trailing hair, shoulders and bosom that was properly formal. 'Oh, thank you!'

Philip was left to exchange glances with Frank, which relaxed the situation momentarily. Frank seemed to have grasped the mood in the room. He had a better sense of the personality of the pianist he admired and was more careful.

'Philip's upset about the review.' John rubbed his eye.

'Of course,' said Frank. 'The review is bunkum.'

Philip looked up in surprise.

'A critical travesty penned by a mincing cretin. Those goons all have their petty agendas. I mean these days it's all "my prose is purpler than yours". Maurice Venables, for example.'

'Maurice is fine. Maurice likes me,' said Philip.

'He was probably on holiday, and Andrew Dungface farms you out to those snapping curs Baldwin Cocker or Patrick Peabody. Cocker is a waffle merchant, and Peabody a hatchet man.'

John shook his head in amusement.

'You've been lucky, hitherto. All the gods get desecrated sooner or later. Look what they said about Horowitz – "a mere show-man". Brendel – "too intellectual". Kempff – technically "not quite world class", according to some arrogant German bureaucrat posing as a critic. Bolet was "too measured" when the poor old bugger was in his seventies, Richter "too hard". Perahia "too hygienic"; Kissin too God knows bloody what. They're always trying to flip the apple cart. Daft eunuchs, the lot of them.'

John laughed out loud.

Philip smiled, in spite of himself.

'It's a great recording,' said Frank. 'It only adds to my determi-nation and excitement. Listen, John will go over the details with you. I'm using a new business model. You become a copyright owner in the disc, with a say on packaging, and reissues. I've got foreign distribution all sorted. We move faster and lighter on our feet than the majors, who are so busy firing people they don't know what's going on, and my team are first-rate. There's a new tech-nology initiative through a subsidiary company and we're hooking up with this Williams chap, who designed these extraordinary speakers.' With a grand gesture Bulmanion plucked the music remote from his side table and clicked it in the direction of the wall.

Piano sound erupted from the loudspeakers. John was suddenly alert, Ursula startled.

The image was gargantuan, crystal clear, the surface immaculate. Waves of arpeggios rolled up and down in the bass. A trumpet-like clarion came in in the treble. Semiquavers showered the air like particles of light. They were immersed in sound, surrounded by glints and sparkles, a stirring envelope of shattering piano tone enhanced to an unbelievable degree so that one seemed to be in the centre of the composer's mind, at the teeming source of inspiration, and as the texture became more complicated, the myriad skeins were held in high-resolution clarity by the astonishing loudspeakers, an interlocking tracery of brilliance that dazed and confounded simultaneously. The music came to its first cadence, like a detonation of grandeur, before releasing the right hand, which now swooped off with spread wings, soaring on its path like an eagle cruising the thermals and gusts of an immense canyon, whilst the left hand rose in pillars of golden sound beneath it.

Bulmanion listened with transfixed radiance. John shook his head in near disbelief. Ursula was rapt, as though enslaved by a masseur's masterful hands. Philip, too, was utterly captivated. He was listening to himself.

When the track ended, John burst into eager applause. Bulmanion clicked off the player and put the remote on the table.

'That was you, wasn't it?' said Ursula.

Philip could barely acknowledge this.

'Yours will be the best-engineered CDs in the marketplace,' said Bulmanion sonorously. 'In a hundred years your recorded legacy will sound crystal clear and be the pride of connoisseurs.'

John looked at him with brilliant eyes, urging him to embrace the vision.

There followed some talk about the speakers. Frank had gone into the matter thoroughly before writing a cheque for two hundred grand. John nodded sympathetically. It was a pleasure to discuss very expensive things on apparently equal terms with Frank.

Philip was paralysed by the playing of another self, a self he hardly recognised. The recording was fifteen years old and blazed with temperament and technique. Everything was so shaped and definite and confident and it frankly amazed him that he had once been the pianist who played like that. The strength of the playing lingered in his mind, overlapping something half forgotten, as if a torch from the past had been aimed at the present and amongst the shadows was the lost outline of what it had felt to be thirty-five, with a younger man's fresher connection to the music. Listening to that earlier self he realised how much he had changed, and how irretrievable were the reflexes and impulses of early confidence, as though the means to play like that was driven by a need to express that was now less acute, or more qualified by a subtler sense of the music. The past was more cut off than even he had realised. The man who had achieved that sound was somebody else, someone he could be no longer. He felt a curious surge of rivalry with his younger self. He could do as well now, could do more. By different means he could achieve that powerful unity of effect. It would take a lot, absolutely everything, but this was the thing he was born with: the will to try harder, to make, once and for all, an indelible impression.

He had a need to be on his own.

'I hope you'll come to the concert,' he said suddenly.

John looked at him in disbelief.

Bulmanion smiled. 'I booked my tickets long ago.'

Philip rose from his seat quickly.

'Thank you for seeing me. I apologise for my ill temper. It's a very attractive proposition that you offer. I'd like to discuss it, obviously, with John and perhaps we can come back to you shortly.'

Bulmanion stood up solemnly. 'It would be a privilege to work with you.'

John's beaming face glistened with relief.

Philip turned to face his agents. 'John, you're the best. Sorry I've been such a handful. Ursula, I don't deserve you.'

She smiled at him with lovely warmth.

'Jeremy will take you wherever you wish to go.' Frank guided his guest to the door.

Soon he was on the back seat of a Mercedes. The big car made its smooth way along Villiers Lane. Philip listened in his mind's ear to the Rachmaninov prelude that Frank had played to him, as if he were playing it now.

Chapter Seven

THE DAY OF THE concert started with a phone call from Cynthia Erhardt. She wished him luck and begged him always to relax the upper body and foot arches, so that energy could 'come through to all of us'. He received flowers from the John Sampson Agency with a note from Ursula, voicemails from Laurent Mattier Brzeska of the London Piano Competition, and from Olivier Desormand of the Conservatoire in Paris. Everyone knew about the concert. The Guildhall's Alistair Banville said his pupils were coming. There would be London-based concert pianists, Frank's production team, sundry figures from the British musical establishment, critics, the public, and friends.

He rose late and wandered around his bedroom getting dressed. He was neither confident nor nervous. He was in the pre-concert groove of strained determination, a familiar state. One sleep-walked through all the intervening stages of the day incapable of doing anything except become tensely ready. He booked his cab, checked his shirt and tailcoat.

For the last three days he had practised without break, dawn to dusk, an onslaught. He wanted to be absolutely fit, as assured as possible in the technical security of his playing. Inspiration would come if it chose to, and if it chose not to he would take his own advice to Vadim and get through it anyway. Because you had to keep playing. The best-prepared concerts could misfire. If preparation were no proof of success, self-doubt did not mean failure.

He had not allowed himself to think sideways or backwards. Sleep had come to him steeply and profoundly on the Saturday night, and after rising late on Sunday he had begun to feel his old self again. He practised with a consuming attention to sound. He allowed his hands to reacquaint themselves in super slow motion with the topography of each piece.

'What d'you do on the day?' Derek had asked him at their last lunch. Derek had wanted to film the behind-the-scenes run-up to performance as part of their pitch to the BBC, but Philip had declined, not wishing to be distracted for so trivial a cause.

He had practised, of course, limbering up with exercises before the final run-through at QEH. And mid-morning he went to the bookshelf and took down a volume of Chopin portraits. He turned to the Bison daguerreotype, taken months before the composer's death. Chopin was posed in a photographer's studio, seated with his hands on his lap. Even in the mottled grey of the picture his illness was blatant. The looks of a thirty-nine-year-old man had almost vanished behind the swellings of oedema and the tension of pain. He was mentally and physically ravaged by consumption. Famous, but too young to die, Chopin faced the camera with the barely suppressed despair of one who knows the awful significance of a formal portrait in this state of health. Peace would come before very long, he knew; death would release him from the burden of illness and incurable nostalgia. This he bitterly accepted, and was letting it be seen. But Philip saw something more in the faded old photo, something he had never really noticed before. Although on edge with discomfort, it seemed as if Chopin, when the shutter fell, had wavered a fraction, his sternness faltering, his eyes following the train of a thought on its way across space-time into a realm that pain had never obliterated, the secret sanctuary of a poetic distraction from which, in the short space of his life, he had drawn immortal inspiration.

Philip closed the volume gently. He sat at his desk for several minutes.

He arrived at the South Bank by cab at a quarter to seven. He came through the lobby of the Queen Elizabeth Hall and made his way through the empty auditorium to the dressing rooms behind the stage. There were people in the anteroom moving chairs and shifting music stands. He checked in with the floor manager before disappearing into his room. He unpacked shirt, tailcoat and anti-perspirant. His cigarette pack he put carefully on a shelf, together with house keys and spectacle case. He could see from the clock it was ten to seven. The room was a comfortable cell: upright piano, vinyl chairs, ashtray, wall mirror.

He stripped down in the washroom and showered. The tingle of water on his skin brought everything to the surface. His naked body was like the essential self he would bare on the concert platform.

At ten past seven he stood in his bathrobe smoking a cigarette. Every inhalation banished nervousness for about thirty seconds. He dressed carefully and methodically. The shirt was fresh and cool; his tailcoat eased on comfortably. He fixed his cuffs and combed his hair, checking the results in a mirror. The whiteness of the shirt improved the colour of his eyes. He polished the lenses of his spectacles and slid them back on.

After a moment's hesitation he sat in one of the easy chairs and bathed his face in his hands. He had no inclination to touch the keys. Instead he swallowed, felt his heart hammering against his chest. Adrenalin seemed to attack him in squirts below the midriff, and then in warm waves of sensation – a diffusion of aches. This was the sickness of his profession. He inhaled and exhaled deeply, rubbed at his fingers and palms.

There was a knock on the door.

'Come in,' he said, rising.

Arthur England bared his teeth in a jovial smile before the two men collided in a hug.

'Traffic's ghastly.'

He could smell the old composer's suit: mothballs and fusty wool.

'Didn't expect to see you.'

'Wouldn't miss it for the world. Great Scott, what a journey! There's absolute blind buggery on the A34 at the moment. You're looking sharp.'

Philip smiled as best he could. One was supposed to manage well-wishers through the riot of nerves. He would always make a special effort for Arthur.

'I won't come backstage afterwards if you don't mind. I'm too old to stand in a queue.'

'Is someone with you?'

'Oh yes, nurses and doctors and chairlifts and Zimmer frames. I'm fine, actually. Can still hobble about. I've got my driver, bless him, one of Oswald's young swains.'

'You're looking fantastic!'

Arthur smiled with doddery pride. 'Ninety, to be precise.'

His face had been pink for years. His moustache and eyebrows were well groomed, making up for the gizzardly neck and snaggly teeth. His buoyancy was illimitable.

'Philip, I want you to pay me a visit in the next few days. Three-line whip.'

'Love to.'

'I'm having a shindig for Konstantine Serebriakov end of next week.'

Philip struggled to concentrate, his nerves surging. 'I had no idea you were friends.'

'He's a relatively recent acquisition. Nineteen sixty-four, I think. Pretty good at the ivories, old Konstantine. He gave the world premier of my piano concerto, as a matter of fact.'

'How wonderful!'

'It's his birthday and he's not well. But we'll have an amusing time if you come and see us. Oswald will cook and prattle gaily. Fine wines, stiff walks for the under-eighties. Usual form. The grounds are lovely at the moment. May blossom everywhere. God, but isn't London diabolical? Suppose I'm too old for this lark. I'll slip off now. I can see you're straining at the leash.' He put a hand on the door. 'Project my way. Back of the stalls on the right. Bring the house down, as usual.'

He waved and went out.

By now the crescent-shaped foyer of the Queen Elizabeth Hall would be thronged with people and smelling of ladies' scent and filter coffee. Queues at programme kiosks. Last drinks at the bar. Members of the musical middle classes cruising around, spotting friends, snaffling cake. And now the gong at last, yanking up his pulse, the final tolling. A thousand men and women would take their places in the next few minutes, bustling in, getting adjusted to the space, the sense of occasion, the view of a lone piano on the stage.

His hands were sweaty and freezing cold. He dabbed them with a hanky and stared at the upright and seconds later was groping for the volumes in his case, suddenly convinced that all those notes would fly out of his mind if he didn't have a look at the score for the millionth time. He sat going over it, like an actor whispering lines backstage.

Going on to the platform was like dying. No one went with you. The stage manager knocked on the door and peeped in.

Philip's head cleared as he stood. His hands felt clammy. One had at least to *seem* confident.

He got himself ready while the stage manager stood outside, walkie-talkie in hand. He had the thin lips of a men's-store shop assistant and smiled economically as Philip emerged. He spoke to the auditorium usherettes and to lights, coordinating the final count-down as they went along the corridor and across to the stage door. Philip touched his bow tie and fiddled with his cuffs as he walked, squeezing the hanky in his pocket to dry his palms. They came up to the curtain slowly, waiting for the all-clear. His heart beat faster at the familiar noise of the audience – a muffled din – beyond the curtain. One could tell from the weight of sound that the auditorium was packed. He inhaled deeply against the final crisis of nerves. Suddenly the house lights lowered, and the aery swell of a thousand voices sank in layers to a respectful murmur. They were ready for him.

He stared at the curtain.

The stage manager took up position, hand at the curtain's edge, all set to pull back.

It condensed inside him.

'Doors closed. OK, thank you. Ready, sir?'

He pulled the hanky from his pocket, dabbed his forehead.

He was giddy, not feeling good. Not the right feeling.

God, he thought.

The stage manager nodded in confirmation, he nodded back.

The curtain opened for him and he strode across the threshold, into another dimension, the roof of the hall zooming up, the rear stalls rising way back, and as he strode up the ramp into the spotlight haze he could see a multitude of hands rising to greet him, and he could hear the crackle of applause beginning on the right and rippling across the auditorium sideways, like a wave, rebounding and redoubling into a barrage of acclamation as he reached the edge of the stage. He saw the instrument standing there like an Andalusian bull, rollers glinting, keyboard shining.

The greeting increased in volume, reaching its enthusiastic maximum as he came centre stage, an outburst of sound, almost violently partisan, and as he turned towards the rising tiers of faces, going all the way to the back of the hall, he sensed the presence of friends, a congregation of fans, an audience very consciously devoted to the sight of him, his live presence. He looked at them all, heart pounding, temples throbbing, and bowed gravely, hand on a corner of the piano. He saw smiling faces, familiar faces, all staring back at him, and still they kept on, frantically clapping, determined to bathe him in a long and demonstrative approbation, and he bowed again, to the right, to the left, to the centre, and nodded in acknowledgement, and felt the din abate, a sudden drop, a steep decline, the spasm over, tension returning, the gap of a few moments in which he would sit down and adjust the stool, and they would watch in readiness, and the noise of welcome would taper to a hush.

He stepped back, turned to face the instrument, found himself sinking on the stool, flicking his tails, placing his juddering foot by the pedal, taking his hanky from his pocket, clenching it again. There were muffled coughs and throat-clearings to his right.

He looked at the white keys, felt the attention of the audience as a searing heat on the side of his face, sensed the moment coming at last. He stared swimmingly at the Steinway logo on the keyboard lid and breathed in deeply, seeking a centre. And then he knew, he knew easily. A morbid relief went through his limbs, which gave him a kind of weak will, a weary strength. He looked at the shiny keyboard as if to be dead sure, once again, and then rose.

He walked dizzily to the edge of the stage, legs weakening. He looked up at the audience, capturing every pair of eyes. The place was packed.

'Ladies and gentlemen.'

The sound of his voice was diffuse, bodiless. He could hardly hear himself.

Hundreds of people were staring at him.

'For reasons that are impossible to describe, I have decided that I cannot play tonight. I ask your forgiveness and understanding.'

There was a mass exhalation. He could see the shock in people's faces.

He walked across the stage, eyes averted, and as he descended the ramp one man clapped in solidarity. Once through the curtain he ran to his changing room. He needed to be out of the building before anyone caught up with him. He grabbed the music off the upright, chucked things in his case, switched out of his tailcoat and into his jacket. Down the corridor to the right he found an escape door, pushed the bar and slipped out. He hesitated on the concourse. He madly feared someone would be pursuing him. He walked swiftly along the esplanade past the doors of the Royal Festival Hall and ran up the steps to the footbridge. He covered the Thames at a brisk pace and was soon breathlessly descending on the Embankment side. He took out his mobile and clicked it off, wound off his bow tie and loosened his shirt button.

A few minutes later he stood at the bar of a pub, cigarette in a shaking hand, whisky on the counter. There was television laughter and jukebox din and the roar of regulars all around him. He took deep draughts of the cigarette and looked at the backs of his hands hardly knowing what he had done, and then it hit him like a sledge hammer, a drowning tiredness that made his temples pulse and seemed to pack his forehead with cotton wool, so that he no longer cared what had happened, or knew what he was doing, but was content to stand on his own, lost to the world.

Chapter Eight

THE LIGHT IN HIS bedroom was extremely beautiful. Wind played in the curtains, which gently swelled, manipulating the influx of sunshine. He lay awake for an hour, staring at the ceiling.

He ate breakfast at the small table in the kitchen: egg and bacon, a mug of coffee. He went through the food quickly, con brio, and it was only after a certain fullness set in and he was looking at the yolky residue on the plate that he realised he had come to the end of his life. He stared through the kitchen window at the tree outside, and felt the coffee lift him into an empty trance.

Later, he stood still in the music room, registering the quiet emptiness of his house and the hollow cheerfulness of morning light on bookshelves. He picked up the telephone and listened to his messages: three calls from John, a message from Laura, kindly reassurances from Derek and Arthur, neither of whom could conceal his alarm. Someone from the surgery asked him to fix an appointment.

He trailed through Regent's Park under the tresses of weeping willows. His legs carried him across football pitches and over ornamental bridges and all the while his thoughts became thinner and vaguer and his head airier, as if the sight of pendulous planes and fluorescent tulips syphoned all sense from his mind. He stared at strolling Arab families, at Japanese tourists taking photos, at pinging joggers evangelically perspiring. The day was violently bright and colourful with sharp outlines and resolute shadows. He would not be found out here.

In the afternoon he ambled around the West End, aware hazily of Dorothy Perkins and Liberty. He had no idea where he was going or what he was doing but needed to keep moving. He looked in a trance through the windows of jewellers, stared in fascination at lingerie mannequins, halted abstractly at the corners of roads, wondering where to go next. Busy hordes milled past him. Traffic thundered by. On roads and pavements everything was bustle and purpose. Existence without energetic direction, he realised, was a kind of sleep. Simply to breathe, to walk, to drift, was hardly to live at all.

Around four-thirty he came to, and found himself sitting in a side-street café. His mind was working furiously now, breaking down the waves of guilt, marshalling arguments, trying to find some thread of justification. Explanations were required, apologies. He had done the worst thing, for himself and everyone else. All that he could say was that suddenly on stage he knew it was impossible. What those pieces cost he could not pay. His life had been parasitised by an unsustainable perfectionism and enough was enough. The old Philip Morahan had made an executive decision not to be mediocre and now, as he sat with his teaspoon and a crumbling Amoretti between fingers, the bravery of that decision amazed him.

The pressure of thoughts was suddenly unbearable. Grand gestures begat new crises. He was alone with his music, but more alone without it. How could a man reconstruct his life at fifty-two? What remained but drift and boredom when obsession failed? A failed artist had nowhere to go. Music, already, was a kind of last resort.

He wondered in a panic how quickly he could clear this up. All kinds of prostrations and grovelling were imperative to get John back on side. Bulmanion was a write-off but, if he could just pull himself together and do the next two concerts, he would have a life. The Royal Academy would let him off. Pupils would understand. He could return to routine at a lower level of ambition, holding on to what he had and not expecting much. The past would lead to the future and this episode might soon be forgotten.

He ached. His feet ached. His head throbbed. He sat at the metal table breathing the trafficky air, listening to the warble of city pigeons, and it seemed to him then as he lit another cigarette that thinking itself was pointless. Thinking would not contribute.

Mid-evening he was back in Chiswick. Walking along the pavement to his house he felt like going to bed and sleeping for ever. Reaching for the keys in his pocket, he pushed through the front garden gate and rose up the step to his porch. He worked the key in the lock and was about to go in when somebody called his name. He looked over his shoulder.

'Philip!'

Ursula stood on the pavement. She stared at him timidly.

He looked at her in astonishment.

She came closer, almost cradling herself.

'Are you all right?'

His heart beat hard. He had not banked on seeing anyone.

'Sorry to . . . I've been waiting for hours.'

'Waiting?'

'In the car. Over there.'

'Did John send you?'

She was distressed by the idea. 'You're not answering calls.'

He stared at her.

She looked at him almost bravely, as if to show the depth of her concern. She was flushed with agitation and a kind of embarrassment.

'I wanted to see that you were OK,' she said.

He nodded vacantly.

She smiled with painful relief.

He was not at ease with her concern.

'I'm OK.'

'Can we talk?'

'Don't worry.'

'Philip!'

'I can't talk, really.'

'Of course.' She stepped towards him. 'Of course.'

She was tall, almost precarious, her neck willowy under the weight of thick hair, tucked inside her collar.

'I'm not here because I'm your agent.'

He stared at her.

She came even closer.

They exchanged a look.

'Please!' she said.

He tried saying something but had no will to resist her. He turned, twisting the key in the lock, and let her into the house. Once inside, he gestured her into the front room, catching the smell of her leather jacket as she passed. He followed her in, almost as if this were her home now.

Ursula came into the drawing room with a kind of reverent watchfulness. He circulated behind her, switching on lamps and pulling curtains, and she stood by the piano as he fetched a wine bottle and glasses from the kitchen. She gazed thoughtfully at his Steinway and then took herself across the room to consider a landscape painting. Her arms were folded protectively.

Philip glanced at her as he opened the wine bottle. Both of them knew she had exceeded her brief and that their professional relationship could help neither of them. Not that he wanted help. He wanted to lie down and go to sleep. He gave her a glass and crossed the room to a seat. After a moment she followed his example and took herself to the end of the recamier, where she perched.

They sat across from each other silently for some moments. He regarded her expressionlessly. Her being in his room was not his doing. He felt he was staring at a stranger whose solicitations he was too exhausted to repel. For a while the anomaly of her presence was strangely absorbing. Behind the mask of his face he was sinking. Ursula's unexpected manifestation held him at least to the moment. He was prepared to stare at her indefinitely.

She sipped her wine, waiting for him. She was not exactly at ease. Whatever she thought she was doing, she was doing it for the first time.

'I intended to play,' he said, monotonally.

She shook her head, signifying an automatic acceptance of whatever he would say, the matter being absolutely beyond accountability.

'Till the last second.'

She nodded carefully, acknowledging the sentiment, the reality of his feelings.

There was a pause.

'I wasn't really surprised,' she said.

He made no reply.

'After Saturday.'

Philip rubbed his eyes and then stared at her without expression. 'The moment I met you I knew something was wrong.'

He took a sip of his wine. He was shattered.

She looked away. 'I know you think I'm inexperienced, but I've been listening to your CDs for years. I went to your concerts as a teenager. Apart from the fact that I love your playing' – her colour rose – 'I feel I know you quite well. In fact, when we met the other day you were exactly as I imagined.' She glanced at him sincerely. 'When you said you wanted to cancel I was so struck.'

She took his silence as permission to continue.

'I noticed . . .'

Her gaze was intense. She had been working up to this.

'When you looked at me . . .'

She blinked and glanced away.

He watched her in silence.

Ursula moistened her lips, smiled apologetically. 'A frightened boy. The look of a distressed child.'

Philip could only raise his eyebrows in mild amazement at this declaration. He had no idea how to respond. Her sympathy was undeserved, uninvited. He had not expected to reckon with the piercing concern of a young woman at this hour of the day.

'You reminded me of my brother Paul,' she continued.

He stared at her.

'Paul was eight when my mother died. I was fourteen. It was terrible for me, but for him . . . He lost something of himself.'

Strangers had been intimate with him in this way before. It was as though they believed that he as a pianist could be entrusted with tragic confidences, could purge the woe of the world in his playing.

'When you . . . didn't play . . . it was like a confirmation.' She rubbed her eye. 'Of . . . Oh, I don't know. I'm sorry. Excuse me.'

He waited.

'You must think I'm very intrusive.' She smiled courageously.

He shrugged. 'No.'

'You see, my mother was a pianist. We listened to your records all the time. My father took me to your concerts in Berlin. There was always music in the house. When Mother died we'd play her favourite records. She listened to your Kreisleriana, and your Brahms violin sonatas with Wolfram Eckert, and so my family was always passionate about your records, and when my mother died, so united by them.'

Ursula smiled again with the relief of confession.

He pulled himself up a little, almost to displace his embarrassment. Ursula's declaration filled him with humility. What she told him explained a great deal.

'My father is still alive,' she added. 'He's a novelist, actually. Diederich Kaustner.'

Philip inhaled deeply, feeling the wine strike at his tiredness. He sat in the chair for a while, wondering what to say. He frowned, touched his forehead delicately. Ursula's solicitude was so penetrating. 'I reminded you of your brother?'

She looked at him in pity. 'Because you lost your mother?'

He smiled to cover his unease. She was being so distressingly sympathetic. 'I never knew my real mother. For all I know she may be alive.'

'Then you lost having a mother.'

For a moment he sensed the inscrutability of his own feelings. 'She was Irish.'

'Your mother?'

He managed to sit up a little. He sipped at his wine and cleared his throat. He was suddenly overcome with the crushing sense of what he had thrown away last night – his reputation, his entitlement to respect. He had abandoned his audience at the height of their expectation.

'Your mother was Irish?'

'An Irish nurse,' he managed. 'She worked in a hospital in Manchester. I was the result of a broom-cupboard romance that may have been one fuck long.'

He had no idea why he was telling her this. There seemed a need to offer something in return.

'You were adopted?'

'By a grammar-school teacher and his wife. Few years ago I tried to trace my mother through an agency. No luck. My father lives in Australia. He was a consultant eye surgeon until quite recently. I wrote to him for the first time when I was thirty-five suggesting we meet up. He replied saying that he had his own family who knew nothing about me, and didn't think it was wise.'

She nodded carefully. 'Were you disappointed?'

'I never expected love. What . . . depressed me was the lack of curiosity.'

'Did he know of your success?'

'I didn't want that to be his reason for seeing me.'

'And your adoptive parents?'

'I loved them and they did everything to support my music and to help me get on. They're both dead, but I think of them a lot. I held on to their house for a few years after they died, then sold it and put the money in high-tech stocks. Lost everything, actually.'

There was a long interval of silence. Philip gazed at the floor.

'D'you feel cheated of your birthright? A parent's love?'

He gazed at her intently. She wanted to know the givens. He could tell her the givens, but from what standpoint do you evaluate a life that has been the only one possible for you?

'Whether and how I feel it, I don't know. My destiny was to become a pianist, and almost everything about that destiny means a life outside normal human relations. But yes, one craves normality. Music is very rewarding, and one leaps into it, but when I see happy families, happy parents, happy children, I wonder what it would have been like to be unexceptional, and tied into life in the usual way. Music abducted me at an early age. It takes over your mind, your body. My closest allies were dead composers. My fantasy life a score. To say I was lonely is untrue. I was dangerously self-sufficient. To have a *raison d'être* at the age of seven is quite something. The child is suddenly partaking in a grown-up mental world, though what happens to the child in all this, I don't know.'

Ursula nodded. She passed a hand inside the lapel of her jacket and eased it over her shoulder and arm. With a neat shrug she released the other shoulder and arm. Her coils of hair sprang loose and she had to tame it with her fingers, drawing it back around her ears, flicking it off her collar. She wore a gypsy-style shirt with puff sleeves and bare arms; a necklace of beads and a silver bracelet.

He saw shapely arms, fine wrists. He was aware of her breasts in the contours of her shirt. Ursula had flamenco possibilities in the line of her neck and shoulders.

She recollected the wine glass, ran its stem between her fingers. She looked suddenly thoughtful.

'Why are you so miserable?' she said.

He looked at her in surprise.

'Something has happened?'

He reached for the wine bottle, topped up his glass.

She regarded him with contemplative intensity, as if divining something.

He actually found it impossible to speak. To begin to explain was to head off in a direction he could not face. He could hardly describe, let alone define, and just to make the attempt was somehow to parade so much vulnerable feebleness that he would rather it stayed trapped inside him. As he sat there, biting his lip, staring blankly at her bare foot, which had discarded its shoe and risen on to the sofa, he felt the old resentment growing – against his weaker self – that he could not share these thoughts with another person and satisfy her sympathy.

'Konstantine Serebriakov was there last night,' she said.

'What!'

'In the audience.'

'No!'

'With Arthur England and Jean Rose. John spotted them.'

Philip smothered his face in shame.

She was dismayed by his reaction, watched him closely.

'Apparently, he's very ill.'

He massaged his eye-sockets, defeated by this latest news.

'People were moved by your speech. Everybody is desperately concerned about you. There's no shame, Philip.'

With a sudden burst of energy he ejected himself out of his chair. 'I'm holed beneath the water-line,' he said brightly.

'Why?'

Her look held a quality of sympathetic overflow, of ready amazement, showing the depth of her talent for dramatic participation. He faced Ursula, looking down at her as she gazed up at him, and saw in her lovely face the expression of a woman who could generate the most turbulent excitement from her body, whose bare arms and neck were maddeningly responsive to touch, whose high-strung sensitive involvement derived from a physical intensity of being.

He turned away, compressing the idea into a tight corner of his mind. He steadied himself at the mantelpiece.

Philip waited. A special effort was required, which he could barely bring himself to make. He sensed that she was giving him an opportunity. 'Two years ago I split up with a girlfriend. Laura. She wanted to marry.'

Ursula looked up at him.

'Anyway . . . um . . . anyway, we keep in touch. She told me recently that an old girlfriend of mine got pregnant as our relationship was ending, and had a termination.' He looked down. 'How did she find out? Don't know. Why did she tell me? No idea. I just couldn't get it out of my mind.'

He was adrift for a moment.

'I felt that in ending that baby Camilla was somehow terminating me. Another generation of Morahans stymied, as though we're not wanted in the world.' He managed to look at her directly. 'Me or my child.'

She nodded carefully. 'Why can't you have a child with someone else?'

He was almost amused.

'If that's what's missing in your life!'

'There speaks a twenty-six-year old.'

She frowned at this tack.

'I'm a knackered old bachelor, Ursula.'

'Bachelors are supposed to have fun.'

'What you don't know about men of my age!'

'I like men your age.'

'God, you're charitable.'

'I'm not being kind.' She moved her bottom, looked at him levelly.

Philip reached for the wine glass. He could not conceive that Ursula was flirting with him.

'If a man my age is single, there's usually a good reason.'

'Maybe you haven't met the right person.' She looked at him innocently.

Philip felt more alert now. He took a sip from his glass.

'One needs talent, I think, to spot the right person.'

'And a passionate nature, which you have.'

He looked at her suspiciously.

'Oh, come on, Philip! It's not that difficult, making babies. Falling in love.'

'Relationships can be difficult.'

'But is that destiny or luck?'

He smiled. 'In my case incompetence.'

'You want freedom, but you need love. There's got to be a way.'

He raised his eyebrows. How simple life could look from the twenty-six-year-old end of the telescope.

'Can I tell you something?' he said, after a moment.

She smiled.

'About something else?'

'Don't be too defensive,' she said.

'I'm not being defensive. I'm changing the subject.'

'That's what I mean.'

He decided to ignore this. He looked at her for a moment. She leaned across a pile of cushions, legs curled up.

'The other week, I had a student here. Girl from the Academy. I try not to have students in the house because they chatter away and you can't get rid of them. She was Russian. Twenty-two or -three. She played the Funeral March Sonata. The piece I was supposed to play last night. When I heard what she did with it I couldn't speak afterwards. It was quite overwhelming.' He grimaced in recollection. 'Chopin wrote the march itself in 1836. The plight of Poland, the death of his sister. He had enough good reasons to pen a funeral march. Two years later he and George Sand went to Majorca for some sun, but he got bronchitis and started coughing blood and only just survived. Back in France he composed three further movements around the funeral march: the Opus 35 Sonata. Well, I knew all this, but I had always seen the work as a young man's measuring up to death, with a touch of Gothic rhetoric. A walk around the graveyard, not a flop into the coffin. When the Russian girl started I had the sensation of actually being Chopin and feeling what I can only describe as terror. You see, when Chopin was in Valdemosa, I'm sure he thought he would die. And though he survived, he had the taste of death in his mouth. The whole sonata is his creative struggle with the memory of that abyss. I think he realised that he'd written a funeral march for himself. It was an unconscious musical premonition that became, in Majorca, almost a reality. With a terrible insight. Because after the funeral march, what comes next? A return to life, spring? Some ethereal threnody conducting us to a place of peace? Not for Chopin. What you hear in the last movement is the absolute end. A soundworld beyond human life. The unspooling of consciousness itself.'

He looked away. He was now ready to make a declaration. He felt somehow stronger as he spoke the words.

'An unwelcome elegy for the death of an unborn child, I thought. It reminded me of something known for a while but not yet felt. When I die there will be nothing left of me, nothing that precedes or succeeds me. No parents or siblings or cousins. No wife and children. I am the beginning and end of the line. Anticipated by nothing. Returning to nothing.'

He gazed into the mirror above the mantelpiece, saw his reflection, saw Ursula's.

She held his eye as he looked at her reflection in the mirror. Her expression seemed unfamiliar, as though the reversed image of her face in the mirror showed another self.

He looked darkly at her. She was being drawn into the contradictory world of his mind, a place where external reality is alternately overpowering and non-existent.

Slowly he came back to the armchair. After a moment he sat down. The wine, as he sipped it, tasted strange.

She remained still. She had the look of a person whose role is to wait and to listen.

Philip allowed the silence to play out. He feared that his candour would be alienating. He was not an easy man to reassure. He regarded Ursula with sympathy. Her revered pianist was in dire form today.

'Why can't you have children?' she asked.

'Oh, that again.'

'Because you can't fall in love any more?'

He stared at her.

'This Laura. You weren't in love with her?'

'She says I'm a claustro-agoraphobic. Can't bear to be alone. Can't tolerate intimacy.'

'Isn't playing the piano all about love in some way?'

'It's all about everything.'

'When you can do it?'

'I play the piano to move myself, Ursula. The audience attends, and hopefully the audience is also moved. Human love is a matter of practical compromises and sharing. It's a loving enterprise that delimits artistic freedom unless your partner is a doormat, and God knows there are some. So you make a choice between going it alone and harming no one – what I've done – or inflicting your inability to compromise on a partner, which seems selfish. Or you give into the demands of marriage and parenthood and become a more connected human being and less yourself. Good for partners and children. Bad for your art.'

'What about the heart, Philip? The heart needs sustenance. How can you be human and cut out tenderness and passion and all the bonds that enable people to be happy and to care about each other?'

'Classical music doesn't come from happiness. So much of it is so fundamentally tragic.'

'But this musician,' she burst out, 'can't play the piano any more. The romantic artist hero has gone on strike! If music is the great love of your life, you've just been dumped. What now?'

He glanced away.

'You're miserable,' she said, 'because you need more of life and a lot less of art. Music has dried you up in some way. I don't believe this emotional current you're talking about stems from turning your back on other people . . .'

'I don't . . .'

'If music is about everything, it's about everything in life!'

He covered his brow, as though she were striking him.

'You need to live a little, Philip. The piano is part of something much larger. You have to find a reason for living beyond all this.' She gestured at the shelves of music.

He regarded her with tense admiration. Ursula's appearance belied her true nature. The collapsible lissomness of legs and shoulders, the fine eyes were upstaged by her rigorous certainty, which somehow sidelined the feminine.

He shook his head. 'What do you recommend then?'

She shrugged. 'Very easy. Cancel the series.'

'Cancel the series?'

'Postpone Bulmanion.'

'This is my agent speaking?'

'Put everything on ice.'

He was amused. 'And do what?'

'Time out. Find yourself away from music.'

'I have commitments . . .'

'Escape everything to do with music.'

'And then?'

She smiled brilliantly, almost teasingly. 'Have a romance.'

'Oh yes?'

'Food, sex, travel.'

'You have a touching faith in my . . .'

'I honestly believe a good woman will sort you out.'

He blinked. 'I'd like to find a good woman.'

'Many fish in the sea.'

'Very helpful of you, Ursula.'

'I believe in keeping my clients happy.'

'Thank you for your professional attention.'

'My pleasure.' She gave him a half-humorous look and tossed the hair off her face.

She ran a fingernail over her knee, finessing her composure in a new position on the recamier, which produced more leggy slants and the roll of her hip.

Philip maintained a look of introspection whilst allowing his mind to be compressed by the alien notion that Ursula might find him attractive because of his fame or artistry or the residue of some teenage crush garnered at a concert when he was ten years younger and which somehow still flickered on in her head despite his present state. The idea was incongruous and not to be dwelt on, and probably deluded because how could a woman of her opportunities feel anything more than respect for a man of his age? He was not a sexual player any more, not in his own mind. Ever since Laura, he had censored the idea of another relationship; if that one had failed, it was impossible to imagine another could succeed. Certainly he was inhibited by a fear of repeating the past, inflicting disappointment on somebody new and loathing on himself.

He waved it away, as if to release himself from her attention.

'You get off the train at my stage of life, you might never get back on.'

She gave him a look of pert reproval. 'The train's already crashed.'

'Well . . .'

'Regenerate, Philip. Get on another one. A better one.'

He leaned forward, setting his glass down. 'Where did they teach you this happy-clappy born-again guide to mid-life crisis?'

'We don't have time to be depressed.' She almost smirked. 'We barely have time to sleep!'

'Prozac and Viagra. That's your philosophy, I take it.'

'No!'

'Life is short and shitty, so let's party and laugh.'

'I didn't say that.'

'If I knew how to regenerate, I would. Yeah, sure, fool around like some menopausal twit desperately clutching at the wisps of lost youth. Take a holiday in Florence, coming to terms with middle age over the crossword puzzle and a glass of Chianti. Read pop psychology and self-help manuals to get in touch with my inner fluffy bunny.'

She was crossly amused by his horrible parody.

'Because this ain't no dress-rehearsal!'

'Shut up, Philip.'

'And I'm a talented bastard, so I shouldn't complain. Is that it?'

She gave him a gravely forbidding glance.

'An attitude makeover?'

'Yeah, maybe. Lighten you up a bit.'

'No, I don't think so. You see, things can happen that change your mind on this.'

'What things?'

'Bad things.'

'What bad things?'

'There's no need to say.'

'Yes, there is. What bad things?'

'Things happen out of the blue.'

'What happened?'

'People . . .' He swallowed.

'Somebody . . .'

'Friends. Close friends.'

She waited.

He averted his eyes.

'Which friends, Philip?'

'Does it matter?'

'They died?'

His face grew pale.

'When was this?'

'An old cottage. Went up like a . . .'

'When did this happen?'

He looked at her starkly.

She moved her hand, rose slightly.

He held her gaze, drawing her in, fastening on her.

'What is one to make of that? Yes, a tragedy. Now what? These things happen and one has to carry on, sure, but carry on to what? I mean something like that can't be "understood" or put in any kind of box. How can anybody come to terms with arbitrary disaster? I get no help from religion or philosophy.'

She looked at him with grim understanding.

'Life is so much sadder than we can bear.'

She averted her eyes. 'When did this happen?'

'Regeneration is not so simple, except in the dumb sense life goes on, replicating endlessly.'

'I only wanted to help you,' she pleaded.

'You're kind.'

'It's not pity.' She was sudden. 'I believe you're a great pianist. That means something to me.'

'My therapy is to ignore and forget. Something disgusting happens. Blank it out. Why grant victory to fate? It's enough that fate happens. Stand back and let the scythe come swishing in. It'll be my turn next.'

She sat there still and thoughtful, immersed in what he had told her. It seemed there was no come-back. She had wanted to help, believing that she could. Often, in the past, he had seemed intractable to the sympathetic. He presented opportunities for redemption, and this drew women to him who were then dismayed by his incapacity to be tamed into happiness according to their instincts for love and nurture. His moods were part of an emotional constitution that worked well in relation to music and badly in relation to his personal happiness. Happiness for Philip was subsumed in obsession. How to give perfect realisation to a musical work, an abiding concern: happiness through thinking, practising, listening, playing, discovering, uncovering, inhabiting, performing, realising and sharing a score to the umpteenth degree. Ursula thought, perhaps, that the emotions she experienced, listening to him play, related in some direct way to his passions as a man. She was drawn by the sensibility of an artist without considering that the quality she loved was elicited by music. The energy she witnessed grandly exerting itself at the keyboard music unleashed. Philip had often pondered the correlation between a pianist's inhabiting of emotion in romantic repertoire and his ability to love another person whole-heartedly. Did feeling stem from him, or was he merely the vessel through which it passed? Emotion in music was nobody's property. Emotion in performance was variable, mysterious and strangely sourceless.

She drew herself up, and then she looked at him. She parted her lips, and looked at him. It was her way of getting around words, of cutting away ideas and explanations and recalling him to the fact of her presence.

He inhaled slowly, as if taking in a haul on a cigarette, and at the bottom of the intake she got through. What he experienced was not so much the sudden truth of her arresting beauty – a kind of jolt to the system – as the force of will projected through that beauty, making him realise directly and instantaneously the strength of her mission: to appeal to a complex and sensitive mind, almost to excite him as a piece of music would excite him, to be an experience that he could neither resist nor comprehend because Ursula was so determined and surprising: the incalculable total of different orders of value paradoxically focused on him.

Eventually she looked away, though whether the spell had passed or was broken he could not tell.

'You're beautiful,' he said.

She was not ready for this.

'And perceptive.'

She leaned forward with a pained expression, returning her wine glass to the table, but then she laughed, and met his gaze with a confident directness.

Philip considered his hands. Probably he had said the wrong thing.

She gave him a more settled look, and now her demeanour was rather different, as though she had the full set, suddenly, a recovered sense of her power, and with it the dynamic of opposites she liked to work within: male and female, youth and maturity.

'What are you thinking?' he asked.

'That it's probably time for me to leave.'

He felt a pang.

She pulled her jacket back on, making to rise. He rose, too. She moved without hesitation into the hall. They went to the front door, and as he followed her his heart sank.

In the hallway she turned, all zipped up, hair in her collar, and gazed at him half humorously. She had known a great deal about him, and found out more. Now he knew a little about her, too.

'I'll call you tomorrow.' She kissed him lightly on the cheek and let herself out.

Chapter Nine

HE CAME OUT IN a daze from the doctor's surgery. Traffic criss-crossed in front of him, a hurtle of cabs and cars reflecting bright sunlight, festive summer light. A rap wagon throbbed on the kerb; a shuffling woman and a dog passed him.

The GP was a locum, Asian, the waiting room crowded. Philip sat in a corner reading *Hello* magazine amidst people with preoccupying medical conditions and doomed faces.

His test results had not arrived, or been mislaid, and were then found. The locum sat at his desk checking the notes on screen, clicking and scrolling whilst Philip sat on a chair with his hands on his lap. He watched the doctor's face, busily concentrating. He was asked to unbutton his shirt and take a seat on the couch behind the screen. His abdomen was palpated, chest tapped, tongue examined. A nurse came in. Words were exchanged about another patient.

Philip reclined meekly as if diagnosis were simply the means by which professionals caught up with what was already factual in one's body.

John Sampson had phoned him in the waiting room. Philip reflexively answered.

'I'm at the doctor's.'

'I need to see you.'

'Let me call back when I'm out.'

'Where's the surgery?'

'The surgery?'

'Give me an address. I'm coming right now.'

After the examination the two men resumed their seats at the doctor's desk. The locum rummaged around with papers: Philip's

86

results or someone else's. He made a further appraisal of the clinical notes from the last consultation. After a moment, he drew his chair closer to Philip's and looked at him directly. His expression was different. His brown eyes sought a link with Philip's before he spoke.

'Um . . . listen, it's not bad news and it's not good news.'

Philip's heart quickened.

'We're missing one of the blood results, which is infuriating. My apologies. The ultrasound shows a shadow, which could be various things. The long and short is that you need more tests and probably a keyhole biopsy.'

Philip frowned.

'Straightforward procedure.' He seemed to shrug. 'The consultant will advise on the test results, obviously.'

'Right.' He had not expected this. His chest was tight.

The doctor looked at him carefully.

'A shadow, you say?'

'There's a shadow.'

'What's that?'

'Discolouration, maybe nothing, maybe scarring from a viral infection.'

'But the biopsy?'

'I don't want to alarm you unnecessarily.'

Philip stared at him.

The doctor seemed to wait.

'Some kind of growth?'

'Well, this is precisely what we have to investigate.'

'Because of the shadow?'

'Because of the bloods.'

He nodded.

'Mr Morahan, it's a possibility we have to rule out.' He looked away quickly. 'I should be able to get an appointment for you in the next few days.

His heart was racing now. He noticed how the doctor would not meet his eye.

He was sent back to reception, asked to leave a further urine sample. It took an age to relieve himself into the plastic bottle in the gents. He was light-headed, weak at the knees. On the wall of the waiting room was a poster entitled 'Menopause Whenopause?' and another advertising antenatal classes.

He came through the electric sliding doors to see John Sampson parking his car on a double yellow line. Philip stood on the kerb and watched the traffic pass as John undid his seat belt and pocketed his mobile before jacking open the door and springing out.

John's office move was going on this week and his eyes were puffy with tiredness and stress. 'You're liable but Bulmanion will pick up the tab.'

They stood facing each other on the pavement outside the doctor's surgery.

'Need to get some sort of medical opinion, doctor's certificate.' He swallowed. 'OK, no venue's going to sue a major artist, but people need to claim insurance. Best course is to phone Frank, say sorry, you've had a major crisis in the family, make it up, doesn't matter what.'

His head was burning. He felt weightless and weak.

'It's not in your nature. But you need to bend a little. That way he can deal with the insurers. Plus I can spin it. Might do us some good.' He glanced around nervously.

Philip grimaced.

'Just say yes!'

'Can we . . .'

He raised a finger remonstratively. 'You've dropped a thudding great turd on your career.'

He looked away. He was feeling dreadful. He needed to sit down.

'I've had a ton of angry calls and I'm thoroughly hacked off. Meanwhile, you loll around having a nice little flirtation with Ursula, your phone off the hook while I shovel shit.'

He shook his head contritely. 'I wasn't flirting, John.'

'You don't explain, apologise, communicate.'

'I'm sorry . . .'

'Can you imagine what it was like sitting in the stalls at QEH, surrounded by the music establishment?' He was distraught now. 'I should have known my client. Should have realised that when you told Frank you'd play you were pulling the wool over our eyes or totally deluded. I don't pretend to understand what's going on in your mind and that's a failing, but nobody exists in a vacuum.

You're in a community of relations with the venues, the audience, the press. You can't treat this infrastructure like an army of court flatterers . . .'

'John!'

'. . . by cancelling at point-blank notice. Nobody does that. Nobody needs to. It takes a certain kind of naivety or grandiose arrogance to dunk everyone in the piss pot after the moment of no return!'

Philip felt his eyes smarting as though he were about to cry.

John shook his head, seeming almost to feel sorry for himself. He pulled at the skin under his eyes, grazed his cheek with his fingernails. He looked sallow, and exhausted.

Philip had no strength for confrontation.

John faced him and sighed deeply.

'I'm so sorry, John.'

The agent hung his head. He was briefly in remission from the throes of apoplexy. 'I don't know what you're going through. You won't share it with me. I accept that.'

'I need to go home or sit down.'

John pointed to a bench on the pavement. Philip sat down and John perched on the end.

'I'm sure there are people who can help.'

Philip nodded dutifully. He wanted to appease John's anger.

'What I can do is hold the structure in place, give you continuity. So when you snap out of it something is there. I want to keep our options open. That's all.'

As he sat there on the street bench it welled up inside him, a terrible pity for himself that made his eyes water. He had a shadow inside him, an undefined manifestation that might have been nothing, or the finger of death. He was drained, enfeebled and horribly humanly vulnerable, his worries and woes subsumed in dread. He could barely make the effort to sit up.

'A couple of calls, a couple of gestures, a little bridge-building. We're insuring the future. You need to be allowed to make music, give concerts, record repertoire. If that is taken care of, your other concerns will sort out.'

John tapped the back of the bench with his palm. He took in the faces and backsides of passing girls. His eyebrows arched. He blinked.

'I'll draw up a press release. Tell Frank – uh – death in the family. You know, milk a bit of pity. Square off the South Bank. I can darn out the wrinkles if you'll promise to play the next two concerts.'

Philip nodded carefully, as though in full agreement. 'I can't really promise anything.'

John turned to face him directly. His mouth worked a little before he spoke. 'Even if you played like a crippled pig on acid you'd do less harm to your career than cancelling again.'

Philip looked into John's eyes, the irony dawning that he might have the perfect excuse.

John was not a safe recipient of such news. Later, he wondered if it was the prospect of John's 'profound sympathy' he could not stomach, or the visible dawning in John's eyes that his client was history. He suddenly felt cold, withdrawn. It was too much to be subjected to this pressure. John's insistence grated on him, and at such times one had to be forceful.

John nodded. 'What d'you say, then?'

Philip swallowed. 'Don't let's fall out over this.'

He shook his head, annoyed by the tone. 'No agent in the world can function this way.'

'I understand. There's nothing I can do about it.'

'I can't believe you're saying this.'

Philip sat rigidly on the bench. 'Please leave me alone.'

John smiled in disbelief. 'I don't just walk away, Philip. Your problem is my problem.'

'Shut up, will you!'

John stood abruptly. He was full of energy, almost cocky with the sense of rectitude. He tugged at his trouser belt, flicked a hand through his hair.

'I've seen this existential heebie-jeebie rap with a dozen clients. I don't get sucked in. It doesn't behove me to be gentle and caring, because you don't employ me to be gentle and caring. I am here to be positive and effective, and if possible amusing; and whatever I say – and I'll always be blunt – because I refuse to be the victim of mass artistic temperament, you'll remember it was me who secured the concerts, the sponsorship, the record deal, by exuberant pro-activity and regal dynamism of an ilk rarely seen in this industry. And here I am again, the managing director and principal share-holder of a company with twenty-two employees, one hundred and fifty clients, and an annual turnover of four million pounds, sitting on a pigeon-shit bench in Marylebone, having driven through syphilitic traffic, talking to my dear Philip, whom I love and admire deeply, because I would do anything for you, trying to solve your latest crisis not with cocoa and commiseration, which you can get from that tramp over there – but with practical suggestions which I'll deliver on a nod. I can endure irritability, the slings and arrows of ingratitude. I am not some sensitive floral creature. But even I can't ignore self-destruction, and for you to brush me off . . .'

'I'm not brushing you off!' he shouted.

'Sack me if you want, but I can't change the way I work, and while I'm your agent I'll say it straight, because there's no value to you if I'm pulling my punches.'

'Oh, punch away.'

John's expression was suddenly serious. He came closer to Philip, sat down slowly on the bench.

'I don't quite know how to say this.'

'Yes you do.'

His cheek muscles bunched against unsavoury thoughts. 'Frank tells the truth.'

Philip shook his head.

'No reflection on anything. Just career dynamics.'

'What!'

'You're fringe.'

Philip smiled bitterly.

'Wednesday didn't help. Wednesday was ostentatiously unhelpful. Even so, we have a couple of days to lock in the miracle that is Frank. Before he pulls the plug, and you're left with a shitty review and a cancelled concert and no record deal and no sponsor and nothing on the horizon!'

'How can you talk to me like this?'

'Because it's true. There's hundreds of pianists out there struggling for the limelight, whose best work is going unrecorded, whose careers are languishing. The big time is just a handful of names. Hordes fall by the wayside. But you've been given a chance.'

'I just can't . . . I just . . .' His temples were pulsating. He felt contaminated by the things John was saying.

'And I have to tell you, I have to be honest, I'm just being completely above-board . . . if you drop out, Vadim's in line. I don't want it to come as a nasty surprise.'

'What!'

'Breaking news. Your protégé is the hottest thing in town, because Paul Harringay at Classique is banging on to everyone about his new Rachmaninov disc, which is truly awesome, and the majors are wading in. If you drop the concerts, Vadim will grab them, and Bulmanion will be on to him like a flash. He'll get your deal.'

Philip gazed at his agent in a trance of wonder.

John gazed back, watching the effect of his words.

'I have no choice because Vadim is the only person who could hold those dates.'

'You're diabolical.'

'Cobblers! I'm doing my job.'

'You're pressurising me.'

'Hah! Join the real world.'

'I can't . . .'

'It's last-chance saloon, old man!'

'My reputation doesn't stand or fall on a concert.'

'Oh no? Ashkenazy and Pollini are busted flushes. Brendel's getting old. Argerich is history. There's phase-outs everywhere. Zimmerman and Perahia are gilt-edged but corporate. Hamelin and Volodos are around for a bit, Hough's holding up, Schiff's dug in but, as Frank says, you're almost a legend, and if you let yourself fade into musical history . . .'

'Shut up!'

'. . . turning sepia before our eyes, Vadim et al will take over.'

'He'll take over anyway.'

'In this rat race, damn it' – John banged his fist on the bench – 'you have a duty to promulgate your art!'

'For Christ's sake . . .'

'Can you imagine Franz Liszt relinquishing his crown? Or Rubinstein, or Horowitz flinging in the sponge? Letting some other pianist steal their thunder? You have to be magisterial, Philip. You have to get in there and show them you're the fucking best. You have to fling the rabble aside, because this is not some well-mannered cultural Utopia of egalitarian mutual respect between caring, sharing touchy-feely hard-working humble pianists, worker ants in the garden of music, this is a battle for supremacy. Greatness needs to impose itself. Needs to prove what greatness in music means. Otherwise the geeks and the technocrats will crawl all over the shop. You owe it to your art, Philip.'

'Oh, fuck my art.'

'If you really think that, fire me now.'

'I'm going mad listening to you.'

'I can't represent has-beens.'

'I'm not a fucking has-been! I didn't get to where I am by making compromises. If that's going to jeopardise our relationship . . .'

'Relationship! What you call a relationship is a one-way street of ego-massage and damned hard work in return for the immortal blessing of your music when you feel like it on your terms.'

'Then, let's call it a day.'

'Nobody else will take you on.'

'Ursula would look after me better than this!'

John's expression hardened. 'She won't get the chance.'

Philip looked at him in confusion. 'Are you trying to get rid of me?'

'What!'

'Because of Ursula?'

John was adrift for a moment.

'You'd throw me away out of some misplaced sense of jealousy?'

'Jealous! I'm not jealous.'

Philip stared at him. He could see it in John's eyes. John was jealous. Jealous of Ursula's sympathy for him, the fact she had gone to his flat and waited for him in a car all day. John had forced Ursula on him and now he was jealous of her concern.

'You insult me because you want to get rid of me.'

'I've never heard anything so ridiculous.'

'Because you fancy Ursula and want to promote Vadim?'

'If you believe that . . .'

'Go to hell!'

He turned on his heel and walked away fast.

'Philip!'

He walked rapidly along the pavement, not looking back. He crossed the road at the intersection of Dorset Street, and headed round the corner and out of sight.

'Philip!'

He was light-headed and sweaty around the collar. Iron palings flowed past, fan lights and window grilles to his right, sapling trees in squares of earth and parked cars on his left. A drilling din erupted: side-street roadworks. The sun was pouring down over car bonnets and the smooth, dry belly of the road. He pressed on only half aware of the launderette and the sex shop and the aubergines and sweet potatoes coming out to greet him on grocers' stalls. His legs carried him on, rescuing him from the dementing pressure of the scene he had left behind; but when he turned into Devonshire Street a new sensation developed hailing from a telephone booth, the sight of which filled him with dread, as though the world were stained from the top of the sky downwards, causing him to catch his breath and panic. He reached out to steady himself and was suddenly going down like a nine-pin, a twisting collapse, legs buckling, elbow raised before he hit the ground and blacked out.

'No, I'm fine.'

A man and a woman were helping him stand. He was ropy but clear-headed. They kept in position, firm hands under armpits, and brought him to a table outside a Greek restaurant, where the proprietor fetched a glass of water and called a cab.

He nodded his thanks and sat there feeling weird, concentrating on his water and trying to calm down. He stared at the fabric of the blue cotton tablecloth, watched a pair of businessmen eating meze on a nearby table. When the minicab arrived he put a pound coin down and let himself be guided by a waiter to the door of the cab. He collapsed on to the back seat, hauling his mobile from a pocket.

'You OK, boss?'

'Camberwell, please.'

She was not there at the office, which gave him hope as he dialled her home number. He glanced out of the window watching the street ease by, anticipating the sound of her voice. The number rang and rang and he held on tightly, panic rising. He screwed up his face, made himself redial. He stared past the driver's headrest, mobile cupped to his ear, and thought how peculiar it was that this dizzy foreboding had been in store for him all these years, and that his tightly wrought life should start to unravel now. The cab bumped along, finding its way through the midday traffic of

Central London, and Philip's expensively acquired mastery of the piano seemed a wraith-like thing.

'I'm falling apart,' he told her.

'Philip!'

'I need a shoulder to cry on.'

'Where are you?' she said.

'I'm on my way.'

'You're coming here?'

'Laura, thank God you're in.'

Chapter Ten

LAURA, IN THE EARLY days, had been his George Sand, sans cigar. She was almost rotund, a cuddly bun of a girl, with hips that curved well when she lay on her side and a bottom that improved and improved as she bent over. Her neck was short, her arms plump, her waist a little vague. Nature had not shoe-horned her into the easiest shape for kindly consideration, but her eyes were so dark and holding that it was impossible to look at her and not be captured by something depthlessly feminine. Her gaze offered involvement, soft curiosity and, when he played the piano in her drawing room and she curled on the chair listening to every breath of sound, those eyes of hers became sightless with recollection.

He had found her gentle and robust at the same time. Her thoughtfulness was a kind of armour. Responsive and susceptible, she saw people with a true eye. Laura enjoyed what life yielded easily and sidestepped the rest, being a centred sort of person with an instinct for survival. She coveted solitude, but social people needed her. She attracted the decent, the noisy and the over-wrought, drawing in all types, but without quite belonging to their worlds. He found her freely expressive but never talkative. He had to listen carefully because she said so many things that were so well put it was easy to miss quiet gems. She noticed language, the rum adjective in someone's tale, the force of an unfamiliar word. Her feel for what people meant when they tried to express themselves was for Philip profoundly companionable. At last, he felt intelligible as a man rather than as a musician.

Her social circle, which included Derek, was ideally devoid of professional musicians; and if it sometimes appeared that Laura's friends needed to smoke and drink and relate more intensely than he because they lacked his channel of musical expression, it also seemed that their sharing of ideas, their playfulness and wit enlarged social contact to something he had not enjoyed before. Her friends were at the early, unfailed stage of promising careers, but their day jobs were left at the door, like brollies in the hat stand. Philip found himself appreciating the independent-mindedness of people who worked hard perhaps, but didn't make work into everything. Laura's barrister friends he found particularly amusing. Rodney and Colin Wyatt were brothers at the Criminal Bar with lumbering pinstripe-clad figures, big voices, bigger appetites, and a monstrous knowledge of classical music. Romantic souls were trapped inside their bloated public-schoolishness, rendering them double anachronisms, of which they were wistfully aware. They were honoured to meet Philip, referring to him as 'Maestro' with an appreciation beyond irony. It was only when Philip heard them addressing another friend as 'Deity' and Laura as 'Principessa' and someone else as 'Imperator' that he realised these terms were tokens of affection rather than an index of his musical stature amongst the educated public.

Laura's solidity of character appealed to his need for freedom. He could tour, practise, travel, and when he returned she would be getting on with her life but ready to absorb him. She took quiet and immense pleasure in her new boyfriend. In the early weeks of their romance she came to one of his London concerts, and having known little about his standing in that world, and being a newcomer to the experience of a piano recital, she was struck to see him on stage, aghast that the sensitive man who had come into her life was so brilliant and the object of so much devotion. In the dressing room afterwards, amongst a crowd of well-wishers – some of them famous – she glowed with pride.

He was honest from the start. Even before the first kiss he explained that it was impossible for him to get married and have a family. He liked children. He enjoyed domesticity, but he had always known music would come first. It was unfair to inflict the absences and the obsessiveness of his calling on another person, equally impossible to compromise. Marriage without flexibility was not marriage. In the end he knew he could not be beholden to another.

She had listened to this carefully, advancing as far as she could towards his point of view, gaining his confidence by not arguing the point or questioning the finality of his self-knowledge. She took him as he was. And later, when the romance had started, and Philip was spending the night with her three times a week, and flying her out to meet him on tour, she found it hard to imagine the line beyond which their relationship would become too much for him, too limiting, or consuming, because everything they did together went so easily and so well, and the terrible moods that he hinted at, the seething maestro fits, never happened. He felt at home in her ground-floor flat, and liked having her to stay in his house. She could work on his computer there, and he was happy to practise on her upright. Although their time together was shaped by his diary, his busy round never stopped them doing the couply things: week-end lie-ins, wine-bar trysts, art-gallery outings. He practised, boy, did he practise, but the habit was so ingrained it seemed nothing could disrupt him. Their moderate social lives blended easily. Philip passively enjoyed the company of more relaxed people. He cherished the musical judgements of Rod and Colin Wyatt, gloriously irreverent as they were. The brothers knew every artist, every recording, every anecdote; they were comically erudite. They had gone to a thousand concerts and could talk musical shop with the bluff confidence of those who have never touched an instrument, let alone performed, but have listened devoutly for years and know what the main thing is. Whilst duly humble where appropriate, the flick of a cigarette, or the twiddled stem of a wine glass might see off some world-class pianist whose efforts they deemed ordinary. Rod tended to sit at the end of the table, giant legs parked to one side, his broad face beaming in candlelight like a post-prandial Henry VIII; Colin struck profile between Laura's female guests, exuding intensity of aspect and listening judicially to his brother's intelligent balderdash.

Rodney had once turned to face Philip with a look of encyclopedic finality. 'You "own" the Chopin Studies. In the way Horowitz "owned" Rach 3, or Cortot the Chopin Preludes.'

'I agree,' nodded Colin, raising his glass in tribute.

'Everybody else can just buzz off.'

Philip had smiled wisely. Like most pianists he distrusted approval as much as he resented criticism. He made it a point of honour never to condemn fellow musicians or to admit praise, however sincere. In general, the brothers' discussions he found both amusing and depressing. 'Face it, Colin,' said Rodney on another occasion. 'We're hooked on music that's a century out of date, with no status in the mainstream. Our one abiding passion is a hangover from a bygone era, making us into walking dinosaurs.'

Colin was not happy with this description. 'I don't think you can put classical-music lovers on the same level as trainspotters or S & M collectivists. We're not a quaint fringe. We are keepers of the Grail in a time of cultural darkness. Our taste is far more important than the mass taste of the age.'

'Oh, come on, Col!'

'I refuse to be culturally irrelevant just because I'm civilised and sensitive.'

Rod smiled dangerously. 'Just because your CD collection is not quite the honey trap for young lovelies that you hoped.'

'That's irrelevant.'

'But true.'

'Call me snobbish, elitist and a fogey,' insisted Colin.

'We will.'

'But not because I adore classical music.'

Rod nodded and turned to Philip. 'We are your followers.' His eyebrows peaked nobly. 'The Knights Templar *de nos jours.*

Laura accommodated him without surrendering and he was increasingly dependent on her. He experimented with the idea of marriage, nurtured fantasies of a proposal that never became plans. Though he was tied up with her there was some element of true love slightly around the corner, which he could neither define nor identify, except by its absence, and the more he came to ask of himself what this missing element was, the more absent it seemed, like vanished lust, inexplicable but unarguable; and as he reflected on the issue, as he felt he must, for her sake, his lack of certainty began to irk him. She was ten years younger than he, ten years firmer. When did he kid himself he would find more than this in a woman? And anyway, it was not an issue of content or type or the sum of any female quality that she might represent, because he already loved her for the very thing she was. He loved her, he felt sure, as much as he could love anyone.

The demise of their relationship was a terrible thing. Her hints were so gentle at first, so painfully reasonable. If, as he said, his love was complete, how could he deny her the fulfilment of that love? How could marriage and children be anything but a natural extension of their fondness for each other? He would listen and nod, feeling her view with care, even tenderness, whilst his heart twisted. Her reasonable questions exerted suffocating pressure. She was probing into an area that he did not control or understand. After such exchanges, an abyss opened between them – harrowing for Philip. He needed so much to feel close to her.

His special pleadings about the life of a pianist wore thin. Nothing could be more important than a central relationship. Laura herself pointed out that an art form that depended so much on the humanity of its practitioners could hardly prescribe that its practitioners sacrifice something essential to that humanity. When he tried to explain his need for freedom, for separateness, she told him he was already enmeshed with her, that the need was a delusion. When he tried to describe the missing element or un-certainty, she said that he had no model of Miss Right, no archetype on to which any girlfriend could superimpose. He had never known his mother and his adoptive mother was quite different. He had, instead, to value the reality.

They coasted along, hoping in a way that the relationship would simply subsist. Then the deadlines began, the signs of a terminal toughness. Philip had to face the well-meaning enquiries of her father – the dear old man meekly hoping to clear things up for Laura's sake, and putting his foot in it with both of them. He was shamed by the old boy's love for his daughter and fondness for him. His hopes for Laura's future happiness and his own peace of mind as an ageing father rested on the match and Philip felt acutely sorry for the family heartache their separation would cause. He suffered the kind remonstrations of old friends. Peter and Clarissa were devoted to Laura. John Sampson heaped praises on her. She had the double thumbs-up from Julius Robarts, his American colleague. 'Great PR for you, my friend. It's like your aura's had a makeover.'

All he could do was feel guilty and selfish and incompetent, whilst recognising it was up to her to get rid of him. Whatever she said, he would not make the break. The onus was on her to get so pissed off that she left him, and this he probably exploited, knowing she would never give up.

He was wrong about that. Laura had shockwaves of rancour in store. It depressed him to see this final backlash and he believed it when she said he had ruined her life. He was her undoing, the curse of a man who cannot commit and who comes at an age when a woman has few remaining chances. Without him her prospects were more hopeless than ever. He had cheated her of vital years, a happy future, the chance of a family.

She foresaw this in the doomed last months of their years together and the injustice of it drove her to an extremity of contempt for him. He took the punishment like a man, feeling that, if she had suffered from his emotional incapacity, he should be made to suffer for it, too. In the end, of course, his pity had limits. One could not be forced to marry. Her haranguing and beseeching became tedious.

The break was sudden. One morning in his house she gathered her possessions into a carrier bag and left without a word. He stood by the sash window in the living room, looking down at the street as she came out of the building, and watched her hail a cab without a backward glance.

Thereafter she wrote him a letter that poisoned his sleep for weeks. It was a declaration of the most desperate love and it paralysed him completely. Everything good about Laura breathed in the lines of this letter. Even her handwriting moved him: so feminine, so genteel, so lovably old-fashioned. Her phrases were full of life and intelligence. In language she conveyed the beauty of a woman's ardour. Her appeal washed away all the rancour between them so that he could see again the calibre of feeling he had attracted. All her qualities shone in this letter and for days he struggled with the conviction that, if he did not take up the challenge and offer to marry her, he would be letting something of inestimable value slip through his fingers – a fine woman's love. He expected her to call as the days passed, but Laura knew better. This was her parting shot. The situation now had a bitter clarity and it was up to him to respond. If he could bear to live without her love, she had done the right thing. She had wanted him to know exactly what he was throwing away: a part of himself. For six or eight weeks the world was a bleak place for Philip. He had the certainty of a wrong turn, but was powerless to do anything. He decided to suffer and survive. He despised himself, of course.

Two years later they met by chance in Harrods. Both were Christmas shopping and it seemed the civilised thing to have tea upstairs. That went well enough and a couple of weeks later he invited her to a gallery preview, which she attended. Now forty-two, Laura was an archivist working for Channel 4. There was no hint of a boyfriend and yet she seemed to have moved on, and somehow or other they found a groove that did not insult the strength of their previous bond. There followed sundry meetings, strangely autumnal in character. She had not quite forgiven him, nor fallen out of love with him, but habits had changed, and the same dignity that compelled her to leave him allowed her to enjoy his company without expecting too much. She took him as she found him and kept herself in rein. Perhaps it pleased her to sense he still needed her. On one of these occasions Camilla's name came up. Laura had discovered a friend in common with Philip's old flame. That friend had told Laura about the abortion, and Laura now passed this on to Philip. At the time, he was so surprised he hardly noticed how she slipped it into conversation. It was the kind of news that came from nowhere but was impossible to forget.

Chapter Eleven

HE STOOD IN HER front room.

She had a plumber in the flat, so was out in the kitchen. She gave him a whisky the moment he arrived.

He had spent many evenings in this little drawing room with its Victorian fireplace and stripped-pine floorboards. He recognised all her things, moved but not replenished: the heirloom Bechstein against the wall, lid closed; the alcoves of bookshelves showing the same faded spines; the tired chaise in the bay, dried flowers in the hearth, boudoir throws on old armchairs, even the fat candle on the mantelpiece with its hint of convent solace. A dead fly lay on its back on the windowsill. The room was faded and smaller than he remembered. It was a cosy enough place six years ago. She should have moved on by now.

He remained standing because he needed to stay on his toes. He was apprehensive and absolutely ready to cave in, and guilty in advance because he had come to be mothered. He needed to be dosed with sympathy and Laura was the only person he could turn to. Beneath the need, however, was something else. He was more shaken up than he realised and wondered in dread what either of them could take from an encounter in this state. When she came into the room, eyes wide with concern, she seemed already to understand that something serious had happened, and that this was something she might have predicted and even known about: a moment of reckoning that flowed from everything that had failed to happen in his life.

She took his hand with the care of a nurse, gazed into his eyes.

He was distressed by her touch. It brought emotion to the surface. His eyes prickled and he let out a deep sigh.

'Sit down then.'

'OK.'

'Let's have a cigarette.'

He subsided into the armchair, like Frankenstein sitting down, a palm on either knee.

'I've left mine . . .'

'I've got some in a drawer.'

She was soon sitting near him, leaning across the arm of the chaise, watching him smoke. He sipped his whisky and puffed gratefully and thought what a blessing it was when you were miserable to let someone look you in the eye, as though the main thing, first off, was to let the bad feeling be registered. Her dark eyes were so subtly knowing.

He waited for something to occur to him, a way in. He had no idea where to begin.

'I heard about the concert,' she said.

'Oh.'

'Sounds awful, Philip.'

He nodded in agreement. That was one of many awful things, and now they were all mixed up.

'I've just cancelled the series.'

She did not react.

'Think I've sacked John.'

'Did you row?'

'Yes.'

He could see that she was unsettled by this. Whatever he might tell her, the consequences of a rift would seem worse than the cause.

'Gosh,' she said softly.

'I can't trust him any more.'

He looked at his whisky. He hated more than anything the idea of going back to hospital: long corridors, waiting rooms, grave faces.

'How are you?' he said quickly.

'Fine.' She smiled.

'It's nice to be here.'

'Lucky I was in. I've hardly been back recently. It's all very musty and dusty.'

He frowned. 'Oh. Right.'

There was a pause. He drew himself up in his chair, and then the realisation dawned. His head cleared suddenly. 'Have you . . .?'

Laura looked at him in a certain way, to prepare him. Her face was tranquil, the outer effect of unfamiliar happiness.

He swallowed.

She smiled again, ironically bunching her cheeks and then releasing them.

His heart was sinking, an unprecedented feeling.

He glanced away for a moment, as if to fortify himself. He could not rise above an abrupt sense of loss, a landslide of the spirit: and yet this was inevitable.

'Somebody from work?'

'Someone new.'

'Rodney!'

She laughed. 'Course not!'

'Colin?'

'Don't be ridiculous. He's married.'

'Colin's married?'

She half-smiled and shrugged. 'One bachelor less in the world. True love, actually.'

'You?' He was tense with emotion. 'Or Colin?'

She looked away, drawing on her cigarette. 'Maybe both of us.'

Philip averted his eyes. His ash hung long and crooked. He felt as though he would never get out of the chair.

'Nobody you know,' she said, after a while.

He nodded.

'Think I'll have another drink.' She rose and then leaned across, bringing him the smell of her scent. 'Another?'

He heard her talking to the plumber along the corridor. She was chirpy and light-hearted, her voice ringing, and when she came back into the room, a glass in either hand, he could see her expression changing back a gear, as if to protect him from the sight of her happiness. He noticed her hips as she came towards him. She had developed a way of walking, an unaccustomed ease of movement that asserted a right to her new sense of attractiveness. It suited her.

He was now less sure where to start. His preoccupations seemed endless. His life's orderly scheme had been abandoned and yet he had no idea how to live without order. As she took up position near by, softly settling on the chaise, he was struck by the sensation of her being so easily close to him whilst belonging to another man. He savoured the surprise unpleasantness of this emotion, noticing a strange jealousy in the mix. He was becoming the master of retrospective regret.

Her words of comfort could not mean the same now.

'What did John say?'

He shook his head.

'He's very fond of you.'

'I need to know.' His throat was dry. 'Why did you tell me about the abortion?'

Her face changed colour. She put her glass on the table.

'Why did I have to know that?'

'Why?'

He rubbed an eye.

She shook her head.

'What good would it do me?' He could not bear to look at her.

'Sorry. I couldn't keep it to myself.'

'I confronted Camilla.'

'You what!'

'I went to see her.'

'God!'

'She has two lovely children.'

Laura was ashen-faced.

'She didn't deny it. She made her reasons absolutely clear and that was that.'

Laura digested the remark without reacting. She was concentrating hard, measuring what might and might not be said.

'You knew I'd be devastated.'

'I didn't.'

'Bull's eye, Laura.'

'Don't be ridiculous!'

'Why else, then?'

She was suddenly crestfallen, as though he had shamed her. 'I thought if I knew, you should.'

'I see. You imparted this information to make me realise how profoundly I was rejected by Camilla?'

The accusation seemed so unfair. 'Camilla's been married for ages, Philip. She was a lost cause years before I came on the scene.'

106

'Yes, but you thought I hadn't accepted that. So I needed to hear about the abortion to make it crystal clear.'

She looked at him with painful honesty. 'I was never jealous of Camilla.'

He got up from his chair, walked across the room. 'You wanted me to know how much you suffered when I refused to have a family. Payback time. I can understand that.'

'Think what you like.'

'You wanted this information to have an effect.'

She frowned, overwhelmed suddenly. 'Why not? It's your information. Your life!'

He turned to meet her head-on.

'It should have an "effect",' she told him.

'I needed to suffer in order to rise to your proud level of emotional maturity. Is that it?'

'Blame me all you like. It's not true. Have you tried to understand why this revelation is so upsetting?'

'I'm sure you can tell me.'

She looked away. 'Philip, I've said enough.'

'About our relationship, sure. You needed me to be something that suited you, and when I failed to be that thing, you had no interest in the very thing I was.'

'Why are you here?' She was almost angry. 'How can I possibly be of help to you?'

Her strength, once bared, cowed him. She was no longer bound up with him and he could never return to her again, and this was suddenly stark. His anger was beside the point and so were his accusations of bad faith.

He passed a hand across his face. No one could partake in his misery. He felt foolish, deflated. 'What's wrong with me, then?'

She shook her head, knowing it was neither the time nor the place for this. 'You're in a state.'

'No! No! What has always been wrong with me?'

She looked at him squarely for a moment, and then shrugged.

'Very difficult for you to be objective. I'll take that into account.'

She raised her glass, swigged back the whisky. 'It's not fair to ask me.'

'Tell me the worst. With knobs on.'

She laughed, shaking her head sadly at the same time.

'Because you left me,' he said. 'You were the one that left!'

She gave him an odd look. This interpretation did not please her. 'That's what happens when a man won't commit. The woman has more faith, and then more courage.'

He raised his hands in frustration. 'Yes, but why can't I commit? Why am I such a basket case?'

She heard the plumber calling in the corridor and slipped outside to pay him. Philip looked around in a turmoil of embarrassment and dismay. He had not meant to ask this question; it just came out of him. He had come here to be comforted, to feel loved.

He waited in suspense, and as he returned to his seat he felt more like a friend whom he had once made the mistake of pitying, Michael Connelly, an Irish theatre director. Michael's romantic activities were tiringly ceaseless and repetitively futile. He had once been invited by a married couple to join them on holiday in Portugal. Other couples and plentiful children were present in a scene of uxorious contentment. Connelly was duly relieved when one Robert Burlap turned up. Also in his forties and militantly unmarried, Burlap had hired a sports car. The spectacle of so much fulfilment was tiring for both men. They decided to slip away to Lisbon for a couple of nights 'on the town', as a one-in-the-eye to the marrieds, 'on the town' amounting in all probability to two sedentary restaurant-bound evenings of swapped gossip and mutual solidarity in the forlorn existentials of bacherlordom. Michael was hoping for an exchange about the odd sensation of being middle-aged, barren, slightly depressed and fixated on younger women. Robert would surely drop his guard and wash down a clubby platitude or twain with a good bottle of Dao. Why were they so high and dry, so unwilling to commit, so enervatingly incorrigible? It was time for a few statesmanlike reflections that would place their rather dubious behaviour in a wider context, alleviating any sense of guilt or responsibility, not to mention seediness, as if commitment-phobia and two-timing were a zeitgeist bugbear victimising them as much as the poor women they strung along. Robert, alas, would not be drawn. Michael's enquiries were deflected. His frank and occasionally compromising admissions were stonewalled with a curt smile. Burlap kept it light and general with the result that two men with a rich kinship in emotional incompetence found it impossible to communicate. Michael told Philip, when the holiday was over, that Robert must be hell to go out with. 'Conversation can never get personal. He's a sphinx without a bloody secret!' Philip had suspected that Robert could bear to hear neither his own evasions nor Michael's lies. For neither man was self-knowledge a palatable option. Emotional depletion begat a kind of cognitive circularity. Whatever their starting point they would end up with themselves as they were, not as they might be, which after a third glass of port was beginning to resemble destiny. Whence real passion at their age? The biological clock was a woman's problem. Men had the emotional clock to fret over and Robert and Michael had just twigged this valuable and compassionate concept when, for both of them, it was two seconds past midnight.

Philip looked at the pattern on the rug. He waited awkwardly. He was being examined in every way at the moment. Other people were running tests and making diagnoses or reviewing him judicially. All his life he had been dissected as a pianist, his every career progression had been approved by someone other than himself: examiners, jurors, music critics, audiences. His art had been written about and subjected to comparison, but as a man he had never been quantified; his moral nature was undefined, known to intimates perhaps, who had only ever been able to take him as he was – a law unto himself.

She came back into the room and settled on the chaise.

'Remember,' she said, her voice tight, 'that you requested this.'

He swallowed. 'That sounds so ominous.'

'It's only my way of understanding you. Probably very shallow.'

'I doubt it, Laura. I doubt it.'

She passed him a look that was gentle at first, almost questioning. She seemed to reassure him of good faith. The look was a reminder of all that had gone on between them, and supremely of her loyalty to his best interests, but in her eyes he saw a strange superiority. She knew her mind; she had a view, and this was a view she could only impart in full.

He was determined to hear her. He wanted to know what he was up against, the full interpretation.

'I used to think that music was your strategy for avoiding the pain of human relations. If you devoted yourself to the piano, you could

109

reach people on your own terms. Music was a means to keep the world where you wanted it. At arm's length. It was an obvious strategy because you're so gifted, and as an only adopted child it must have been great to have this world that you could escape into. That's how I understood it in the early days, when you spoke of your commitment to the piano, like vows. Here was a man trying to hold himself together. Sudden intimacy would engender the terror of separation.' Laura frowned intelligently, gathering the thread. 'Before then, I never understood men who couldn't commit. With you I had to form an understanding. To be deserted or let down by a lover . . . I could see that was an unbearable prospect. I never believed you were indifferent. Self-protective, rather.'

He sat with crossed arms, gazing into the fire grate.

'Then I met Edward. I realised how natural and uncomplicated it is when you meet the right person, even though meeting that person is a fluke. All the important things can be so simple. But without having those things – love, trust, security – you just haven't developed.'

'Is this you talking, or your shrink?'

She was sudden. 'If I hadn't met you, I wouldn't have needed a shrink! You were the most complicated thing that had ever happened to me. I was determined not to be fucked up by you, Philip. Because unlike you I had no international career to go back to, no cheering audiences and famous friends. After my three years as your girlfriend I had no fall-back position. And without a decent future, the future I deserve, the past is just OVER.'

He shook his head.

For a moment she was subdued, depressed all over again.

'I hoped that if I was constant, always there for you, that if I poured love into you' – she wiped her nose with the back of her hand – 'you would gradually heal, and some inner place would thaw, and the love that I thought was trapped inside you would get out; and eventually we could get married and have a child. I played a long game, Philip. And lost. Something you will never do. In fact, giants of the keyboard have no idea what ordinary people put up with to find fulfilment. They have to be patient. And strong. So strong.'

He avoided eye contact, but she was in any case downcast with reminiscence. She paused, as if to gain strength for what was to come. She had lived through all this. Talking it through required courage and concentration. She had to say what she thought, and she had to trust what she said for both their sakes. 'But then I realised I had fallen in love with the artist and not the man, and that these two things were not the same. Your beautiful playing was not a gift to me. It was a gift to the world. What I got to myself was only the man.' She looked at him with pain. 'The man was not enough. I could have gone on hoping for the best, because people develop and you had a history to overcome, but . . .' She had lost all colour. Her lips worked the bitterness of a thought. 'After the fire, there really seemed no point.'

He had not expected this and was suddenly at sea. It hit him in the vocal cords so that when he spoke his voice was trembly. 'What d'you mean?'

'You are cauterised, Philip.'

He smiled uncomprehendingly. 'I wish I were.'

'In your heart you are.'

'You'll have to justify that.'

Her jaw jutted and her eyes glinted. 'Dead inside.'

'You condemn me but you don't help me!'

'You don't need help. You've got exactly what you want.'

'I've got nothing.'

'I couldn't believe it.' She grappled the end of the chaise. 'When Peter and Clarissa and the children died, you didn't react.'

'I reacted!'

'Philip, you didn't go to the funeral. You didn't write to his parents. You froze up. I remember you flying off to Stockholm for a concert the day after we heard. When you came back, you wouldn't even talk about it. And he was your best friend!'

He guarded the side of his face with his hand. 'I was . . . he was like a brother to me . . . I was . . .'

'You never shed one tear,' she declaimed.

'I coped with it in my own way.'

'Because you hate strong feelings. Better to have no feelings at all than to grieve someone's death.'

He was tortured now.

'Your heart is a sliver of ice.'

He tried to think straight. 'I couldn't assimilate it . . .'

'Assimilate! What kind of word is that? Your friends died and you didn't flinch.'

'I didn't . . . I couldn't get my head round it. Couldn't understand . . .'

'Because people mean nothing to you. You're so wrapped up in yourself that nobody else is quite real and when they die you don't really notice.'

'What is one supposed to do?' he shouted. 'There's more to grief than tears. One minute they were there. Then they were . . . gone. I couldn't figure it.'

'Figure this. Understand that. You're all brain and no heart. I saw the coldness and I wanted to get out.'

'I do have feelings, Laura.'

'What use are feelings if nobody ever gets the benefit of them? They might as well not exist. No feelings. So no wife. No children. Nothing.'

She was overwhelming him.

'No wonder you can't play,' she said.

'Oh, don't!'

She was formidable now. 'I mean are those bad reviews just a coincidence?'

'I only had one bad review.'

'God, why are we doing this? What's the bloody point? You can't connect with reality.'

'The *Gramophone* guy's an opera specialist!'

She shook her head. 'Rodney said there were three bad reviews.'

He was stunned.

She glanced, suddenly hating herself.

'I didn't know that.'

'Philip . . .'

'Oh . . .'

She looked at him, pausing a moment while the information settled on his mind, and then her eyes grew large. Suddenly, she knew what she meant exactly. 'If you can't be wholehearted in love or grief, how on earth can you expect to move your listeners?'

His face went white. He had to look away and blink hard against the cruelty of her logic. His hands crushed together on his lap.

'You've become narrow.'

He had no resistance.

Laura stared at him concertedly, holding on to the point. 'I think you have to look at yourself. In the past you've made other people unhappy. Now you're the unhappy one. You have a lot of issues, Philip. It's time to get help.'

He felt like a child.

'Are you going to be unhappy for the rest of your life or face up to things? You need to change.'

There was a long silence.

'Change is not easy,' he said softly.

'It's extremely difficult. Very painful. But there's no going back. You have to break the pattern, because the past is over and what you could get by on then isn't enough any more. The grand bachelor days have led to this, look at you, this ruined figure. And now you're desperate and miserable because you've been living your life in a way that doesn't work. Get some help, get your own therapist. Do the job properly. You're too old at fifty to have delusions about the quality of the life you're living. It's now or never, Philip.'

He gazed at her abjectly.

'What have you got to lose?'

She rose suddenly. She was done with him.

'Laura!'

She walked towards the door and turned to face him one last time. 'You're right, Philip. You're absolutely right. That's exactly why I told you about the abortion. I wanted to prove to you that even you have feelings deep down beneath that crust of ice and it's bloody well time you acknowledged them!'

'Laura!'

'Go, please. Leave me.'

Chapter Twelve

SEREBRIAKOV – A FACE cut from rock, the jaw, the cheekbones, the ridge of the brow, a face forged by the sufferings of Soviet history, custom-made for one of those banners showing Lenin in implacable visionary mode, expressing how hard Russia was going to have to be to itself, to change; and in that look of bitter endurance, in Serebriakov's case caused by his utter disgust with politics, his refusal to be manhandled by history; in the way he looked up at you with intolerable candour, in that granite glance there were flashes of a suffering so compressed that pain itself seemed hewn in the moulded cast of his cranium. The cyclone of his talent had none-theless protected him from historical reality. During the war he was pushed around in the service of his country: propaganda films for the Red Army, monkey-like performances at state functions, cock-tail piano for Politburo chiefs. He was blackmailed and threatened by the Ministry of Culture, coerced and bugged. His family were gently persecuted and two of his Jewish friends disappeared from their flats without trace. But life was easier for him than for most. The Wehrmacht swarmed over the Ukraine, the Red Army crumpled back to Moscow, Stalingrad became a whirlpool of death and Serebriakov learned new piano sonatas. He transcribed any orchestral score he could find, and gave concerts in blacked-out halls at short notice. Later in his life he spoke of those years with an intractable mixture of sorrow and contempt. Human dignity had been stripped from everyone. To relate all the incredible stories of cruelty and suffering was to share a class of information that could not be felt, being beyond the heart's endurance. And so one pressed on. History was everywhere, regrettable, hideous, but the mission of a pianist was not to oppose or resist. The duty of a pianist was to survive through music and to distribute as widely as possible (on countless tours of the most obscure parts of the Soviet Union) Faschingsschwank aus Wien, Et la Lune Descend sur le Temple qui Fut, Aux Cyprès de la Villa d'Este, Goldberg Variations, and a thousand other pieces 'which they need out there'. In the fifties he played in tiny town halls, churches, old air-raid shelters. He loved the days of travel to reach these places. He was a great walker and never missed an opportunity to explore the landscape around remote towns. Privileged and pressurised in equal measure by the Soviet authorities, his reputation with professionals and his fame across the Union was instantly monolithic; and as copies of his recordings and accounts of his playing eked out to the West, foreign critics began to anticipate from musical Russia something as titanically galvanised as the Cold War superpower itself. What forging of temperament had he endured to become this legendary figure? His Russian contemporaries whispered of something immeasurable, something absolute; and if indeed his first concerts in Europe were received with due hysteria it proved remarkably trying to pinpoint his genius. Felix Weber, the Austrian critic, attended his Berlin debut. 'I went to hear him play sonata of Haydn. At first I think no big deal. A minute later the tears are streaming down my face.'

Since the early sixties he had moved to the West. He was shy but his reputation brought him into contact with kings and movie stars. A recluse by nature, he disdained his own celebrity and loathed most of his recordings. Those who gained his trust he invited to a manor house in the Perigord Noir. Music could be played in an adjoining barn. Despite his fame he lived only for music and it would take many hours of shared music-making or solemn record-listening to gain his confidence. To those who had figured out how to fit in around him he was angelic. He revealed a gift for mimicry and a sense of satire. Serebriakov detested the vain and pompous and knew too many people with these qualities. Occasionally, a satirical rage would convulse him, and then his humour could be lethal.

By the seventies he was a living legend, so associated with the post-war years as to seem almost historic. His mountainous presence lurked mistily behind the new generation of pianists. In a way, his sovereign example was a backdrop to all who followed. Against

Serebriakov you could measure any pianist. He incarnated an absolute musical integrity beyond the reach of ambition or fame.

This was the person who in 1974 attended a concert of Philip Morahan's. Philip had no idea of the maestro's presence during the concert and was stunned to see him in the dressing room afterwards, taking his place in the queue of well-wishers. They had never met before and, when the divinity shook his hand and congratulated him with the tenderest smile, Philip felt he had been blessed.

By then, Konstantine was already a decade into his friendship with Arthur England. Konstantine had fallen like a lover for the landscape around Arthur's home near Bromyard, with its views across Herefordshire to the Black Mountains. He would spend a fortnight there every summer, going on walks, and immersing himself in the music that Arthur lived and breathed: Britten and Delius, Howells and Bax, Finzi and Vaughan Williams. He had returned again this year (possibly for the last time) to celebrate his birthday and make a little music. He was eighty-eight, not well. He had come up from France by train and been collected in London by Arthur in Oswald's Bentley (driven on this occasion by Kevin – Kevin was Oswald's sous-chef and manservant when not chauffeuring the elderly great along Arcadian B-roads). The same driver had been sent to collect Philip two weeks later, and Philip now sat in the back seat, allowing himself to be conveyed along the M40 into the past, as Kevin slalomed in great swerves of effortless velocity between crowded motorway lanes.

He had not been to Herefordshire in years. As they drove through the Chilterns his tired eyes could not escape the scenery: the dramatic revelation of vast fields, sudden stands of beech, the forested capes of commanding hills enshouldering the road. In late May the beeches seemed shampooed. Their crowns were glossy and well conditioned. After Oxford the trees became more furrowed and antique, and as the grand old estates around Ledbury and Tewkesbury kicked in, the rolling landscape was indented by lordly Wellingtonias, and blasted oaks with antlered crowns and old limbs elbowed in cow mud.

He sank lower and lower in the back seat, catching everything, stone houses, the rivers of May blossom, the muffled heads of thatched cottages that came and went. He had nearly fallen asleep when the car pulled to the right and proceeded with reverential moderation down a lane. The lane levelled and broadened in preparation for the drive to Arthur's house, and then the gravel crackled and the palms of a cedar loomed overhead and they were there, approaching the posing corner of Moreton Manor. He watched the Edwardian pile draw closer, with its mock-Tudor chimney stacks and gables, and mullion bays blindly greeting all comers. They came under a gateway on to the forecourt and parked. Philip got out of the car and had time for a glance at the long view to the west before Oswald's cornet greeting cut the air.

He sat with Oswald in the old kitchen sipping tea. Arthur and Konstantine had driven off to Hergest Croft to see the azaleas, and Julius Robarts was upstairs, flat out with jet-lag.

Oswald's lined face and stringy dewlaps and eye pouches were all caught up in the excitement of the event, and twitched vitally as he described the delicacies he had prepared with his kitchen under-lings, the wines that were assuming perfect temperatures, and the distinguished musicians Arthur had conscripted, not just from the four corners of England, but from all over the world.

'We have Lola Montrero, ha ha.'

'Lola?'

'Set the cat among the bloody pigeons.'

'My God.'

'Vyacheslav Chuikov.' Oswald wobbled his jowls compassio-nately. 'Veritable thumb-sucker and nose-picker. Autistic, I pre-sume.'

'Right.'

'Geraint Davies, Cedric Bowles, Aldous Braebourne. Two Royal College professors.'

'Which ones?'

'Damien Baldwin. Lovely Mauritz Wengler all the way from Berlin. Your friend, Vadim.'

'Oh dear.'

'I've put you in that cosy b & b up the road, all expenses paid, so mind you eat your Full English. There's a peer. Some jackanapes New Labour acolyte keen on the blasted arts, would you believe! Couldn't keep him out. Amanda Holcraft. The Ambrose Quartet.'

'You putting everybody up?'

'I'm packed to the rafters. More tea, please, Barry.'

A clean-cut young man emerged from the pantry. He wore a sleeveless T-shirt and had a tattoo on his biceps.

'Give Philip a spot more, too, would you, Barry.'

'Thank you.'

Oswald laughed chestily. 'I'm fortunate in having these paragons at my disposal.'

Philip watched Barry return to the pantry. 'Where d'you get them?'

'They're Harry Ploughman types from the local.' He managed a pursed smile. 'Sweet dullards. But . . . you know . . . decorative!'

'Watch your silver.'

'Oh sure! I'm like a closed-circuit camera with these fickle youths. Follow your every move, don't I, Barry!'

'How's Arthur?'

'Indefatigable. I so hope he notices when I die.'

'You're a juvenile by comparison.'

'A buggered old wreck of seventy-two,' he chortled.

Philip looked in astonishment at the floor. 'Lola's coming?'

Oswald nodded certainly.

'God, I haven't seen her for about twenty-five years.'

'Lovely girl. Julius said he calculated she must have smoked seven hundred and fifty thousand cigarettes since they last met. Doesn't look a day older.'

'She's remarkable.'

'Very great pianist and a total maniac.'

'I'm glad Julius is here.'

'He's a dear. Apparently he qualified as a chartered accountant before getting the piano bug.'

'Oswald!'

'Well, you know what I mean.'

Oswald was a doughty satirist of musical types. Whereas Arthur presented a timeless patrician serenity that was a bit out of date, but just about plausible given his vast age, Oswald had appointed himself court jester. He found musicians to be an extraordinary and ridiculous bunch: 'People whose talents so far exceed their social skills that sometimes I feel I'm conversing with a pair of hands attached to a life-support system.' Oswald prospected for the one foible or characteristic which would make it impossible to take a great musician seriously again. He would look at you and say: 'Seven hundred and fifty thousand Marlboros. They call her Rola,' and that was it for the tumultuous Montrero. Oswald liked people to the extent that their conversation allowed him to recreate himself as wit and sophisticate. Someone described him as the gargoyle on Arthur's cathedral, but Arthur relied on his camp alter ego for everything, and the two had been inseparable for years. 'Thirty-five years, actually, which is a lot longer than some of you promiscuous heterosexual bods.' Oswald had private means. 'Based on biscuit tins, or something. Bloody catering. Look at me now. All I ever do is cook meals for people.'

'How's Konstantine?' said Philip.

'Oh.' Oswald looked away, blinking. He shook his head sorrowfully. 'He's not got long.'

Philip glanced at his lap.

'What will we do without them, Philip, these grand old boys?'

Philip spent the afternoon walking in the lanes. He heard rustic voices carrying in the wind, the cranking sound of farm machinery. The verges were dense with celandine and greater stichwort. Old trees looked young again, the wooded hillocks more buxom. He would take in the long view to the west, towards the Welsh hills, visible as a blue line over the interceding countryside, the soft patchwork that rolled from Moreton Manor across the Golden Valley to the Black Mountains, a rural Eden of meadows and parkland and cider-apple orchards glinting in the afternoon light.

He sat down at the foot of a hornbeam and gazed at the tracery of hedgerows, and out of nowhere he pictured Katie approaching him in the long grass and raising her hand to show him a pair of mating butterflies that had settled on a forefinger. They had sat together in the ragged shade of a hawthorn and watched in delight as hares bounded all over the field. He remembered walking back with her through a wood, and when they emerged the three-year-old pointed to a glider hanging over the far fields like a hovering gull, sheet white against azure.

Memory weighed on him. The past was all around him now.

Today, he felt no pain, merely the actuality of things.

After seeing Laura he had purchased the offending magazines: *Hi-fi News* and *Record Review, International Piano, Classic CD.*

He read the reviews in the privacy of his drawing room. He was satisfactorily numb. They were not terrible. They were certainly not good. The magazines slipped off the chair on to the floor as he stared at the writhing shadows of a tree on his ceiling and walls.

He had accepted Arthur's invitation right off. He was not presentable in any sense, just a shell of a man now, but a couple of nights in Herefordshire would help eat up the wait for the test results; and Konstantine he could not refuse. In his present knackered straits it moved him to contemplate the old boy's incorruptible purity, his allergy to compromise, his dogged perseverance. He had never been commodified by the record companies. No impresario had tamed him. Throughout a bustling musical life he had never let go of the main thing, the simple sense of how to play a piece. He knew. And what he knew was unfathomable. Philip dared not play his best recordings too often. He was not invariably attuned, but when in the mood he found himself experiencing something beyond insight or interpretation. It was like sharing for a moment a physicist's mentalisation of space-time or subatomic particles, as though Serebriakov divined the music of the spheres and made them audible. The celestial order of his playing induced a kind of ravishment – so beyond one's means to reproduce as to reek of total genius.

Serebriakov would simply say he followed the letter of the score.

Philip lay on the bed in his room at the b & b until six-thirty. He then got up and strolled back to the big house, as instructed. He came through the porch into the hallway and was shown to the main drawing room by Kevin. The room was full of evening light, which lifted its mahogany gloom to a twilight of fluttering blues and parchment oranges and deep warm browns.

Oswald hovered pleasantly over champagne and glasses. Arthur took his ease on the settee.

In the high-backed chair by the fireplace sat Konstantine Serebriakov.

Philip came forward solidly but then hesitated at the spectacle before him. He felt a qualifying respect that delivered the initiative to his host, as though he were waiting for a kind of acceptance into the group. The elderly gents were still recovering from their walk, and had only just sat down. Arthur took a while to register that Philip was Philip, and then greeted him from his seat.

'Konstantine, it's Philip Morahan!'

Oswald smiled from his station, and Arthur relapsed into his cushion.

Philip hesitated, not knowing whether to offer a hand or to nod. The old Russian tilted his head, as if better to hear. His eyes were large, vague. He seemed not to recognise Philip.

'B & b OK?' said Oswald, handing him a glass of champagne.

'Yes, thanks.'

Oswald sidled out of the room and Philip made to sit down between the two old boys. He was shaken by Konstantine's appearance. The old pianist was a ruined figure now, bald as a stone. There was something so vulnerably skeletal about him. The planes and curves of his skull had been tautened and harrowed by age. His hands lay on his lap like manacles, patchy with liver spots.

Arthur tweaked his pipe.

'Did you . . . did you have a nice walk?' he asked.

The old man was wide-eyed.

Arthur cleared his throat blusterously. 'Hergest Croft is lovely this time of year.'

Oswald swung back with a tray of smoked-salmon tidbits. 'Were the azaleas absolutely glorious?'

Konstantine looked up, more in response to movement than sound.

Philip scratched the side of his head. He was sitting next to the greatest pianist in the world and had no idea what to say. What could he ask him?

'Were the azaleas glorious?' said Oswald in a very loud voice.

'They look good,' said Arthur. 'Can I have one?'

Konstantine blinked. 'Azaleas?'

'Were they glorious?' said Oswald with a continuing expression of joyous enquiry.

Konstantine brought an old hand up to his breast pocket and drew out a handkerchief. He shook it open and let it dangle from forefinger and thumb. He stared at Philip, as if posing a question.

Oswald gingered around with the canapés and frowned patiently.

Konstantine's eyebrows were arched enquiringly.

'Handkerchief trees?' said Philip.

The Russian cracked a smile. 'Free in May.'

'They do a great job up there,' said Arthur, administering his pipe. 'The colours are heavenly.'

'The azaleas were obviously superlative,' said Oswald, presenting the canapés to Philip. 'Where are my servants?'

'I saw Kevin lingering in the hall,' said Arthur.

'He's very good at lingering, is Kevin.'

'He lingers rather well, I've always thought.'

Philip gazed steadily into his champagne glass.

'You did not play!'

He looked up to see Konstantine gazing at him.

'I'm sorry,' he said, involuntarily.

Konstantine waved a hand, brushing it away.

Philip had no idea how to continue. Somewhere along the line he had lost the power of speech. He sat there like an idiot.

'You are brave,' said Konstantine, dabbing his mouth with the handkerchief.

'It wouldn't have been easier to play,' he managed.

'I think for you at that moment it was harder to play one note than for me to climb Eiffel Tower.

Philip caught Arthur's eye.

'He hadn't done enough practice,' said Arthur. 'Must remember to ask for my money back.'

Oswald chuckled. 'Nobody ever got their money back from a temperamental keyboard lion like Philip.'

Philip blinked.

Konstantine continued to stare at him, expecting more. He was incontinently interested.

'I couldn't face the Funeral March Sonata,' he said lightly, quickly.

The Russian made some business of clearing his throat.

Arthur and Oswald seemed pretty uninterested in the exchange. Arthur was in a quasi-vegetative prepreprandial state, and Oswald had catering stratagems on the brain.

In profile Konstantine looked more haggardly ruminative than ever. He used every furrow in his forehead to shift thought. 'But,' he said, swallowing and blinking at the same time. He made a special effort to look Philip in the eye, to advertise his reply with the most saucery glare. 'This is only the Second Sonata. Then you go up. One half-tone to Third Sonata. One semitone. Everything is different.'

'Is that Julius?'

'Julius!' cried Oswald.

'Everything changes.'

Philip looked over his shoulder and then back at Konstantine. He wanted to bury the subject before anyone else came in.

'You understand?'

'I wasn't playing that sonata.'

Konstantine took in a gulp of air, frowned at the evasion. 'It's there all the time. Whether you are playing it or not.'

'Hello, gentlemen.'

Konstantine looked up, mouth agape, and discovered the refreshed presence of Julius Robarts in ironed shirt and chinos.

Arthur staggered to his feet to receive the newcomer and bring him over to Konstantine.

'Happy birthday,' said the American, bowing to greet the old man. 'It's an honour to be here.'

Konstantine released Julius's hands and subsided back into the chair. 'From Boston?'

'From Boston and Rach 3 with Marek Nolson. Hi, Philip.'

Philip smiled. He was unbearably tense.

'It was good?'

'It was OK.'

The old man was perplexed. 'What is OK?'

'Five Rach 3s in five cities and five days. OK is good enough.'

'You are modest, perhaps.'

'Cedric!'

The word had no sooner sounded than Konstantine's face transformed. From somewhere he gained the strength to get on his feet and trundle across the floor to an intense grappling of hands and patting and hugging with the seraphically beaming figure of Cedric Bowles, who had just arrived and who took him in his arms like a long-lost friend. Oswald's face was creased with smiles. Arthur was enchanted. Cedric embraced and pressed flesh with all the aplomb of a fifties matinee idol turned geriatric star attraction at the Yvonne Arnaud. A former leader of the Covent Garden orchestra, he had been smiling without let-up for forty years.

Conversation became more general, and by the time Cynthia Cross and Dame Elizabeth Barrett arrived, Philip felt that Arthur had somehow time-warped them back to his heyday in the late fifties. He slowly moved to the edge of the throng, allowing Konstantine the undiluted company of his oldest friends. Before long he had slipped off unnoticed and found himself in the evening air on a country lane, walking easily and aimlessly. He happened on a pub in due course and sat at a table in the garden with a pint and a packet of crisps.

Later, in bed, he could not sleep. He tried to read, and then slid down again into the cool of the pillow. His thoughts rambled and tumbled and turned, and after a while he found himself picturing Clarissa and Peter in France, a scene he had not recalled for years but which now came back in all sorts of detail. He had joined up with them on the third week of their honeymoon in Provence, along with a few others. They were staying in a villa near Cotignac, going out for dips in local rivers. Peter swum around nude, trunks on his head. Clarissa sunbathed topless amongst riverbank grasses, a glass of wine between her fingers. Above the river an escarpment of rock dangled tapestries of vine. He remembered sauntering through the meadow after lunch to a pile of rocks where he sat on his own for an hour, enjoying the heat and the sound of the crickets, and the sense of a past alive with sprites and nymphs and naiads, as though all those classical creatures were the imaginary fruit of an urge to inhabit landscape in the most literal way possible; and as he sat, entranced by the glittering leaves of the Lombardies, he saw her rise from her hide by the stream in only the slip of a bikini bottom, relishing the sensation of air on bare skin as she moved from the rug and the towels and took a path around tall grasses, stepping into the haze of the meadow, a blossomy gauze rising to veil her back and shoulders, till only her head was visible, and then only the sideways progress of her pink headband; and he could tell from the motions of that head, which halted and inclined and remained for long moments quite still, that she was wading with her whole soul into that meadow, allowing the bees and swallowtail butterflies to play around her, and the lavender to brush her calves, and the shadow of a pine to run over her breast and shoulders.

He lay in the darkness of his room embalmed in these thoughts, which developed to things that were purely imagined, Clarissa and Peter coming and going on the villa balcony, Peter reading under the feathery shade of a mimosa; and as these images developed a life of their own and the faces seemed so near and present, as informally alive as the faces of people captured on home videos, the idea of their non-being seemed meaningless. He lay on his side, clasping the edge of the pillow between his hands. Moisture came to the corner of his eye. He would hold on for a bit. He would join them in the tranquil shade of the black river, swimming behind them over the streaming reeds, rolling and turning in the silky water, till their figures blurred and dislimned in the grey shallows of sleep.

Chapter Thirteen

FRIENDS FROM ALL OVER the world had taken time out of their concert schedules to be in Herefordshire on a Sunday morning in May, and as the distinguished, the elderly and the elegant filed through the hallway to the terrace (where silver glinted on linen and flowers spumed from vases) it seemed more like a wedding reception than a birthday party. Sunlight sparkled and danced on the scene.

There were perhaps a hundred people on the lawn, the Russian contingent, antique British musicians with walking sticks and parasols, young conductors at the height of their celebrity smiling gloriously. They arrived with cards and gifts and easy laughter. There was a bustle around those, like Lola Montrero, who had travelled furthest. Konstantine was in heartier form, greeting all comers on the terrace. He made a thorough job of embracing and double-kissing every guest. Tender eye contact with one well-wisher would be followed by a bear-hug with the next, each new person causing a joyous spasm on his ruined old face.

Oswald's young men from the pub circulated in tunics bearing trays of champagne. Oswald himself swooped and wheeled like an inexhaustibly perfectionist maître d', dropping one minute into the kitchens to chivvy caterers, bustling the next past Barry or Kevin with a snap of his fingers at an empty tray or bottle. His elastic face crushed into charming expressions of welcome for arriving guests. He ushered and complimented, escorted and introduced; then slid through a side door to recapture his misanthropy like a gulp of fresh air.

Philip, meanwhile, busied himself on the sidelines. He popped corks and filled glasses and relayed empty trays to the pantry, avoiding eye contact wherever possible. His aim today was to be helpful and to keep on the move.

Arthur was grandly stationed at the end of the terrace. He was sedentarily magnetic, nonetheless, and had drawn to his side a retinue of the amiably ancient. Cedric and Aldous Braeborne were chipping in jokes, and Arthur was chortling pleasantly. 'By Jove, she's here,' he erupted. 'It's Galina!'

Philip turned to see Galina Berberova hugging Konstantine and winking at Arthur, which caused the old boy to launch himself towards the only woman who had ever queered the perfect pitch of his sexual convictions. The insurmountable diva received his toothy peck like a blushing Venus scaled by admirers. Konstantine gazed on in craggy rapture.

Beyond them stood Vadim.

Philip was alert, though he did not move. Too many people were around for him to make an approach.

His heart beat faster. He should have called him before. It was awkward here. The onus was on Philip to take back what he said, but now it was too late.

He glanced around, seeking a refill. The depth of his unease surprised him. It was not so easy to take back the truth, to swallow it up. The truth was his doing, something he had to get out of his system to make the friendship tenable. Apology was impossible, of course. He swigged back his drink and decided to collar Vadim later on. He would have to be sharper and stronger than his protégé, and this was going to be difficult because his confidence was low. Only a kind of numbness insulated him from the depressing sight of so many pianists. Everywhere flocked eminence, reputation, youthful swagger. And along with eminence sauntered glamour. In the corner of his eye he saw a startlingly pretty woman: red mouth, golden locks, long eyelashes. She bobbed in the crowd like a trophy.

Vadim leaned towards her a second later, and whispered in her ear. She took his hand and smiled brilliantly, a scandalised smile.

Philip averted his eyes to avoid complicity. He was pained and embarrassed. Poor Marguerite. If wives could be abandoned so carelessly, what hope for mere friends?

When he risked looking back, Vadim had joined the line-up to meet Konstantine. He was holding a cigarette and a wine glass. Momentarily he glanced at Philip, but without recognition.

There was now a bottle-neck by the door; more pianists, a traffic jam of talent plodding towards Konstantine: Slava Chuikov, Aram Kalajian, Detlev Schwindler, Marganita and Boris Bergamot. They all edged dutifully forward, faces prepared for the moment of greeting. Even the crabbiest oldsters were held in check. Even the great Lola Montrero, who played like no one else, allowed her power to fade a few degrees in Konstantine's immortal presence.

'I hope for Medtner's sake a bomb doesn't go off,' said Julius, at his side suddenly.

Philip nodded.

'The only pianists in the world currently programming Medtner Five are right on this terrace.'

He needed to move.

'Hey, Philip, I liked your Chopin disc.'

'Shall we say hello to Lola?'

'Always a good idea.'

Lola was pleased to see him but more interested in Julius, which was acceptable. Philip separated himself from the duo and had the misfortune to catch Vadim's girlfriend's eye. She smiled quickly, and came over to say hello. Her name was Jonelle. She was an American academic researching a book about pianists, which she pronounced 'penists', and she knew all about him. Philip answered her questions economically whilst looking for an out. A pleasant enough girl, she was doomed to humiliation in Vadim's hands.

Oswald tapped a glass to gain attention, announced lunch, and commended everyone to the placement.

Philip had engineered a seat next to Aldous Braebourne and Lady Carmichaels, neither of whom would ask personal questions or refer to cancelled concerts.

'Kevin!' he called out, as he took his seat.

Kevin turned on his heel.

'Be a sport and get us a bottle of champagne.'

After lunch people strolled around the grounds, or took coffee in the drawing room, easing off a bit before the concert, which started at five. Ten minutes before time a handbell was rung on the terrace, recalling everyone to the music room. People drifted in from the garden and the house, taking their places on the semicircle of seats on the parquet, and waiting eagerly for the music to begin. Konstantine was in the centre of the floor, sweet master of ceremonies, bringing performers to their seats and directing the not-so-agile around the music stands. Oswald adjusted a blind to moderate the afternoon sun, and Arthur moved sheet music on the lid of the piano. The members of the Ambrose Quartet uncased their instruments and readied their bows, and after some good-humoured badinage between audience and those on stage, Arthur came to the fore and permitted silence to fall.

Philip watched him from a seat in the corner. Everyone was present and comfortable and Konstantine sat in readiness, eyes cast down.

Arthur cleared his throat and looked about him.

'What a lovely host of faces I see before me.' He beamed goodwill in all directions. 'Thank you, my dears, for making a dream come true. To see so many wonderful people gathered together in one place is the ultimate luxury. I'm thrilled beyond words and so happy. Because now we can celebrate the joys of friendship, and the ineffable artistry of our beloved Konstantine, who will be eighty-eight in about five and a half minutes.'

There was a burst of cheering and good-hearted applause.

'Konstantine and I have known each other for near on forty years, but on days like today time seems to dissolve. We look a little older, of course, but we've been looking older for a very long time, whereas inside we're just the same. And what remains immutable helps us to remember. What wonderful memories, indeed, are conjured by the faces around me now! Memories of things that passed a lifetime ago. We share them all, and to celebrate everything that we have shared and loved I thought we should anoint this happy occasion with the very thing that drew us together in the first place.'

Arthur smiled, and brought a knuckle to the corner of his eye.

'There is not a person in this room whose life has not been made by music. We take it for granted sometimes, but it's always there. And when you get to my age, and so much lies behind you, and so little ahead, music remains to the fore. Other things fall back. But music draws closer. Because music is infinite, inexhaustible, and in that respect very similar to the persistent genius of one Konstantine Serebriakov, whose gifts have been the wonder of the world for three-quarters of a century, and whose service to music has been unstinting throughout a long life, and who is blushing to the roots of his hair – what's left of it – as I speak. My dears, may we thank Konstantine for everything he has given, and may we rejoice in the dedication of all musicians, who bring happiness to the world, and who make it a wonderful thing to be alive and ninety. To Judith, and Cedric, and the marvellous players of the Ambrose Quartet, thank you so much and God bless you all.'

As Arthur turned there was renewed burst of applause that grew louder and fonder as Konstantine rose and came over to take Arthur's hands, smiling and bowing, and without further ado the two men went to the piano and took seats side by side to play a duet.

Konstantine sat nearest the audience. Arthur leaned across him to dog-ear a page. Each placed his hands on his lap and waited for quiet. They glanced at each other and nodded and then Arthur reached up to start the opening of Schubert's Fantaisie in F minor, a gentle rocking accompaniment to which Konstantine soon added the tune.

The sound of the Bechstein was soft and sweetly ringing. The two old men were so instantly and effortlessly caught up in the business of playing. They gazed with wide eyes at the staves of music and swayed slightly, hands rising and falling, rising and falling; and as the melody moved from minor to major, from the dolorous to the skittish, people settled into positions of comfortable concentration, succumbing to Schubert's melancholy drift with ease. Philip looked into the cups of his palms and then up at the ceiling of the music room, and then slowly and unstaringly around him at the faces of his fellows. He raised his eyebrows at the peak of a phrase, felt the music somehow in his body, let himself regard the performers almost abstractly, taking on something within and without him, the hold of a phrase pulling at him, entwining his heart, so that suddenly he was dissolving inside and had to blink back the moisture in his eyes. He was fortunate to be sitting at the back, alone with his teary incontinence. He swallowed hard and pulled on his cheek, as if to banish the ache, but it would not leave go. He grasped for his hanky and blew his nose quietly.

He was more controlled during the Duparc. Judith Garwood sang and Gerard Philips accompanied, and the vibrant beauty of her voice had an enlivening effect on one's being. Through a gap in the blinds the tilting sun inflamed her hair. Konstantine looked up – as if at a goddess.

Judith and Gerard were succeeded by Konstantine at the piano, accompanying Cedric on the violin. Cedric tuned in a trice, working his fingers on the string, and then at a glance had Konstantine ready and was soon with his eyes shut drawing the bow flowingly across the string, emitting the purest tone, which Konstantine supported with the wispiest sounds on the piano. Philip could see Arthur listening intently, trying to hear his Third Violin Sonata for the first time. Cedric played as though lost in violent reminiscence, eyes shut tight throughout; and Konstantine allowed the piano to sound around the violin's thin thread like running water, an iridescent stream, throwing points of light and reflections into the air.

After the violin sonata, the players of the Ambrose Quartet took up position. Soon the music room vibrated with the united power of their strings as they launched Beethoven's Grosse Fuge. The convergence of energy and purpose was irresistibly involving. Arthur was watchful, caught up, and suddenly in the old man's face Philip glimpsed the unageing artist. So often in Arthur's look one sensed that he belonged to a bygone era, was estranged from this one. One saw the wistfulness of a man who believes he has had his day and is no longer able to change things. Deep into retirement, toweringly old, Arthur had come to seem closer to the remote past of his own childhood than the period of his heyday – the mid-sixties: and whereas he was in the sixties a true contemporary to the age, now that he was really old he seemed the embodiment of something much earlier, almost Edwardian. His persona was gloriously old-fashioned, and this he enjoyed, distrusting the modern. But the outer man was a convention, a bufferish façade behind which the artist furtively lurked; and this artist was always on the look-out, always alert, as now, for example: hearing new balances and tensions in a familiar masterwork for the first time ever, secrets that had escaped his ears until this very moment, thanks to the Ambrose Quartet. Engaged with the thing he knew and loved, Arthur was as timelessly contemporary as the next man.

Judith provided the first of the encores and Konstantine was prevailed upon to finish with a solo, which he cast around for as he sat on the piano stool. He let his head fall to the side before settling his hands on the keys. There was a moment's silence, and then he started to play Siloti's transcription of Bach's B minor Prelude. The audience responded with a collective sigh. This was Emil Gilels' famous and invariable encore, and in playing it Konstantine seemed tenderly to be linking this world with the one into which he would shortly follow his great compatriot.

Philip listened, forehead on his palm, knowing what would go through him when the melody came round a second time.

They were here to celebrate more than musical greatness. They were here to give thanks for a heroic longevity. Konstantine's life transected so much of the last century. Grim past eras were sustained in his memory. Long-dead people lived on in his mind. He was the product of a talent and a history that would never recombine. It was inconceivable to imagine anyone like him ever existing again. Age, experience, heritage and history had concentrated his musical wisdom into something unique, something that would pass for ever when he died. And whilst it was wondrous to find him at eighty-eight still able to convey what music could mean to one who had come through so much, this unique, invaluable consciousness would soon be no more.

They had come to celebrate, he realised, and inevitably to mourn.

Cake was served on the lawn. Philip slipped away down a footpath and through the rose garden. Somebody called after him, but he pretended not to hear. He crossed a stile at the bottom of the garden and disappeared into a wood.

He walked aimlessly for a while, under the leaf-light of oak trees. He sauntered through twigs and bracken, hands in pockets, until he came to a fence. Carefully, he got across the fence and into a field. He kicked against the tufts of grass and aimed for a group of trees. There, with the valley in view, he sat at the foot of a beech, rubbing his eyes and gazing at the folding hills.

After a while he let his head fall back into the grass. His face was creased with sorrow.

He was only halfway through his life. Only halfway through.

He watched an ant cross his hand. In a distant field a tractor moved slowly, like a ladybird.

Ursula stood before his enquiring imagination. She sat down to play. Her arms and wrists were graceful. He joined her by the piano stool and she turned to smile at him. She waited for him to comment. He moved to guide her arm a little and place her hand just so, but she catches his eye and suddenly their gazes lock and she breathes in deeply. But now she is fading as though all this could lead nowhere.

He wants to try again and places her this time on the recamier, where he has seen her before, a memory to get things going. He moves across to sit by her and she seems happy with this and looks at him sideways before shifting and cradling her knees in her arms. She is relaxed. She laughs and smiles, sips at her wine. He leans forward to make a point, his left hand penetrating the space between them. They are alone in the flat and the hour is late. He must be gentle. He must bring her with him. It would have to be so. He is right up close now and she looks at him in surprise. Her eyes this near are enormous, questioning.

This is how it would be.

He is acutely aware of his age as he takes her neck and chin in his hands. She yields a little, not withdrawing, but still waits for his next move; because she has no idea what this could lead to, this intimate moment, or how she would feel when his lips touch hers. He holds the nape of her neck and gazes into her eyes.

And then he is inside her and they are fucking, her breasts swaying with each thrust, her head jammed against the base of the armchair.

He grips her arm, powerfully engaged with her body, which is shockingly beautiful, and she turns into Laura, and the scene removes to Laura's double bed where they are familiarly connected, Laura panting, teeth bared in effortful pleasure. She is willing him to make her pregnant.

He tries to bring back Ursula, but Ursula has gone, and now he holds an infant in his arms. The nurse bends over him, makes a cooing noise. So this is Katie. He remembers very well. This little baby is new to everything, has never existed before in all the millennia man has been on the planet!

He holds a blade of grass between forefinger and thumb, gazes at the sky.

And now they run helter-skelter across the leaves, James and Katie in their winter coats. He follows their freewheeling antics, walking a few yards behind them, his measured steps inversely proportional to their spurts and charges. The children are suddenly alert to a carpet of pigeons on the ground. Someone has dropped a loaf on the grass and the thick birds are bunched in a seething mass. Red rag to a bull, because the children are suddenly charging this bloated target, screaming at the tops of their voices, at first ineffectively because the fat birds won't desert their prize and cling on to the last second, daring the children to risk their ankles in a sea of beaks. But suddenly they erupt from the ground with a sound like gunshot, in mass vertical take-off, beating themselves airborne, into a great flapping cloud that begins to organise itself into a giant circle around the children, going round and round with increasing speed, held in formation by the sight of the bread, which the children are unwittingly guarding; and now something weird starts to happen as the birds revolve in the air, a raucous whorl going faster and faster, round and round as if madly possessed by the sight of the loaf and the need for attack. The children will not shift and the birds won't disperse and suddenly he is afraid that something unnatural will happen; so he runs past the kids, starting a race, and as they rush on behind him he turns in time to see a twister of pigeons sucked down to a clump on the ground.

People in the park thought they were his. He was proud of the attribution, which was near enough. It was a privilege to have charge of rumbustious innocents, nice to be mistaken for a parent.

Philip looked at the grey hair under his wristwatch. The skin on his hands was changing. In the mirror that morning he had seen an older man. One's complexion changed: crow's feet, deepening pores, thinning lips – all this happened slowly. But something else changed, too. The cast of one's face altered according to the body's time code, so that age developed from inside, joining in with the wear of the years, producing someone else to stare back at you.

He reclined as far as he could, and gazed up the skirts of the beech tree.

His mobile rang.

He checked the number before answering. 'Hello.'

Her voice made him blush.

'Where are you?' she said.

He gazed across the field. His heart was beating hard.

She was calling from her flat. He could tell that she was worked up.

'Did something terrible happen with you and John? You know about his son?'

'What about his son?'

'Septicaemia. He's been in hospital for a week. John's in a total state. You mustn't take him seriously.'.

'Oh, Christ!'

'Where are you?'

He could feel the pressure of Ursula's concern.

'In the country.'

'John says you fired him.'

'We fired each other.'

'What's going on? This is ridiculous.'

'Is his son OK?'

'They're pumping him full of antibiotics. It's been really scary. Tell me what happened and I can patch it up.'

She was intense and distressed and had been working up to this call.

'I'll find a new agent. It's no problem.'

'I'm your new agent! You can't leave me just like that!'

'Listen, Ursula . . .'

'John says I can't represent you. Suddenly I'm not allowed to talk to you. This is ridiculous.'

'It's no use intervening.'

'You've been with him for years. You're friends. I have to make you see sense. Can we meet?'

He did not answer.

'When are you coming back?'

'Ursula! Don't do anything to jeopardise your position!'

'Why are you holding me at arm's length?'

He hesitated, unable to think quickly enough.

'He's given the concerts to Vadim. He's blown you out with Bulmanion. This is madness.'

'Vadim?'

'Did you cancel?'

'Well . . .'

'He can't do that!'

'There's bad blood, I'm afraid.'

135

He could feel her frustration with him.

'I'm more trouble than I'm worth, you see. You're better off without me.'

'Oh, don't be absurd!'

It amazed him. She was only twenty-six. He was touched by her possessiveness.

'Honestly. I'm a handful.'

'Philip, you're in a state. You need somebody to help you. Please don't cast me off.'

'You see –' He swallowed. 'I may not play again.'

'What!'

There was a tense silence.

'You'll play.'

'Ursula . . .'

'If I have anything to do with it.'

'I'm so grateful for your concern.'

'Concern!'

He listened, not knowing what to say.

'Oh, Philip!'

'There's nothing you can do.'

'This is so awful.'

'Oh . . . well . . . maybe . . .'

'And I can help you.'

'I think it's too late for help.'

'You need looking after, actually. That's what you need.'

He held the phone to his ear, stared at the grass. He felt goosebumps on the side of his neck.

'Are you there?' she said more gently.

Her solicitude was incomprehensible, overwhelming.

'Can we meet?'

'Well . . . I . . .'

'I can't call from work. When d'you return to London?'

It was too much for him.

'Um . . . I don't think we should meet.'

'What?'

'Not just yet.'

'What's wrong?'

'It's too complicated. I want to terminate the agency completely.'

'I don't believe it.'

'Sorry.'

'Can't we just talk it through?'

'No, Ursula. Goodbye.'

He ended the call and turned off the mobile.

He laid his head on the grass. A breeze furrowed the leaves on the trees. He trembled.

Chapter Fourteen

IT WAS LATE, BUT still people chatted outside on the terrace. Cigarettes glowed in the dark. Wine bottles were passed along. Laughter erupted here and there. Most of the oldies had turned in – Arthur blowing kisses, Cedric shaking a dozen hands and patting shoulders. Konstantine remained at the end of one table, sipping fizzy water and listening quietly. He was glad to be around younger folk.

Oswald's puddings, it was generally agreed, had been out of this world.

Philip was unobtrusively drunk. Sitting at the edge of a group that included Lola and Julius, he had begun to find the shop talk irksome. Subtle rivalries were playing out amidst flip references to great conductors and famous venues, or items of epic repertoire that someone had knocked off in Rio or Helsinki. Absent colleagues were being discreetly downgraded. If someone's career was on the rocks their playing was praised to the skies – no longer a threat. Anybody meteoric – ah well: 'What burns bright does not last.' Excluded from the group chatter, Philip had risen carefully to his feet and strolled inside. Looking for a more comfortable place in which to be quietly drunk, he found himself in Oswald's study eyeing an armchair.

He let himself sink into the deep cushions of the chair. He was tired, but his mind was on the move again. He dreaded the return to London. Being with people was hard; being alone would be worse.

He looked up.

Oswald stood in the doorway, rumly inspecting him. 'Great minds,' he declared, heading towards a similar chair.

They sat opposite each other in the glow of table lamps, amidst polished furniture, embroidered cushions, framed photographs and glass ashtrays. Oswald got his calves up on to the footstool. 'Oh!' He shut his eyes, taking in slow breaths, exhaling peacefully. After a moment he drew himself up in the chair, moistening his lips. Today he had achieved catering greatness. Now was not the time to drop off.

'D'you know I was nine when that violin sonata was written! Oh Lord.' He smiled, his wrinkled face softened by remembrance. 'The gliding years! I must say, my minions behaved impeccably.'

Philip was blank faced. Anguish welled inside him.

'Isn't Galina tremendous! That woman is a beacon to her sex. No spring chicken, clearly. But everything is relative, and relative to some people I'm a juvenile. Of course, you get to my age and realise you might drop off tomorrow, or hammer on into geriatric infinity. I don't know which is worse. How are you, Philip?'

Philip's head was tilted back. For a moment he was unable to speak, and then the pressure overwhelmed him. 'Oh . . . cracking up.'

'Cracking up!'

He could pretend no longer. 'I'm going to pieces.'

'Dear, oh dear.' Oswald was ruffled with the greatest concern. 'I'm extremely sorry to hear it. What can we do about that?'

'A drink might help.'

'Most certainly! Press that bell, will you.'

He pressed the bell.

Oswald urged a silver cigarette box on Philip. 'You'll have a cigarette?'

'No thanks.'

Oswald took one for himself, tucked it between his teeth and snapped on a lighter. He looked enquiringly at Philip, exhaled smoke.

'My dear fellow, what can the matter be?'

Philip's face darkened. Oswald was a dangerous confidant. 'You'd better give me an honest answer.'

Oswald looked suspiciously at his guest. Rarely was he asked to be honest.

'Cub's honour. Hope to die.'

'What's gone wrong with my playing?'

Oswald involuntarily smiled.

'Please be serious.'

'What's wrong with anybody's playing? You are doing what you have come to do, and what you are able to do.'

'I've got problems, admit it.'

'I'll admit nothing.'

He had humiliated himself already. 'Did you read the reviews?'

'I don't read reviews. I form my own opinion.'

'You heard me play last year in Aldeburgh.'

'Very fine, too.'

'Oh, for God's sake! Say what you really think! You're always slagging off other pianists. Now's a good chance to slag me off.'

Oswald was demure. 'I don't slag anyone off. The slag word is not in my vocabulary, thank you very much.'

'Am I falling off?'

'My dear fellow!' He was pained and amused. He had not reckoned on a conversation like this in his private study after an exhausting party. 'Nothing anybody can say to you makes a shred of difference if the main thing is there. If it isn't, you're lost anyway. You have what counts, and the rest is down to managing one's temperament.'

Philip levered himself up in his chair. 'That's unusually diplomatic and evasive for someone with your talent for mockery.'

Oswald batted his eyelids. 'You're in wonderful form tonight.'

'Yes. I know. Sorry.'

'All very cosy in here,' said a voice.

'Brian!'

The broadly beaming face of Brian Bellew peered into the room. 'Hello, hello, hello!'

Philip sighed heavily.

'What impeccable timing,' hailed Oswald. 'Philip, you must talk to Brian.'

'No, thank you. Brian's a fucking critic!'

Brian thought this was most entertaining. 'Fucking critic, eh!'

'Philip's having a crisis about his playing. You'd better join us.'

'Love to.'

'Oh, Christ!'

Brian crossed from the door in the direction of a third armchair. He tripped on the corner of the rug but just managed to keep his balance. He was a burly fifty-eight-year-old with a brainy forehead and glittery, irresponsible eyes.

'You're looking pretty festive,' said Oswald.

'D'you mean drunk, by any chance?'

'Good heavens no, not drunk.'

Brian sank like a deadweight into the armchair. 'Lovely party, my dear. Barry's very attentive, I see.'

'Thanks to the martinet skills of yours truly.' Oswald curled a distinguished eyebrow. 'Were I but twenty years younger . . .'

Brian's torso rocked with schoolboy mirth.

'I was very imposing as recently as ten years ago, I'll have you know.'

'You're imposing now.'

'I'm decomposing now!'

'I think I might turn in,' said Philip.

'Don't you dare!' said Oswald. 'Where the devil is Kevin? KEVIN!'

As luck would have it Barry was passing in the corridor outside. He stuck his head into the room.

Oswald snapped a finger. 'Bottle of bubbly and three glasses for these gentlemen. Philip, stay where you are. We're here to help.'

Barry nodded and vanished.

'Patience, Brian! You'll get an eyeful when he returns.'

Brian gasped at the imputation.

'So hard to find diligent catamites these days.'

Brian burst out laughing. He recovered himself slowly, wiping a tear from his eye. 'Philip, how are you?'

Oswald waved a cigarette. 'Young Philip here wants to know what's wrong with his playing.'

Brian blinked convincingly, commandeering seriousness.

'He's rather concerned about a review.'

Brian was deputy editor of the *Musical Times*. He crossed his legs. 'A review?'

There was a pregnant pause.

'Oh, yes. A review.'

'Is this some kind of trap?'

Oswald smiled dangerously. 'You look pretty trapped in that armchair.'

Brian was profoundly entrenched. 'You'll need a crane to get me out of here.'

'Let's not change the subject, shall we.'

Philip cast his eyes down in embarrassment.

'Did you hear the recording?'

Brian tongued his underlip. 'We haven't . . . I think we haven't done anything in the *MT*.'

'Well, that in itself is cause for concern.'

'Ignore him, Philip. He's being mischievous.'

'You're thick with those bloodhounds at *Gramophone*?'

'What am I saying? I did hear it. Somebody sent me the disc about a year ago. Gosh,' Brian put fingers to forehead. 'Sorry, Philip. No, I heard it. I thought . . .'

'Say some reassuring words, for Christ's sake, man!'

Brian wore his discomfort on his sleeve. 'Well, I . . . what did I think . . . Of course you know I don't do reviewing any more.'

Philip's face was a mask.

'That's a paltry excuse!'

'It was terrific. Technically remarkable. Beautifully refined, voiced, very sharply recorded. I think you've cut away a lot of lazy performance tradition . . .'

'There you are, Philip.'

Brian nodded readily. 'I'm a huge fan of your playing, Philip. Isn't everyone?'

'Not apparently your colleagues at *Gramophone*.' Oswald turned ominously.

Brian shook his head in puzzlement.

'Philip would like to know why.'

'Well, I can't answer for them.'

'What!' Oswald forced himself higher in the chair. 'Are you telling me the profession has no weight of consensus! That you're all breezy enthusiasts with your own opinionated grudges? I mean, is this just a sub-branch of belletrism, or what?'

Brian looked long-sufferingly at Philip. It was getting beyond a joke.

'Can we trust *Gramophone*?' said Oswald acidly.

Brian shook his head. 'Reviewing's not a science.'

'This man is in a state of spiritual despair,' said Oswald, 'because of a beastly review in *Gramophone* magazine.'

'Um . . .'

'Have you any idea what pain your pronouncements . . .'

'I haven't pronounced . . .'

'The pronouncements of your professional coterie cause to practising musicians?'

Brian began to laugh. 'This is a bit rich, Oswald.'

Barry entered with a tray of champagne flutes and a packet of Bendick's Mints; Kevin followed with Bollinger and towel. Brian looked around at the new arrivals, hoping to direct the focus of everybody's attention away from himself and on to them.

'Well trained,' said Oswald.

Kevin released the cork with impressive control and administered the glasses. 'Champagne, sir?'

'Rather,' said Brian.

'Oh, the pleasure of selected vulgarities. Present the mints please, Kevin.'

'Was that a bottle of champagne I saw before me?' said another voice.

'Aha!'

Julius appeared in the doorway.

Oswald smiled fetchingly. 'We're having our own party in here.'

Brian turned in relief. 'Hello, Julius.'

The American pianist looked rather manly and imposing in the doorway. 'What fun! May I join you?'

'We insist. There's gallons of champagne to get through. Barry, be a dear and fetch up a couple more.'

Julius settled himself back on the chesterfield. 'Actually, ah . . . Barry. Would you have something shorter? Malt or . . .'

Barry drew himself up to a level of perfect composure. 'Talisker, Macallan, Laphroaig, Glenochil.'

'You run a tight ship,' smiled Brian appreciatively.

'I'm getting tighter by the minute,' drawled Oswald.

Philip was inert in the chair. A champagne flute had somehow been wedged by Kevin between his forefinger and thumb. From where he was sitting he could see the bulk of Julius's midriff straining on a shirt button. The American pianist was developing weight around his jowls. His eyes were a little piggy. Even the arms of his glasses cut into the flesh of his cheek. He had the temporarily relaxed confidence of a man who has recently seen his double CD boxed set of Fetzler-Rose Symphonic Transcriptions in dumpbins at HMV. His self-esteem had survived a whole day in the company of world-class pianists, and he sprawled back now with the well-earned complacence of a busy professional who knows that whilst others are greater he has made his mark, earned his peers' respect, and is content to take his place in the pantheon with all due humility at whatever level is assigned to him by whomever decides these things, because even if Serebriakov was tiringly the greatest, Lola the most smouldering, Vadim the most exciting, nobody else could get within a mile of his Fetzler-Rose Transcriptions at that level of polydextrous elucidation, and absolutely nothing could take that skyscraping achievement from him. He nonetheless gazed at the picture-rail of Oswald's boudoir with cultural perplexity. What a curiously English place to celebrate the old Russian's birthday! Oswald, it had to be said, he found characterful but anomalous. The classical music world was so small it forced odd bedfellows.

'We're having a lively debate,' said Oswald, admiring Barry's departure, 'about the questionable authority and excessive power of music critics.'

Julius chuckled half-heartedly. 'When they like me, they're right. When they hate me, they're wrong!'

'That's more like it.'

'You can't live with us and you can't live without us,' smiled Brian.

Philip came alive violently. They were skating over everything, burying him in banter. 'You're not taking me seriously.'

Julius looked up.

'You're not taking me seriously.'

'I . . .'

'No you're not. I've been giving concerts for thirty-five years now. I've won a slew of awards. Hundreds of people write to me. Brian, I have credit in the bank, and yet nobody will tell me what is amiss now. I mean, what are we aiming at? Some gold standard held over our heads by dead pianists? Some academic formula of perfection? Some modernist paradigm of interpretative excellence? Show me the path. Don't just scold me.'

'Philip . . .'

'Everybody's talking about Slava. He's had terrible press recently. Five years ago he was God. Has anybody any idea what he's going through?'

'Think of it as a stock-market correction. His share value had become inflated.'

Philip flinched. 'What's happened to my share value? Tell me the truth.' He was suddenly pleading. 'Patrick Peabody said that my performances lacked heart. He said there was a lack of commitment. Have I gone and mislaid something these last few years? It seems I have.'

Brian glanced at Oswald, who was impassively smoking.

Philip looked intently at the side of Brian's head. The pause was unbearable.

'You'd know it if you had.' Brian turned to face him.

'Does Slava know it?'

'You can only answer for yourself.'

Philip wiped his forehead. 'Perhaps I have. I feel differently these days.'

Brian stared at him. Julius averted his eyes.

'Even so, I mean . . . I thought that CD . . . I believed in . . .'

Oswald gazed into the reflections of his champagne glass. Brian looked pensively at the rug. Julius maintained a serious, engaged expression, distilling his own reaction to what had been said.

Their silence was mortifying.

Brian brought his fist to his mouth. He coughed lightly. 'I suppose there are . . . um . . . two perspectives here . . .'

Oswald regarded him coolly.

Philip closed his eyes.

Brian looked around tentatively, as if checking the assent of his audience. He seemed licensed to say something, to engage with Philip seriously. 'There is the modernist view that if you do what the music says and play with stylistic accuracy the music will speak for itself – that meaning and feeling are programmed into the composition; and there's the contrary view that what makes a performance work is an insight into something not manifest in the score' – he glanced at Philip with scholarly penetration – 'into the character of a work, its rhetoric or declamation, whatever, and that to perceive that something a performer's emotional and intellectual experience must be co-extensive with the composer's. He exhaled with demonstrative force. 'If a . . .'

'You're saying I'm an emotional cripple?'

Brian raised his hands. 'I wouldn't presume to diagnose!'

'I want diagnosis!'

Brian stared urgently at Philip. 'I am simply tendering a basis for thinking about the problems you've raised.' He swallowed, aware of the eggshells at his feet stretching as far as the eye could see in every direction. 'Sometimes with Slava's playing . . . one feels that too much is preplanned, that the head has come to distrust the heart. And then one likens music to a horse that's not being ridden properly. Music can be harnessed, but not controlled. A good jockey releases some innate flow and energy in his charge. A bad jockey . . .'

Philip stared into the fireplace.

Oswald frowned into his champagne glass.

'A bad jockey?' said Philip softly.

Brian shook his head, dismissing the implied slight. 'Some pianists, for example, are obsessed with surface and use their extraordinary control of the instrument to draw you into a sound-world of minutely inflected expression – Horowitz, for example – these sort of players assuming that the sum of such moments delivers the totality of a piece's meaning. Relish the detail and the whole will look after itself, because structure is written in. There are others, less distracted by sensuousness, who perceive a composition's unity from above, and this type of player seeks coherence in the symbolic structure of the piece, by which music is given a kind of narrative truth. In the first group interpretation is based on nervous sensitivity, which might fade. In the second, on a kind of cognitive insight, which might fail. In my view there is a transitional process that all great artists make between a subjective and objective view of emotion.'

'Yes, but where does greatness come from?'

Brian was nonplussed.

'A coherence that you can formulate is completely ersatz and superficial.'

'Reviewing is a descriptive . . .'

'You have no idea what it is to fall from grace. No idea what it means to attain grace.'

'I didn't . . .'

'You presume to discern, to calibrate, to compare, but this is all beside the point, because no one knows where this state of grace comes from. You can't source it.'

Brian was alarmed and baffled in equal parts. 'I'm trying to share . . .'

'And no one can explain the provenance of the sublime in music.'

'I don't disagree.'

'The only thing that matters, the only significant thing is how the fuck does one do it? The answer is beyond everyone. Even the performer.'

Brian glanced guardedly at Oswald and Julius to see if anyone else wanted to come in on the argument.

Julius remained thoughtful behind steepled fingers. He knew better than to venture opinions from a mood of relative complacence. Even so, he looked stimulated to speak and was cagily computing how to enter the fray without annoying Philip.

'We're led to a religious terminology,' said Brian.

'Yes, and modern criticism has no concept of the soul.'

'Well, I . . .'

'We are guardians of the immortal soul in music. Yes! This is what we have to be. And who can tell us how to be it? Who can say through what purgatories we must pass to reach this state of grace? That's why I need understanding, Brian, if I've lost the way.'

Brian sympathetically nodded.

'Because you can't fault me on detail. Dynamics, line, colour, perspective. I need to do more. Suffer harder for my art. Some sort of crisis or breakdown, which I'm already having . . .'

'Or sabbatical.'

'Or a sabbatical white-water rafting and eating pulses and soya derivatives and reading the classics . . .'

'Philip . . .'

'To recover the essence of great music, which Konstantine has at his fingertips every morning he rolls out of bed!'

'Hang on!'

'Don't you see? I need support! I'm an endangered species!'

'I . . .'

'You guys already have Solomon, Gieseking, Kempff, Cortot. They had the historic sensibility, the unbroken tradition, the

147

sympathy of an era. To reach their levels I have to live outside history, turning my back on contemporary culture. I have to screen out all the titillating data, the mass-media barrage of fornicating celebrities and Royal Family tat. The middle-class House and Garden fantasia. Become a bloody monk. Then I have to reclaim the emotional hypersensitivity of a consumptive Chopin or a schizoid Robert Schumann to do justice to music originating from a pitch of human experience that modern culture does not generate and can only appreciate passively. I have to go through agonies of preparation for a super-critical audience that barely exists any more. What I'm seeking with such difficulty, what I'm trying to keep alive, hardly matters to most people.'

'I don't know about that.'

'We're a historical leftover.'

'What classical music lacks in breadth of appeal' – Brian was roused – 'it gains in depth of impact.'

'Yeah, but when I lose the plot, it doesn't give me strength to think my life's work means nothing to most people.'

'In the history of the world high culture was only ever a minority affair,' said Oswald.

'The minority isn't helping me. Especially this minority.'

There was a pause.

Philip gazed in strained amazement at the floor. It came to him glancingly – the sum of their reactions – so obvious: that he was mediocre. That was what they thought of him and had done for years. He was long past his best.

'I support Philip,' said Julius, bunching forward on the sofa. 'For a modern pianist it's so hard to connect what you do to the wider world. One's expertise or artistry, if you will, is of such an esoteric nature, geared to the past always, meaningful within a tradition that takes a lot of knowledge and appreciation to penetrate. Truly, we are playing against the age, not for it; and when you're performing in some outback hall rented by a music society, some place with a killer piano and Arctic draughts, and no hot water in the changing room, paint peeling on the walls, a spam sandwich and leaded tea for your rehearsal break, plus when you get on stage, it's spot-the-audience time, just a few old people sprinkled around, who'll snore off in your concert and die the next day before they can tell friends and build your reputa-

tion, plus some attention-deficit kid front row flapping his programme through your most difficult passage, you do think:
Should I get a desk job? Afterwards it gets worse. Backstage they
start to roll in, these old folk, and you shake and smile and hope
they don't croak right there, and in comes some controlling
housewife with a cross-eyed son, just taken Grade One and
amazed by your fingers – 'They were like lost in a blur of speed,
weren't they, Johnny?' or 'I don't know how you keep all those
notes in your head!' – and you do kind of wonder was this
manicured interpretation that cost a thousand hours of practice
really worth it? Even with professionals in the audience you can
play like an angel and get the worst reviews. Or play like a bum
and get buried in fucking Interflora. Bottom line here, Philip, is we
can never know the effect we have on individual listeners, even
when they tell us they liked it, because you don't know what that
means, and you just have to believe it's good for people to hear a
Beethoven sonata played live, or an étude by Stuttgart-Martier-
Berenson.'

'Who?' said Brian.

'You haven't heard of Stuttgart-Martier-Berenson?'

'Julius, you're prodigious!'

'He wrote a suite called the Political Études.'

'That should resonate with a wider public,' said Oswald drily.

'It resonates all right. It's kind of Takemitsu meets Kapustin
meets Pink Floyd. Smorgasbord modernism. Real fun.'

Philip looked askance. Even among friends and colleagues he was
alone. He felt an ache around the eye, tension in his neck. He was so
deeply berthed in his chair that he had lost all power to oppose. He
was just a swivelling head, disagreeably regarding other people as
they tried to talk around him. How mediocre he felt. How un-
dignified! He was allowed to communicate musically, but as soon
as he tried to express ideas no one was interested.

'What you can't face,' said Oswald, looking over Philip's head in
haughty summary, and in a tone of voice that was mock-provo-
cative, 'is that you might be an ordinary mortal, not some pianistic
god. You can't stomach bad reviews, and don't like to be in thrall to
a musical public who may exercise their own judgements. You
resent the fact that applause validates your efforts and that others,
not you, are the arbiters of your reputation. That's why you

cancelled, in my opinion. To get one up on the audience. To show them who's boss: the mighty artist. To put them in their place before they did the same to you. But lo, if the audience aren't cheering and the critics aren't on their bellies in prostration, who is there to applaud your noble dedication? The larger world is not bothered by this anguished little tragedy. Only you, by an act of will, can validate yourself. Alas, somewhere along the way, you've lost the ability to do that. But that, my dear fellow, is the only reason why any musician has an audience. Because he is prepared to take infinite pains, to soldier on, to commit more than ordinary people, to suffer whatever Christ-like ravages and tribulations are necessary to understand the great works, and to keep on keeping on. That slavish devotion, plus the humble knowledge that he serves only the music, that alone justifies the elevated status of the artist; and if the artist cannot survive his own doubts he must get off the stage and join us in the stalls. The whys and wherefores of his quest are no concern of ours, as we are not competent to judge beyond the results. It's all down to you. And if you've lost the plot there isn't much we can do except wish you well and ask for our money back.'

Philip looked at his hands and scowled. He felt an inner sliding or collapse, as if Oswald had delivered the *coup de grâce*. Unhappiness was now in a fixed position, attached to its cause, something one could look at and away from, and still find there in half an hour. He had flaunted his angst at intelligent men who all did their best, but whose moderate reactions and prevarications could make things neither better nor worse for him. He realised only that time was running out. Whichever path he might choose, he still had to survive the time it took to adjust, correct, recover, and time might be short. He had lost all sense of an imperative course. Without the sense of a future, the threads of a life seemed tattered and incomplete. This, perhaps, was the hidden curse of childlessness. Everything else fell away when one stopped doing it, whereas having a child carried one into the future, regardless of success or failure. The best part of his life, he realised, belonged to the past. He understood now. He saw it more clearly.

'Klaus Friedrich.' It came to him suddenly. Almost out of nowhere. This was the moment, surely. There had been a moment, yes, a specific event that robbed him of the will to compete. 'He played terribly for three years. Record company dropped him.

Agent dropped him. Total career doldrums. Everything in his playing had become coarse and exaggerated.' He frowned to remember this, as though recollection itself was a kind of proof. 'I was offered a ticket by a friend of Klaus's a few months ago and had to go along to his concert. My worst expectations in the first half. The playing was brash and coarse-grained. After the interval he played the Hammerklavier. D'you know, I have never heard anything like it. He had the piece by the tail. I mean it was rough-hewn but totally apocalyptic. Very hard to convey what he did except to say that I was riveted by the awesome power of Beethoven's mind. One had to succumb. A physical experience. My whole body was in thrall to a kind of cosmic storm, and it made me understand that the truly great performance takes you to the hot core of the composer's brain, and that Beethoven's brain is like the energy centre of the universe . . .'

He swallowed, looked down at his lap, hands joined together. The others were subdued.

Philip smiled painfully. 'A miracle.'

'Sounds amazing,' said Julius.

'After that, I knew . . .' He had never dared admit this. The truth was a kind of relief. 'I had nothing left to say.'

'That's a common reaction.'

He felt stronger. 'I haven't the talent to seek that kind of epiphany. Maybe I never had it.'

'You do need a sabbatical,' said Oswald more kindly.

'I need to quit.'

'Every one of us has something to say.'

Brian sighed and shook his head sadly.

He put his hands on the arms of his chair to get up. He needed to be on his own now. 'Sorry to have bored you all to death. Actually, it's been helpful. I know where I stand.'

'Philip, don't beat up on yourself,' said Julius. 'Self-doubt is a cyclical given. Hold on to this. I remember listening to your recording of the Brahms Intermezzi when I was twenty-two thinking it was the greatest version I'd ever heard.'

'That was in another life.'

'Do it again!'

'It'll be a relief to shut the lid of that instrument, actually.' He rose. 'Night, gentlemen. Apologies.'

'We're all in this together,' said Brian, straight-faced. Then he smiled kindly.

Philip nodded, eyes downcast.

He made his way carefully around the backs of armchairs and slipped through the doorway to the corridor outside. He had to think twice before proceeding down the hall. He would avoid the crowd sitting on the terrace and work his way through the back of the house and out through the music room. He was more tired than drunk, he realised, as he went along the dimly illuminated corridor. He switched on the light in the music room and passed through it to the garden door.

The night air was fresh, the sky starry. He picked his way along garden paths and through gates to the front of the house and then walked down the drive, leaving the glow of the porch lantern behind. Out on the lane he could see the dark shapes of farmyard machinery, an abandoned tractor, the snout of a saw mill. Even at this hour the guineafowl were making their strange noises, like a set of unoiled hinges squeaking and creaking from their perch on the fence. Moonlight cast a bar of shadow from the hedge across the lane. His footfalls were muffled by the flattened scree of mud and horse-dung.

He could smell honeysuckle, which was drifting all over the hedgerows this time of year, and he found himself breathing harder and deeper as the lane began to rise, taking leave of the hamlet behind him and leading to a point where in daytime the view opened out. He was struck by the depth of quiet, the shadowy stillness around him. He heard only the rhythm of his pulse. He was in command of his solitude again.

It came to him softly, an enveloping certainty that he seemed to walk into; it glided over him, he could not say how or why, that he was going to die. He kept on moving, brow furrowing at the strange sourcelessness of this realisation, which passed through him like a kind of understanding or slow elation, leaving nothing in its wake except the frictionless feel of the darkness all around.

He kept on going, propelled by a need to hold on to the sense of his physical being but without breaking the spell, the colourless certitude. It was like the revelation of something long known, released from the depths of his being.

There was movement ahead, a realignment of shadow. He saw a

gate, a figure. He heard a grunt of acknowledgement, and as he went closer, to where the dark margin of the hedge was broken by a gap, he saw a man draped on the bar of the gate, gazing across the night landscape.

'Hello,' he said, involuntarily.

'Philip.'

He recognised the light, dry voice. He was staring at Konstantine Serebriakov.

He remembered later how he had walked over to the gate like a somnambulist caught in the same dream, crossing to see the view spread out under moonlight. Konstantine clung like an old rag on the gate, his attention fastened on the strangeness of nocturnal light, the phosphorescent fields, the mysteriousness of visibility without colour. He held fast and still as the layers of countryside revealed contours to the eye – shadows denoting landmark trees, hills insinuating their presence, the character of everything subtly modified by monochrome.

Philip let the coldness of the gate run into his fingertips. He inhaled deeply, trying to capture the scents and tangs of the field, needing more of something specific to bring back a suddenly accessible memory, the first memory, sliding always to the edge of recall, that went with this scene, linking a depthless well-being to the sight of landscape, the stoic peace of the sinking hills, a childhood acquisition based on a kindling imagination.

For a long time they stood at either end of the gate, averse to any sound or movement that would break the spell, and as Philip dwelled on the branches of an oak tree that had long since died, floodlit by the moon, wondering how many decades it would take for the brittle tusks of that tree to fall apart and decay in the ground, he realised that both of them were looking into the night with the tranquil fixation of people who would never see this – this apparitional luminescence – again, and that Konstantine's rapture was a form of leave-taking, a slow tribute to all that the scene recollected, a culminatory *Mondnacht* to be relished for the last time. If he were to die soon, then this moment was as crucial as any left to him. One's imminent departure deepened the present, because the future had no horizon, and the only category of time to be invested in was the present, which when studied closely, revealed itself in layers of suggestion.

He marvelled at the limitless particularity of what would survive him.

Later, in bed, he felt no pain. Physically he was aware of nothing. His body seemed at peace with itself. But something was going on, a deterioration or corruption, some silent process that he might never have known about. He shut his eyes, trying for sleep in the memory of Konstantine's voice, which had broken the silence softly, as though his thoughts had become gently audible. He carried on where they had left off in Arthur's drawing room. His ideas were like a stream that had gone underground in the interim and now resurfaced in Philip's presence, more delicately prepared for his ears alone.

'. . . this second sonata . . .' Philip smiled to remember the creaky Russian accent '. . . you cannot see as the last word so much as a preliminary view of death. Very close. Very angry. How different with Beethoven March Funèbre! Nothing in music comes like this. The fate of the soul! Kaboom, *fini*! But, but the composer gets a little better, comes to Nohant, very good in the country, and even if you believe' – he raised a finger in the darkness as he spoke – 'Chopin knew he would not live before many years, it is for me as though he had understood his *immortalité* and had made a victory over creative challenge of death. So. Then. Up one step. To B moll. Third Sonata. On the edge of C, where everything begins again. And listen, for Chopin B *major* is so comfortable, so . . . at home. This key is for him satisfaction. You have in the first movement the most beautiful nostalgia. For life. Fulfilled, rich, and strong. In the scherzo he revisits his youth. He is still virtuoso. In the trio, reminiscence. Not without the pain of lost time, but with the idea that all time is eternal in music. And from here you can contemplate eternity. So, Philip' – his voice was a whisper – 'by slow movement, listen, this is the trick . . . consolation has already happened. The soul now looks on life with serenity. The soul is safe and when the tune – da, dee da, dee da, dee da dudeededadadee da dum – comes in the last page we have a berceuse for final sleep. The last chords, this is fate cadence. The acceptance of death. Yes?' He swallowed. 'You understand! And then! But what? What can come after this? On with life, of course, on with future. It's a rondo because in life everything returns, same struggle, the whole story of the future going on after the individual dies. We have so much reminiscence in his music, so much sadness for the past. But this sonata sees the future, and the future is the spirit of man overcoming and winning. You don't know till right at the end – dee, da, da Taaaah! This is triumph. *La gloire*.'

Konstantine chuckled. He placed an old hand on Philip's forearm and squeezed hard.

Chapter Fifteen

MOVING AROUND UNDER THE shade of the apple tree, Peter carving, Clarissa pouring Orangina into children's cups, Philip spooning out potatoes, beans on plates, everyone impatient to sit down and tuck in. Behind them the cottage, doggedly ancient, with its furrowed timbers and panels of flint, and pretty surround of rose-beds and brick footpath. Beyond the apple tree a brook, and then a fence and field, which ran up the hill to a grassy crest set off by an oak tree that leaned against the sky, shoving great spits of dead wood into the air. Hedgerows intersected the fields, puffs of crack willow followed the line of a ditch. Here and there was a cow.

They sat and ate and drank before the view, and when the children had run off to play, deckchairs awaited them. Clarissa would subside into a shapely cat-like curl on the rug, paperback under the compress of her flowing arched hands; Peter and Philip would almost expire on their seats, wine glasses slackly dandled, heads averted from the confronting sunlight, which now, p.m., cast deeper hues across the fields and caused new distinctions in the landscape, like patches of orchestral colour drawn to prominence.

It was much the same for all their visitors. Newcomers to the cottage received the identical surprise. You drove off the main road two miles back. The lane ebbed away into the valley, hills rising all the while, and suddenly the hedgerows seemed lusher, the meadows glossier, the cow parsley more abundant. One was travelling out of time into a rural past and who could say where on the windy lane the spell was cast. At the bottom of the lane one turned right along a drive overhung by willow and ash, and came to a gravelly opening in front of the house. One parked, and clambered out, all eyes on the cottage with its mossy roof tiles and brick buttresses, and was suddenly aware of a view to the right, which opened out between slanting alders, much broader than expected and delightfully arresting because of the vista it opened across the most beautiful countryside, and suddenly one was gaping in marvel at the levels and lines of distance, the tumbling woods and swooning dells, the timeless figures of solitary trees. One dropped one's bags, knocked for six, and Peter and Clarissa came out of the house to hug and greet and pat children on the head. And later, one explored the plot: the orchard, the brook, with incredible elation. The whole fantasy of childhood was brought back in this garden of wicket gates and staddle stones and stumps covered in emerald moss.

In the summer they would have picnics by the stream under the fissured bows of sally trees pushed cock-eyed by the '87 gale – and still dropping spears of dead wood into the soft earth below. Tea was set out on the upper lawn, where one could sit with a newspaper, momentarily gazing at the wood across the field, listening to bees and zizzers and the cawing of crows. Visitors would amble along a footpath or across a meadow and find themselves on the edge of an eerie wood, or on rising pastureland, the hills receding hierarchically about them, the cottage itself sinking to a ruddy smudge in the distance, the poplars one had noticed from the garden as a distant queue of drumsticks suddenly turning up, clamorously rearing, their glittery leaves surging in the lightest wind. He had walked up to that point of vantage many a time – on the edge of a field – and watched the wind pawing at the barley, furrowing its coat, or seen the shadow of a fast-moving cloud scudding towards him, trailing a blaze of sunlight in its wake that crossed the crops and lit up trees and eventually bathed him in its warmth.

He was always welcome. They loved having him around. He amused them, brought stories of the big wide world, and was helpful, too. He would split logs, or Flymo lawns, or dig a trench to channel flood water. He knew about plants and flowers and pruning and planting and was lithe with a scythe when the time came to slay the battalions of stinging nettles that rose around the brook every year. And he was good at fitting in. One summer he stayed for a month, sleeping in the barn on a sofa bed, and joining them for meals. He knew when to come forward in the ebb and flow of family life and when to recede, offering kitchen services or keeping the kids entertained, as required, and then disappearing on long evening walks so Peter and Clarissa could have their privacy. Peter's upright was stowed in the barn and occasionally Philip would fancy a bash, to their delight, making something rather beautiful of the old instrument. He preferred not to play or think music on the whole. His main aim, when he came, was to indulge the children. He made a tree house for little James and purchased track to add to his train set, toasted in over orange juice and Budweiser.

James was a confiding child who brought constant news from the world of play: tree-house dramas, train-set dilemmas, imaginary-friend updates. The boy had rubbery fingers and big brown eyes. He was amazingly gallant towards his little sister, calming her down when she freaked at a video, soothing her when she hurt herself. Katie was more assertive than James. She felt quite at liberty to switch mood as the pressures of the day dictated – from angelic to demonic. A wealth of frowns and cross looks was meted out to parents, toys, passing animals – all in the service of a healthy independence. Despite a certain shortness of fuse, Katie was endearingly suggestible and sweetly responsive to the sights and sounds Philip showed her on their trails through the wood. His appeals to her imagination would be rewarded by that little hand that came up to grasp his when they came to a stile, or entered a field with a resident cow nearer than she required.

Peter he had known since music-college days. After three years playing cello in a professional quartet, he backed out of music and trained as a solicitor, an incongruous switch that suited him down to the ground. All his great qualities as a musician, qualities of flow and exuberance, generosity and verve, were manifest in his character generally, and Philip envied his freedom from practice and performance. Peter had proved that you could live on a lot less music and still be fulfilled.

When he thought of Clarissa, Philip pictured a loveliness that flowed from her smile and light-brown hair, as she looked fondly over her shoulder at life – at the warmth and admiration that readily flowed back towards her and her lovely behind. She was easy and sexy and domestically laid-back, casting her happy spell over house and garden. She extended her motherliness to Philip, not minding much if he caught her nude in the bathroom by accident, as if there was plenty more of that on offer if anyone wanted it. And when he came down with the flu, she moved him to the guest room, and brought him consommé and crackers, and cooled his forehead with a flannel, like her very own child. He remembered the dove-soft call of her voice as she checked on him before bedtime, coming in in her nightdress with a jug of barley water and a packet of pills to sit on the chair and dab his brow; and then Peter came in, too, and they both looked at him with such tender concern.

A couple of nights later he was a bit better, taking it easy. He lay in bed listening to the beams and pipes creaking all around him. There was a bump, and then a giggle. He concentrated on his book, taking it firmly in hand and turning on his side. A few paragraphs later he heard deep breathing. He glanced up at the door. He had not witnessed anything quite like this before. The breathing itself was pretty loud and rather strange from the point of view of mere inhalation and of course he knew that they were making love in their room and that, quite blamelessly, tucked in bed, paperback in the crook of his thumb, Laura Ashley wallpaper all around him, he was privy to a moment of passion, which he could not screen out. There was an eventual gasp, a falling-off, the twang of a bedspring as bodies rearranged themselves, followed by the familiar creaking door and soft padding to the bathroom.

Philip smiled to himself. He did not mind in the least. It was so nice to know that the people he loved loved each other in this way. The house was happy, its strongest desires fulfilled within its own realm.

The last time he saw them was over New Year. He went down with Laura. Clarissa's brother Jack was there, too. The weather had turned bitingly cold and he treasured the memory of an evening gathered around the television set watching a black-and-white version of *The Hound of the Baskervilles*. They sat in armchairs and sofas, passing the chocolates and a bottle of malt, relishing their snug cosiness before the wood-burning stove and the shadows thrown by candles on the beamy ceiling. Clarissa clutched Peter's arm with girly fright at the sound of the hound, and Philip smiled at the demonic vitality of Peter Cushing's Holmes. Jack flung a log on the fire and spun the lid off a bottle of Talisker with practised ease, and even as they cuddled in their seats, snow was piling up outside, rising on window ledges, drifting against the barn, smothering the garden in white felt, which dazzled the whole house the next morning – a brilliant festive winterlight – sending the children into a frenzy. Porridge, bacon, coffee, then woolly socks, wellingtons, mittens for the kids. Peter, Jack and Philip were out in the barn before you could say 'Who'll clean the dishes?', pulling sledges and toboggans on to the drive, crunching across the snow with childish glee, Katie and James venturing more cautiously into the deepest drifts they had ever seen. Snowballs flew at the women as they came out in their coats. Horrible revenges were taken later. Before long they were trooping off to the top of the hill and the mother of all tobogganing sessions.

The snow was drifty and sparkly and then suddenly sparse. The fields were frozen and knobbly underfoot. There were stiff cowpats and slivers of ice, mercilessly scuppered by James's heel. Peter tested the thickness of ice on the edge of the lake, masochistically relishing the fright when it cracked and moved underfoot. Jack had his eye on the steepest incline for tobogganing and soon they were aloft the hill, gazing across white-carpeted fields like a scene from Brueghel, and girding themselves for the downward plunge. Jack went first, zipping through spats of wild turbulence and then creamy speed. Peter tried his luck on a plastic toboggan that shuddered all the way down and evicted him into a drift; then Philip pitched off, Jamie in front, finger-steering to hold course as they swished at an almost scary speed to the bottom of the hill and came to a halt with perfect dignity. 'Again! Again!' cried Jamie, and Philip turned to see how far behind they'd left the others, specks on the hill. He remembered climbing up the slope with a gratifying sense of exertion, smiling as Laura belted past, and gaining the top with Jamie, gazing in boyish delight across the whitened panorama of countryside, raised to a dazzle by the cobalt sky and splintering sun.

Later, when they were exhausted and cold and coming home to what Jack described as the 'obligatory' whisky mac, he looked up with satisfaction to see the cottage, stuck there in the white land-scape, a Hansel and Gretel dwelling with a wisp of smoke curling from its chimney pot.

They would sit around the kitchen table, slicing leeks and scoring sprouts, sipping whatever concoction Jack pressed into their hands, and after lunch the children played outside, and Philip gathered logs and stacked them in the inglenook and there they sat in the heat of the stove, reading and snoozing, Laura making intelligent conversation with adults and children alike. It was this wood-burning stove that set the house ablaze two months later.

Neighbouring farmers said you could see the conflagration from a few miles away. By the time the fire engines arrived the flames were leaping high into the night, casting a sparking orange glow into the black sky like a Guy Fawkes bonfire. The roof collapsed on one side before the fire was brought under control. The old buttress on the north wall was left free-standing. A whole section of the first floor had been consumed.

Chapter Sixteen

THE CAMERAMAN SAT IN the back of the car: Ed, a human tripod, gangly, with a vulture hairmop and pointy chin. He was a 'very nice man', claimed Derek, classic film-crew material, indeed, hard-working, salt of the earth with a tavern smile and a trouser pocket full of Rizlas. He'd left the wife, unfortunately. 'She's a bit mad' – frown – and now, advised Derek, he was knocking off some Italian bird. 'Giovanna, is it?' 'Yep. Giovanna. Quite a handful. In every sense.'

Derek briefed Ed as Philip drove the car.

'We're retracing footsteps to a place of special inspiration. You'll want to cover hills, trees, tweeting birds, the property in long shot. We'll mic Philip outside and follow him up the drive like it's memory lane. Hold on Philip closely as he explains what this place meant to him.'

'OK. Sort of retreat, is it?'

'Should we be thinking in terms of a particular piano concerto or Debussy-type thing?' Derek smiled at Philip. 'I know I'm a philistine.'

'Not really.'

He drove carefully, hardly aware of the others. He had planned to come anyway and then Derek had phoned and offered to film the trip. BBC 4 had signed off the documentary on a tiny budget.

'This was my retreat from music, actually.'

He had not been back for several years, he told them. He made no mention of the fire.

'You came here for breaks, away from the madding crowd?'

Philip wanted Derek's reaction, his first-time reaction, and he needed somebody around.

'It's a very beautiful stretch of countryside.'
'Do I need a boom, Ed?'
'Bit of a fiddle, to be honest.'
'The leads on the fucking camera are about three feet long.'
'We'll be jerking each other around like a pair of Siamese twins.'
Philip was calm. He felt ready at last.

They parked on the lane.
'I'm going to have to push and pull you into available light, but try to ignore Ed. Get him side-on.'
'You'll be asking questions, though,' said Ed. 'Better to have me on the right, light side, and then you put questions sort of over my shoulder.'
Derek frowned, adjusting his earphones.
Ed delicately attached the mic to Philip's jacket.
The sky was blue: a light wind rustled the leaves overhead.
He turned to walk along the drive.
It was the same: same light fall, same bustle of greenery.
Derek caught up with him as they came to the barn. 'Places like this are going for eight hundred grand these days. Friends of yours?' He ushered Ed across. Ed's PD 450 was incongruously small, a hand-held bird of a camera.
'Yes.'
'Expecting us?'
'Not here any more.'
'Aga-saga novelist, more like,' said Ed, with a crooked smile. 'Derek will charm them.'
He wielded the camera in a pan around the back of the barn, the drive, the trees, the side of Philip's head.
'This was a special place for you?' Derek seemed officially to begin the documentary.
'I had my childhood here.'
'What? When were . . .'
They came to the end of the drive, the barn wall receding to expose the house.
'Oh!'
Derek's expression changed, humorous consternation. He looked at Philip to check his reaction.
'Is that . . .?'

163

The house was a charred wreck. The roof had collapsed on one side, the window frames were blackened, weeds growing out from within. Debris lay on the flower beds.

Philip went up the footpath towards what used to be the front door.

'It was a fifteenth-century farm cottage. In fact, I think bits of it were earlier. Absolutely ancient. No foundations. It just sat on the clay.'

Frowning, Derek came alongside. Ed followed, his camera see-sawing to take in the ruin. Philip leaned on the empty window frame. Glass lay on the sill.

They peered inside at the tar-blackened remains of the sitting room, just a shell now, the rear wall a parapet of rubble, the inglenook intact, the floor covered in soot, slivers of glass. He looked up through the vanished ceiling to the sky.

Close up he could hear Derek's breathing.

'When did this happen?'

Philip remembered the arrangement of furniture, the grouping of chairs around the fire, the pine chest, a bookcase above the TV set, all vanished, melted away by heat.

'Some years ago now.'

Derek hesitated. 'Was anyone hurt?'

Philip moved on again, around to the back of the house, as if in search of something particular.

'We used to have breakfast in this area here. There was a trellis smothered in wisteria.'

The trellis had been crushed into a flat mess by half a toppled chimney. Segments of brick lay on the paving stones. A cascade of roof tiles covered the doorstep.

He stepped through a hole in the back wall. There were stumps of masonry on the living-room floor. The soot was impacted, solid underfoot. The ceiling's thick main beam lay on the ground burnt to a spindle of carbon.

'That might not . . . doesn't look too safe in here.'

'They all died.' He turned.

Derek stared back at him. He stepped into the living room, shared a quick glance with Ed.

Philip gazed at the remains of the stairs – a series of charred posts zigzagging up the wall. The tongue-and-groove panel behind the downstairs loo had burnt away.

'You could get it for less than eight hundred thousand now,' he said.

Derek nodded slowly. He was pale. It was taking him a moment or two to recover his presence of mind. There was an acrid smell in the room.

Philip stood by the foot of the incinerated staircase, looking up at the landing. Katie's bedroom was at the end on the right. Peter and Clarissa's bedroom was just sky now. He felt strange. He touched his stomach where the pain came from. The house reeked of dank bitter smoke.

Derek guided Ed towards Philip.

Philip frowned as the sensation passed.

'How does it feel to be here now?'

They waited for him to answer. He looked up at the ceiling.

'The heat was intense. Nobody could have survived, you see.'

'A family?'

Philip turned to face the camera. 'Apparently a passing driver saw the blaze, called the emergency services on his mobile. He saw a man running round the house with a hose. The man was naked.'

'This was your friend?'

'You're pulling on the camera, Derek.'

'Your best friend?'

'Hard to work out what happened. Maybe he jumped from the bedroom window. He got out and then he went in again. Didn't make it. Nobody came out.'

Derek blinked, looking up at the half-roof.

'Timber frame, wattle and daub.'

Derek hooked his finger at Ed.

Philip surveyed the wreckage around them.

'Why have you come back today?'

'Oh . . . uh . . .'

'D'you mind standing . . . That's it.'

Behind Philip was a section of ceiling that had buckled and cracked open, its wires and pipes jutting out like the innards of a severed limb.

There was the sound of breaking glass from under Ed's reversing foot.

Derek tried again. 'Isn't this rather traumatic?'

Philip imagined Clarissa peering from the kitchen door, looking around to see where the children were.

'So you wanted to come . . .'

He swallowed. It was gathering now.

'Please.'

He felt a cold tingling across the back of his shoulders and neck. The room seemed to colour itself in again, filling up with furniture, the curly top of Peter's head in the chair below him, Clarissa coming from the kitchen; and then it released back into the mess in front of him.

'I came to acknowledge something,' he said, turning to Derek. Derek drew close, adjusting his earphones.

'Can you leave me for a moment?'

'Oh! . . . Sure . . . Sure. Come on, Ed.'

Ed lowered the camera, looked around grimly.

It felt strange to be alone. He stood quite still, let his eyes wander. He was waiting to feel something. He expected the emotion to come suddenly, a welling and glutting, the original agony. He was so close to its source, stepping into the past every few seconds, coming back to the spectacle around him.

They seemed absent. Their spirits had deserted the place, leaving it doubly desolate.

He forced himself to picture things: the stencils on the loo wall, the spider plant on the mantelpiece, Peter's slippers by the fire, the children's toy box behind the armchair, the pale light from the window falling on chair covers, Katie's plastic mermaid tucked under the valance.

Nothing came to fill the emptiness inside him. He exhaled, almost frustrated, like a woman in labour making slow progress. Nothing would come into him, nothing would invade him except silence and emptiness and things that were not.

He trod out of the building.

Derek and Ed sat on the grass amongst buttercups and daisies. Ed had retrieved a flask from his shoulder bag in the car and was taking a swig. Philip walked across the lawn and sat down next to them. They took it in turns with the flask, circulating it two or three times. The vodka had a bracing effect on Philip, a hint of heartburn.

Derek started to laugh. He seemed quite shaken.

Ed raised his eyebrows. He was similarly affected.

Derek's voice was thick now. 'You took us by surprise there, Philip.'

They started to giggle. Ed leant on his arm, averting his gaze.

Derek wiped an eye and held his hand over his brow.

Philip focused on the view. He felt a frisson. Time was not straightforward. Every particle of the view settled exactly on memory.

He laughed softly and then crumpled down sideways, his head falling into the grass. For a moment he watched the flask changing hands, saw Ed's chin and cheek against the sky, then he looked at the grass – out of focus – close to his forehead.

He guessed at what he would have to go through. Nothing so simply agonising as grief. A calamity had happened out there in time and he had somehow to find a way of making it happen inside his head. He had to find a way of allowing it through his mind like a toppled tree being dragged, branches and all, through the middle of a house, scratching and ripping at floors and furniture, detritus everywhere until the damn thing is hauled through to the other side, and then the damage is done. He was daunted by the concurrency of this problem with his everyday life. This had been going on for years, side by side with his plans and routines, bulking larger all the time; and now here he was at the centre.

He sat up again, took a rolly off Ed, checked the garden, what could be seen of it. Beyond the drive the lawn had turned to meadow. It was a green haze of thistle and dandelion. The gravel was carpeted in grass. All the roses and shrubs were overblown. The hedges tottering. On the edge of pastureland it took no more than a couple of seasons for nature to scramble over everything, choking borders with nettles and bindweed. The barns seemed embedded in the sloping ground.

Only the fields beyond were the same – fields manicured by chomping cows and nibbling sheep.

Ed was behind him as he walked through the thick grass to the orchard. The camera was not intrusive. There was nothing to intrude upon. He tracked and panned, following point of view, but Philip was drifting now, almost unaware of himself. He had no objection to the documentary. Self-consciousness had deserted him. The public were welcome to whatever they could gain from this spectacle.

This was where he had stood before, between leaning apple trees in autumn, noticing with a crush of pleasure a cluster of rosehips against the blue sky: red on blue, sharp in the morning light, a hyper-vivid miracle. It was a solitary moment, allowable then, a childlike discovery. They had parented him, he knew that, but the house and its garden seemed to nurture him, too.

He wondered by what means they had allowed him to share in their Eden, offering him the run of the place *en famille*, and the right to survive their fate.

He found a sapling Metasequoia suffocated by grasses, reduced almost to a trellis by rampant weeds, its needle clusters thin and sparse. He had planted it and now he disentangled the branches with tender futility.

They were present all of a sudden, as if he had seen them yesterday, Peter coming across the lawn with his tousled hair, white shirt and jeans – a Pan-like figure; Clarissa wafting around the house, snipping rosemary and thyme. They displayed the happy purposefulness of people who had found their nest and had the talent and temperament to make the most of it.

Derek peered out from behind a giant hogweed. He seemed troubled by the abundance of vegetation. He raise a thumb at Ed and framed with his hands the idea for a shot over Philip's shoulder towards a hump-backed hill. 'Elgarian. Sort of.'

Derek was more sensitive and poised now. His movements deferred, drew on, yielded. He had the dissimulated alertness of someone who has caught on and is nervously determined to get the goods.

'D'you have photographs of this place?'

'Probably.'

'Then-and-now effect?'

They paused at a gate, Philip wondering where to go, where to look.

'Why come here today?'

Philip opened his mouth, shook his head. He felt a little giddy.

'This happened a while ago.' Derek looked over his shoulder. 'It's odd to rake it up. What made you . . . all of a sudden . . . want to come back?'

'I . . . I owed them a visit.'

Derek appeared to digest this. He nodded, bit his lip. 'You think of them as still here?'

Philip was open to the suggestion but could not confirm it.

Derek waggled his finger at Ed, who was side-on a few feet back.

'The sudden non-being of someone you know is mysterious,' said Philip.

'Hard to accept?'

'I couldn't have come here before now.'

'Too painful?'

'Of course it was too fucking painful!'

Derek suffered the impatience without blinking. He seemed ready to be given something.

'I mean . . . either you say, "Shit happens." Forget it, get on with your life, because there's no point . . . Or you say, "I have to acknowledge it. Until I let it overwhelm me, I can't say I've survived." '

They stood, the three of them, on the drive, shade playing in their faces. A pair of dragonflies jiggered past.

The shadow of a branch swayed against the brickwork of the barn.

He was crying now. He fingered away the tears, panted in air, against the sobs trapped in his throat.

Derek drew the cameraman away, averting his own eyes.

Philip gestured, hoping the gesture would help him, but nothing came of it.

Derek glanced along the driveway, debating something.

From here the house was out of sight, concealed by the barn. The three men gazed at the light-shot opening beyond the canopy of trees.

Philip moved off along the drive, slowly drawn back. The other two stood behind him checking their equipment. Eventually they followed at a distance.

This time when he cleared the barn and the fringe of willow leaves the house looked more simply awful than before. Some builder should by now have bought the plot and redeveloped it. He went closer, feeling strange pity for the house.

He gazed through a kitchen window at the dim mess inside, walls flaking and peeling, like a degenerating womb. He glanced back at the men and slipped in through a door to the annex, former scene of wellington boots and curls of mud on the floor. In the kitchen the ceiling plasterboard hung loose and gaping in places. The counters were intact, Formica curling; the floor tiles were covered in a scree of dust and rubble. Over the sink there was a trap-door-size hole in the ceiling. Philip came under the aperture and looked up at the rafters of Katie's bedroom. It seemed as if the squarish manhole had been neatly cut by firemen to gain access to the room above. He levered himself on to the counter, stood up on the old units and made his way around to the sink to get a better look. Standing on tiptoe his eyes came just above floor level. He was nose to nose with the leg of a bed. As far as he could tell the fire had not penetrated this room. The walls bore smoke-stained wallpaper, but the door had shut out the flames from the landing. The massive central chimney stack had protected this chamber from the worst of the heat.

He braced his arms and levered himself up, boards creaking, plaster crumbling away and clattering on the sink. He pulled through slowly, wedged a knee on a rafter and rolled sideways on to the bedroom floor.

There was the same smell of smoke, but as he got up, dusting his knees and elbows, he saw that the room was intact. He looked around in a kind of dull wonder, and slowly he realised what he was staring at. Everywhere there were toys, children's books, fluffy animals. Her possessions were on the chest of drawers, the shelves, the mantelpiece. Sticker books, a fairy calendar, a pink plastic hairbrush, the bedraggled queue of toy rabbits and giraffes, sitting patiently on the floor. He turned with a lurch in his heart to see her dressing gown hanging on the back of the door. The men had come in to get her, come too late, of course, taken the poor thing out through that hole, but nobody could face climbing up again to clear up her things. He caught his face in his hands and sat slowly on the end of the bed. The room had been waiting for him all these years, waiting for him to come and see what had happened.

He sat in a trance, as if trapped by a spell, the cluster of memories coming at him from every corner of the room, through stale air that still carried a bouquet of the past, so close now, so concurrent, so rivingly familiar. His eyes rested on everything in turn, every single object he could find to notice and take in. She was there in his mind so suddenly, and this was the difficult thing. These little icons of childhood were imbued with her child self, the lilac toy mobile, the scrap of ribbon, the crayon. How real she had been, little Katie, having her crack at existence with such zest! He could hear the sound of her singing to herself between bossy mutterings as she managed the mermaids or the rabbits. His heart had flowed towards that little girl, whom he thought of as his child only because he loved her so much for herself; he loved the premise of her character, the fact he had known her since day one, had seen a brand-new original human being enter the world, and what was excruciating now was the vividness of this child in memory. She was there. In his mind's eye she was seconds away.

One could almost believe the rest of the house was intact. He dared not open the door on to the landing: a black cavern, no doubt. He noticed how a clothes-rack pole slanted across the wall, barring the window and rescue.

He realised, this was it, yes, because he could not remember, not voluntarily, could not bring himself to picture them, the whole dear family in this house, in this garden, until he had seen for himself that they were gone. Until he had forced this charred ruin into his mind, this rank shell, this dusty, musty death-trap; until he had seen with his own eyes how things stood in reality, and got into his head the stark fact of their awful deaths, the past was closed to him, an unreachable dream. He could not even do Katie the justice of calling her to mind. Had not been able to, had not dared to. And yet in his mind they were everywhere now, so close, just the far side of a corner in time.

He lay on the bed, lips parted, caving in slowly, mildew hanging in his nostrils, dust in his hair, silence sitting on him like a press, a weight that would ease the breath out of him, a flattening weight that crushed away thought and sense and self.

When he opened his eyes, he felt not quite himself. He lay on the mattress without turning his head.

Before descending through the hole he put his hand on a fluffy rabbit and waited a second. He stroked the rabbit but left it where it was. Sliding down into the kitchen the smell of smoke hit him like a wall, a bitter stink you could almost taste.

Outside on the lawn the brightness was dazzling. Everything seemed whitened by sunlight. Ed and Derek were standing in the grass by the stream. They were talking and nodding easily.

A cow in the field flicked its tail.

They looked at him as he came out, but he kept his distance, crossing to a gate by the field.

Ten minutes later he was up on the hill, the poplars behind him hissing like surf. He stared at the wide yonder of fields, catching his breath. The hills were a lattice of light and shade. Woodland tributaries flowed off the slopes and met in the valley. In the flat distance the limbs of a beech tree magnificently erupted. He stood there with mouth agape, letting the emotion run out of him, sorrow out, sensation in, a glut of it, his tears flecked by the wind.

He gazed up at the long length of the poplar's trunk, to the net of leaves and to the burning blue above.

Chapter Seventeen

THE CONSULTANT HAD BEEN slow and careful, leading in gently, placing the results before him as evidence to be made use of. His face was alert to the impact of words, his forehead lined with sensitive concern. He spread his hands across the papers on his desk as if conjuring prognosis from an array of sources. There were results, and there were inferences, a joining-together of the elements in a picture. As he spoke and Philip listened he somehow managed to convey the normality of a life-threatening illness, describing it in terms of wear and tear, as though Philip's body were the inside of a used car and the consultant a mechanic who knew what he could and could not do.

He was full of restless energy. It was a beautiful summer's day outside and he wanted to be in Hyde Park walking across the grass.

'Look on the angiogram here. These vessels are tumour-specific. Obstruct them and you starve the growth.'

He touched the translucent sheet with a forefinger. The vessels were like a mesh of steel wool around darkness.

'By surgery?'

'And subsequent therapy.'

He inhaled sharply. One had to be grown-up about these things. 'So keyhole's out?'

'Given the shape and distribution of tissue, yes. We'll need to open you up and have a proper look-see.'

He nodded slowly. It was all very intelligible.

'Is the operation hazardous?'

'Twenty years ago these sorts of interventions were impossible. Nowadays more is known about the vascular structure of the organ. It's relatively routine.'

There was bedside reassurance here. The dark mystery of the body, its secret deeds and processes, science illumined with daylight clarity. The situation was drastic but Philip had allies. Dr Lewis was a veteran in the wars against cancer, wise to the wiles of his adversary. He had the knife, chemicals, radiology, scanning superiority. His team could frazzle tumours, napalm metastases, smoke out rogue cells. He was a doughty fighter and a shrewd tactician. Of course there were outcomes other than victory in this sort of conflict. Against that particular foe one might not survive valorous battle. Doctors were warriors of a sort, but threshold guardians, too. Cancer treatment hovered ambiguously between steps towards cure and strategies in a process of dying.

'How long do I have to wait?'

The consultant coughed. 'Two to four weeks.'

He had a call into Ursula. This development would make things easier to explain.

'Recuperation?'

'The incision can be sore for a week or so. You'll need to take it easy for a bit.'

He felt the G-force of violently accelerated mortality.

'Then chemotherapy?'

He nodded. 'Then chemo.'

Philip patted his leg. The oncology wing of a London hospital was not a club he wanted to join. The in-patients belonged no longer to themselves but to endgames of sickness and the curriculum of terminal care.

'What are my chances?'

The consultant seemed to acknowledge this was a necessary question. 'We'll know more after the operation.'

He was impatient now. He wanted to be doing something else. 'How little time might I have?'

'Mr Morahan, I think you should be positive.'

'I'm a concert pianist. I make commitments years in advance.'

'Make your commitments!'

'I need a timeframe.'

'I can't imagine a prognosis worse than six to nine months on any set of facts. The more likely scenario is two to five years. As I say, my hope would be for a full recovery.'

He let the information travel through him. 'Thank you.'

Out in the corridor he took the up lift instead of the down lift and got wedged behind a trolley and two paramedics. Up on the fifth floor sunlight rushed in through the plate-glass window and dazzled him. He stood aside as a pair of surgeons walked by. He pressed the lift button and waited impatiently as more staff sped the other way. A nurse with succouring body-curves under crisp uniform held a bag of plasma to her chest as she reversed through a door.

Back on the ground floor he found himself trailing past a shopping mall of coffee machines and sandwich vendors and confectionery stalls. Patients from a ward at the end of the corridor were shuffling past with expressions of institutional self-pity. For a moment he had no sense of the time of day. He stared at his watch, unable to concentrate. This was his predicament: a succession of acute and unfamiliar mental states that he would need to ignore. One had to press on and stick to the plan. Action would help him metabolise thoroughly bad news, which anyway he had expected.

He crossed the lobby and went through automatic doors into the city air, past the cabs on the concourse that led to Praed Street. Light cut across the upper floors of neighbouring buildings, throwing huge diagonals of shadow over the hospital wing. Pigeons hopped on the pavement, a black porter stood over a drunk, who had fallen on the entrance steps.

He felt momentarily bodiless. He kept going, senses greeted by construction noise, the colours of advertising placards, the acridity of exhaust. He decided to walk down Edgware Road, past the Arab banks and Lebanese restaurants, the Halal stores and casino fronts. In the park he strolled around, gazing at the ruff of trees that collared Park Lane between Marble Arch and Hyde Park Corner and at the hotels and embassies rising above the tree-line, crenellating the sky unevenly.

He would collect some sheet music from Boosey & Hawkes and go down to HMV. He wanted to see what Serebriakov recordings they had. He remembered to switch on his mobile. Ursula might call at any moment. It was a long time since he had felt the urge, let alone the capacity, to be charming. John would be more difficult. His agent could dissimulate forgiveness and fellow-feeling if pushed, which he would be. Unfortunately for poor old John he must do a lot more than hug and brush away a tear. He must think the unthinkable and get on with it.

He was dizzy now. The walking made him feel light-headed. Serious illness was so preoccupying. One had to sidestep back into the routine feel of things. Too easily with this kind of news everyday reality lost its immediacy. Plans and interests went flaccid. One felt poorly, persecuted, weak-willed. The solar plexus cracked up. Not for him. None of that nonsense for him.

Fifty-two years of memory, of experience, of living personal history and mental culture, the streaming individual mind was supported, it turned out, only by the frailest wisps of bodily health.

Striking back across the park he recalled Peter's line about heaven, and the likely absence thereof. How to have your heaven in this life was the issue. Without the lure of a hereafter all that Protestant work-ethic propaganda went out the window. Unhappiness, loneliness, angst. Leave all that to the grave and beyond.

Heaven was now or never, he had said.

Chapter Eighteen

THE NEW OFFICES WERE a mess: unallocated computer screens, BT handsets, half-emptied cartons, technicians on their knees pulling cables, props from the last office shoved against partition walls (potted plants, chrome chairs). The central floor space was an open-plan zone for secretaries. Hogging the window-light on either side were cubicle offices for the agents. Philip sat in reception on a low-slung sofa gazing at a sea of music journals someone had atmospherically flung on the table. Beside him on the floor sat a box of client photographs destined for the lavatory wall. Clipboarded posters were stacked behind the reception desk (promotional stuff that John had collected down the ages), some a little out of date by now: Arturo Moroni in his LSO days, shirt studs glittering, toupee going strong; Yono Hasaki modelling chiselled fingers against a black backdrop; Therese Stimmerman lost in a halo of adoring soft focus, as though she had already died and gone to heaven, which in fact, now Philip came to think of it, she had.

Or hell.

The receptionist wore jeans and a fluffy polo-neck sweater and was somewhat thrown by the switchboard, jabbing this button and then that to retrieve a lost caller.

In his briefcase he had a present for Ursula and champagne for John. Neither had returned his calls and it was not difficult to see why. The place was in chaos. He was apprehensive but he had to impose.

The receptionist managed her station with some glamour. He heard her speaking discreetly into the phone.

'I'm pretty sure he's busy,' she said afterwards, sympathetically. 'Please try again.'

Philip had spotted John crossing the office and entering his cubicle. His door was still ajar.

The agency was expanding: new personnel, new computers and offices. Sampson was on the Haymarket at last, his career flourishing. How little difference the fate of an individual musician made to organisations like this! Old clients faded, new ones burst forth. John took strength from the virile talents of people half his age.

She tried again. Whilst she was speaking he could see John's door closing from the inside.

'Sorry! He's a bit tied up at the minute. D'you want to make an appointment?'

'Is Ursula free?'

The girl was pained. 'She's got a meeting, too.'

'I can wait for a bit.'

'We're all at sixes and sevens.'

He glimpsed familiar faces in the open-plan area: Phyllis, who ran accounts, Bob Collier the bookings manager, John's assistant Serena. He had known these people for years.

'OK. Thanks.'

He rose, as if to leave, but instead walked out of the lobby into the open-plan zone, heading for John's room.

'Can I help?' somebody said.

He pretended not to hear and made his way across the space swiftly.

'Hi, Philip,' said Serena, calling from her desk, a note of alarm in her voice.

'I've come to see John.'

'I think he's . . .'

'Right here.'

Philip got his hand to the door handle and twisted it sharply. 'Excuse me,' he said, as the door swung wide, revealing John on a chair and a girl on the sofa.

'What!' John jumped to his feet heading Philip off. 'We're in a meeting. Francesca!'

'Can . . .'

'No you can't!'

The girl started.

'Stay,' said John, palm out flat.

'I have to see you.'

'I'm not available. Make a time.'

'Shall I come back?' she asked. She wore a pink blouse and a check skirt.

'Sorry to interrupt,' said Philip.

'What the hell!'

'It can't wait.'

John went to the door, opened it wide. 'My work's equally important and it can't wait either.'

His heart was beating unpleasantly hard. He had to go through with this; it was one of the things he had to go through with. 'I don't blame you for being angry.'

'I don't care whether you blame me.'

'This is an emergency.'

'Take your emergency to some other agent. Far as I'm concerned you're not a client.' He leaned across to hit the buzzer on his telephone console.

'Francesca!'

'I know you're busy.'

'Get out!'

Philip laughed. 'What I'm about to tell you will make you feel a whole lot better.'

'Am I going to have to chuck you out of here!'

'I'm dying, John. I haven't much longer. I need your help.'

John's frown deepened. He squinted at Philip, tongue running around his underlip. He gasped, indignation arrested, put a forefinger and thumb to the bridge of his nose.

Philip glanced at the girl, who was now rising from the sofa.

John caught the exchange of looks. He waved a hand.

She smiled painfully, took her notebook and slipped quickly from the room.

John sniffed as though suddenly congested.

'Liver cancer,' said Philip.

His agent stared at him with pained care. His handsome face was thickly creased. He had the abject look of someone who senses he has made a fool of himself and is almost too staggered to dissimulate the shock and embarrassment. He wavered for a moment and then shut the door.

'Take a seat.'

Philip crossed to the sofa. He noted John's orderly desk, the

179

intrays and pencil pots, the blue mouse-pad by keyboard and screen. A framed photo of his wife and children leaned against the wall.

He turned before he sat. 'That's why I cancelled.'

John nodded. He was still breathing hard, mastering the shock of it. He moved across to the chair and sat heavily, massaging his eye-sockets. He looked suddenly drained, the latent tiredness of recent weeks brought to the surface.

'Why didn't you tell me?'

'I was waiting for results.'

John shook his head in immediate sorrow. He had no emotional resilience.

'D'you mind if we call in Ursula?' asked Philip.

John sniffed, pulled a tissue from his pocket. There was an extension on the side table. He took up the receiver. 'Ursula. Come in, please. I know. It's Philip. He's here, yup. Just tell Ben . . . tell him to wait.'

Philip reached into his briefcase and pulled out the champagne. 'For you.'

John was pained by the label. 'What have I done to deserve this?'

There was a knock on the door. Francesca tucked her head in. 'Hiya!'

She looked vaguely surprised to see Philip on the sofa.

'Do the honours, will you.' John handed her the bottle. 'Three glasses. If you can't find glasses, tea mugs will do.'

'OK, yah.'

The two men stared at each other for a moment.

'What's going to happen, Philip?'

'Operation. Chemotherapy.'

John nodded. 'Then?'

'Then, after a while, I peg it.'

The agent flinched. He felt the news openly, immediately. 'Is there no hope?'

'There's always hope.'

'You've got to fight the damn thing.'

'I don't think the cancer cares about my attitude.'

'As long as there's a chance' – John was roused – 'you mustn't give up.'

'Leave that to me. I need to talk about something else.'

'Look, I apologise unreservedly. I behaved like a complete tit. I thought you were jerking me around. I'm ashamed, humiliated, appalled.'

Philip chuckled. 'You'll live.'

John's grateful smile faded as the remark sank in.

'That's all water under the bridge,' said Philip.

His agent raised a hand in acknowledgement, wiped a tear from his eye. He inhaled deeply as if to pull himself together. For a moment he could think of nothing to say. He subsided against his chair.

There was a tap on the door and then she came in. Ursula's gaze acknowledged John before resting on Philip. She had not had the chance to prepare for the awkwardness of eye contact. Her look was vulnerable and challenging at the same time.

He had forgotten how tall she was.

'Shut the door,' said John.

'You know I've got someone in with me?'

'So you keep saying.'

She went across to a chair by the sofa and sat down, regarding Philip with a mixture of respect and reserve. She had not expected their next encounter to take place in John's office. She was at a loss and not able to conceal it.

Philip had forgotten how incongruous her beauty seemed amidst the nine-to-five. He was warmed by the sight of her. The advent of Ursula in his life was indeed a kind of miracle.

'How are you?' she said gently.

'Sorry I was short with you on the phone.'

This seemed to her inadequate but sincere. She looked cautiously at John, who sat back in his chair biting the edge of his finger.

'You two have made up?'

Philip admired her directness in asking this.

'Yes, yes,' said John. 'I've been a fool and an idiot and Philip has very kindly let me off the hook.'

She gazed at them both with evident relief. After a while she smiled weakly at Philip.

'Here,' he said, pulling a box of gift-wrapped scent from his case.

She took the present uncertainly. 'What's this?'

'I couldn't help noticing.'

She unwrapped it quickly. 'Oh gosh! Allure.' She was a little put out by the gesture. 'You shouldn't have done that. Thank you.'

'Thanks for putting up with me.'

The three of them sat for a moment in silence. It was Philip's turn to speak but he suddenly lacked the resources or impetus to break the news, as if the news were no longer on his mind in quite the same way now that she was in the room. Ursula's loveliness was restorative.

She waited a little tensely. She had been summoned after all.

John sensed Philip's distraction and was unable to control his unease. 'Philip has some news, Ursula.'

She looked at him uncomfortably, wary of 'news' that might impinge on her.

'Champagne!' called Francesca, coming back in with bottle and glasses.

'Excellent,' said John. 'Over there, would you.'

She set the glasses down on John's coffee table and carefully poured the champagne.

'Enjoy your celebration.' She left with gusto.

John passed the glasses to the others. They sipped and nodded their toasts silently.

Philip turned to address Ursula.

'John,' she said suddenly. 'What should I do about Ben Samuelson?'

He looked at her blankly.

Philip drew himself up. It was a way to explain things, not the only way, but the simplest way.

'I'm quite ill,' he said.

She was alert.

'Don't let's go into the details . . . but I mayn't have very long.'

She reacted with her whole body as if struck by an electric current. She replaced her champagne glass and leant towards him. He could see the swarming of distress behind her shocked expression. He came towards her and seized the hand that she offered on a reflex, squeezing it tightly.

'I just wanted to say sorry to both of you for the fiasco over my last concert.'

She shook her head. She was quite distraught. 'But what . . .'

'John will tell you. It's boring.'

'Oh God!' Her eyes were moist. 'You don't have to say sorry for anything.'

'Lots of things have fallen into place since then. This sort of development can be clarifying, actually. I honestly needed to stop playing for a while.' He was firm. He had to stay firm.

She shook her head, as though denying the credibility of this news. 'How are you feeling now?'

He smiled resolutely. 'Better than before the concert. Once you know, you can begin to deal with it. I'm not saying it hasn't been grim, but I feel somehow or other back in control. I want to play again.'

'Oh, Philip!'

'You know, for a few weeks not a single bar of music came into my head. I haven't actually touched the piano yet, but I know it's going to sound beautiful when I do.'

There were tears in her eyes.

He acknowledged her sympathy with the kindest of looks. 'Ursula's more of an angel than an agent,' he said to John, smiling. 'Don't feel sorry for me. I'm lucky in knowing I'll leave something of myself. Through all this I've realised that in every sense I'm a soloist. I already have all I need or could expect. And I've been able to share that. While I've still got the chance to make music for people I have a reason to be happy. How much time any of us have left we can never know.'

John sobbed, pulling his handkerchief from a drawer and blowing his nose with trumpety plangency. He sighed heavily, averting his eyes and scrunching the kerchief in his hand. He levered himself forward in the chair, gazed glassily around.

'Oh, that reminds me.' Philip dug into his briefcase. 'I'm all presents today. This is for your boy.'

John looked tearfully at the toy car.

'Is he OK, John?'

John nodded with difficulty.

'He's getting better?'

He stood up suddenly, lumbered towards Philip, arms opening. Philip rose to meet the hug; the embrace was strangely healing, genuine emotion seemed to pass between agent and client, as if to confirm that the business premise of their relationship was a structure that housed the full range of human feelings. The driving energies and aspirations of their working lives were entwined. The hug was as heartfelt as John could be about anything – and that was heartfelt enough.

Afterwards John stood back, raised the champagne glass to his lips, and swigged back the remains.

'Your meeting,' he said to Ursula.

She sighed, drained by the idea.

'Don't go,' pleaded Philip.

Ursula glanced at John.

John sat down at his desk, took the phone and dialled reception. He glanced long-sufferingly at Philip. 'Francesca, hi. Ursula's tied up in here, and I need to speak to the guy in her office. I'll ring her extension. Will you pick up and give it to him?'

He rang off and redialled, preparing his face.

'Ben, hi. John Sampson. Hi. Sorry to cut into your meeting. We've got a bit of an emergency here and I need Ursula for a moment or two. Would you forgive her if she rescheduled the meeting? We have ways and means of making it up to you. No, she won't be out in a hurry. I won't bore you with the de – Yeah . . . Ben . . . I know, sure, I know. Yup. 'Preciate that. Yeah, of course. It's important. I wouldn't . . . listen . . . Ben! I'm sure she'll go over that . . . Do me a favour. Please let her reschedule the meeting? Speak to you soon. Thanks. I'll let you go now . . . OK . . . I'm putting the phone down . . . Bye, Ben . . . Good to speak . . . Byee . . .'

He set down the receiver and looked up in frazzled incredulity. 'Christ! What a prat!'

'My fault,' said Philip.

Ursula was haggard.

'I don't understand how some pisswit cellist thinks he can get ahead by wasting my time and trying my patience!'

Philip almost laughed.

'Another day, another absolute tosser!'

'John, please!' said Ursula.

'I have an operation in two or three weeks,' said Philip suddenly. 'Before then I want to play one concert in as big a venue as possible.'

John frowned, externalising his uncertainty quickly.

Ursula responded with interest. She glanced in John's direction. 'Short notice, Philip.'

'I'll pay for the venue, the advertising, everything.'

John nodded more times than was necessary. He bit the edge of his finger.

'I want to reprogramme the Great Sonata series into one concert. I've had some ideas.'

'Could it wait till after the operation?'

Philip responded by saying nothing.

'We'll do everything we can,' said Ursula. Her hands were unsettled, fidgety.

'Sorry to inflict this on you.'

John weeded some dust from his eye. He was struggling now. 'None of the big venues will have a slot.'

'I know.'

John was trying to grasp what Philip had in mind. 'Is this . . . what . . . some kind of farewell concert?'

Philip was momentarily overcast. 'I haven't asked him, but I suppose Vadim might stand down.'

John allowed the irony of this suggestion to colour his expression.

'Bulmanion would forgive me, I'm sure.'

John nodded slowly in provisional acknowledgement. No point in opposing Philip until he had a better idea. 'I'm just thinking out loud . . . maybe we could go bigger.'

'Bigger?'

'A venue to fit the occasion.'

'Don't say what you were going to say!'

'I wasn't . . .'

'Don't anyway!'

'What?'

'Nothing.'

'Why?'

John raised a hand, framing a thought with sudden emphasis.

'I don't want to promote the fact that I'm dying,' said Philip.

'Swan-song recital. BBC 2. You'll hit a couple of million people. That's event scheduling. CD spin-off, Cancer Relief. They can do an obit repeat. Bloody long shot but worth a try. *South Bank Show* did it for Dennis Potter.'

Philip stared at him for a moment. 'I can't play on my own. I need to play for real people.'

'Studio audience, no problem.'

Philip sighed heavily.

'Can you tell us,' said John. 'Um . . . how long have you been given?'

Philip's eyes prickled. It was extraordinary to be asked such a thing. For a moment he could not speak.

Ursula scowled at John, deflecting him.

John shook his head. He was suddenly overcome. 'Christ, Philip!' His voice cracked. 'What's it like?'

Philip looked as though he was about to respond. He twisted his neck, loosened a shirt button with a single pass of his hand, gazed at the floor, utterly bereft. 'Can we concentrate on the practicalities?' he said softly.

John leaned forward, scratching the back of his neck. His directness had become a way of dealing with clients' emotional lives. He needed people to know what he understood and what could be done about it, returning always to the limits of his role. The existential side of things he had a bead on, but was too busy to be existential for longer than was necessary to move the point along.

Now he looked bewildered. He had allowed himself to show feelings only to see them brushed aside.

'Suppose Vadim steps down?' said Philip.

John was slowly recovering. 'Um . . . not a good idea.'

'They were *my* concerts.'

John glanced patiently at Ursula. 'All the ticket holders have been mailed announcing Vadim as your replacement – due to continued indisposition. New programmes have been printed. Hyperion or Teldec are supposed to record the concert. We've just done a press release. Bulmanion's in, thank God. There's a limit to the number of volte-faces a concert-going public can absorb. Let alone promoters.'

'I'll pay.'

John was suffused with unenthusiasm. Ursula watched on tensely.

'I'll pay to have everything changed back.'

The agent's face puckered.

'It's all my fault, but perhaps people will understand.'

John stroked his forehead. 'Sorry. This is a bit much to take on.'

'Well, please take it on as quickly as you can. We haven't much time.'

'What if you're not well on the night?' said Ursula tenderly.

'I'll play.'

'Philip . . . it seems . . .'

'I know.'

John dealt him a flat look. 'Might the strain of the concert make things worse?'

'What have I got to lose?'

'Oh . . . I don't know, ah . . .' John shrugged. It seemed obvious. 'Precious time.'

'To do what? Sit around twiddling my thumbs?'

'Is it so important? I mean, you've achieved it all anyway.'

'No, I haven't. I'm at the beginning again.'

'Even so . . .'

'Don't write me off! This isn't the end of the story. I may not have much time, but what I have to offer now may be the best I've ever done.'

John nodded. Ursula was listening closely.

'I need to perform. Before I lose my nerve. I can't endure the idea that a lousy set of reviews and a cancelled concert is my last will and testament. Do you understand?'

Ursula's eyes had a sheen before the tears were released down her cheek. She looked away, hands guarding her face.

John watched her with troubled sympathy before remembering the Kleenex in his drawer. He passed the box over to her.

'Oh, God, sorry. Ignore me!' She sniffed.

The two men waited patiently as she recovered herself, averting their eyes, but occasionally stealing a glance at the nose-blowing and blinking, and the delicate hand passing its way through ringlets of hair as she tried to compose herself.

Ursula dabbed her cheeks. There was no point in leaving the room

Philip was touched and acutely depressed by the spectacle.

John leaned forward. He had been thinking his way around the matter.

'Vadim would step down. Messy, but fuck it! I can do it. And yet! You know I nearly fired him for messing Marek Nolson around, skiving off rehearsals etc? According to Marguerite he's putting in the hours and practising hard for your concert. I mean he's rising to the occasion, wants to live up to the strength of expectation in your fan base. Do you really want to call him off? He seems to have turned a corner.'

Philip smiled suddenly. He wondered whether his broadside in the Taste of India restaurant had hit the mark after all. Interesting that this update should herald from Marguerite. Maybe things had settled down in that quarter. He felt stronger with this development. It implied that despite appearances he still held sway with Vadim, which would only be the case if Vadim respected him as an artist: a warming thought.

'I expect he wants to show the world he's a better pianist.'

'No, no,' said John. 'Not at all. Far from it.'

'I wish he would.'

'It might be better to let things stand. He's your protégé, after all.'

He was amazed by the depth of his solicitude for Vadim. Something about Vadim called for special terms of treatment, an allowance he was only too ready to grant, given the slightest excuse. If he were really back on the rails it was a lot harder to be selfish and Philip was consumed by the implications of this. Very little could be arranged at short notice. The prospect of his not being able to perform was absolutely harrowing.

'D'you want me to speak to him?' said John.

There was a long silence.

'Um . . . is the documentary going ahead?'

Philip managed a nod.

'Great!'

John's energy was coming back. He glanced at his computer screen, scanning for new emails.

'Best thing we can do now is get cracking.'

Philip's head fell forward. He was in a different realm now.

Ursula reached across to touch his forearm. He took her hand, enclosing her fine knuckles in his broad palm. She squeezed back and the gentle pressure sent a lovely sensation around his elbow and into his shoulder. He looked up sharply, almost to break the spell. 'Would you come and hear me play?'

She returned his gaze with an excited look.

'That's a great idea,' said John.

'I'd love to!'

'I'd be so grateful!' he said.

'Just whenever you want,' she said. 'Call me. I'll come right away.'

John looked on with strained benignance.

'Oh good.' Philip smiled back at her. 'Great.'

He realised that it was now time to rise and move on, and that their business was done. They had an agenda. He must let them get on with it. His eyes prickled as he got ready to leave.

'We'll do everything humanly possible,' said John, hand on mouse. He was tapping in a phone number. 'You heard about Konstantine Serebriakov?'

Philip turned. 'What?'

John stared back at him for a moment.

'He just died.'

Philip glanced away. He was not surprised or shocked but felt the loss immediately, something removed, taken away; the quiet pity of another's death. Dear Konstantine – seen a few days ago, gone now, a dry leaf, fallen. He wanted to sit down, but somehow stayed on his feet, receiving Ursula's look of sorrow almost as an additional token of sympathy for himself.

Later, as he walked through the bright afternoon sunshine that picked out colour everywhere and strolled along Piccadilly towards the leafy gap of Green Park with its sun-shot crowns of chestnut trees covered in white cones and the simmering blue above, it seemed that Konstantine was only fractionally more absent now that he had been for years. The grand old man was a residue of a something that had passed into posterity decades ago. His death merely the perfection of a withdrawal into the domain from which he had come in the first place: the realm of music, a realm of afterlives.

Chapter Nineteen

DEREK HAD DECIDED NOT to use footage from their trip to the cottage. He would not intrude on Philip's grief. The human-interest approach he no longer valued. Instead of filming the pianist's daily routine, or personal story, he wanted to convey his inner life – music as experienced through the mind of an artist.

'We're making a subjective art film that inhabits the sensory, intellectual and musical consciousness of a pianist.'

'Will the BBC wear that?'

'Yes. You need art to address art. Documentary is too literal, too earthbound, too personally intrusive.'

He wanted Philip to recall the history of his musical awakenings, like a parallel biography. He would find a way to match this material visually, providing a sort of filmic descant to a richly scored narrative.

Philip was pleased. It suited him, anyway, to recover first impressions and return in his mind to a period when the musical landscape was unfolding for the first time. He would draw energy from the memory of all that.

Derek meanwhile fastened on images. He was intrigued by the iconography of the piano. The piano was a kind of habitat, its keyboard a stage for all manner of digital dramas, and a sensual surface of subtle resistances. Its rounded end and curving line were suggestively feminine, its soundboard like the inner depths. He became fascinated by the player's lifelong physical relationship with an object of musical furniture. The Steinway in Philip's house was like a companion or familiar. A piano on stage seemed almost bridal.

Derek was correct to linger on the physical relationship. There was indeed something amorous in the player's angle of attack, the way the body expressed itself into the instrument. Every player experienced a need to transmit feeling through touch itself. By the time technique was ingrained musical impulses had become tactile ones. The hand's stretches, the pectoral projection of vibrant chords, the caressing of keys were as much emotional releases as physical means; and although there would be tiresome days when Philip was at war with the mechanism of a piano, there were moments in the heat of performance when he felt fused to it. This precious sensation was the fruit of long partnership.

Even as a child he would have known this instinctively; and just as the piano drew him like an alluring mistress, so sheet music became the herald of forthcoming escapades. He read the literature cover to cover before he could play it. Scores were like journeys through a different dimension of landscape, mapping the physical adventure of a piece and its expressive topography. He would dream of the pages of Schubert sonatas as unending forests in which one could get lost, like the wanderer himself. He remembered gazing for the first time at the jagged semiquavers of Schumann's Presto Passionato, which suggested a pianistic intensity quite different to the mountains and precipices of transcendental Liszt. The Schumann looked crazed and uncomfortable, already patterned with madness. Liszt's Studies, by contrast, were grandly Alpine, as though Liszt wanted to parade unscalable difficulty even in the appearance of his scores.

Derek had the idea of tracking the sheet music of a Liszt étude with a cursor while Philip played through it, so the viewer could witness in notational form the amount of data Philip was processing to generate the music. They picked the central section of Wilde Jagd, using four cursors across two staves to illustrate – first in slow motion, hands apart, and then together at full speed – the right-hand melody coming through broken-chord semiquavers, the echo of that melody an octave lower picked out by the thumb of the left hand, and a syncopated leaping accompaniment which the rest of the left hand had to deliver at huge speed and inconvenience below the 'echo'. 'What you're hearing is a headlong lyrical melody changing colour and direction, gaining in passion and excitement, forcing itself to apotheosis, but what makes the passage so exciting is the complexity of additional information going on around this, all of which the listener is experiencing holistically while the pianist, after a thousand hours of practice, struggles to blend and differentiate as though he had a brain for every finger. In the ideal performance everything must be felt, every note must exist, in balance, in proportion, duly graduated, and what is so madly exhilarating for the audience when the pianist is absolutely fantastic is not the spectacle of dexterity so much as the acceleration of the listener's intelligence. Just as fine prose makes an artist of the reader, so galvanic virtuosity sucks the audience into the pianist's hyper-alert mental field. Suddenly the audience is processing emotionally charged information at a hugely enhanced rate, and it is the excitement of holding on for dear life to this stirring, multi-dimensional outpouring generated by another human being that accounts for the éclat of true virtuosity. Prestidigitation per se is irrelevant.'

Derek wanted to film Philip teaching. Through the Royal Academy Philip got back in touch with the Russian student whose previous lesson he had cut short. He apologised on the phone and invited her to come back again. She was almost dumbstruck to hear his voice, and then nervously eager to fix a date.

She arrived off the street on a Wednesday morning, very composed and gracious, her nervousness under tight wraps, her alert eyes flicking between tall Philip and short Derek. She was determined to seem professional and to master whatever was required for the documentary and she allowed herself to melt a little as Derek explained how very relaxed he wanted things to be. Philip insisted on her taking tea and sitting down while they talked about Moscow, her family, her digs in London, the personalities at the Royal Academy, none of which relaxed her. He said that she had made a very good impression last time, and that today he would talk more and she could play less.

He sat near by at the end of the keyboard. He was right over her, closely engaged with the way she moved on the keys, her hand position and fingering. She fought the distraction of his closeness and started to play Chopin's Funeral March Sonata, almost maximising her gestures to buy space.

Her face was marvellously expressive, frowningly Russian, full of pouting woe and musical surprise. Her shoulders moved a lot. She pivoted from the waist. Music ran through her, from the balls of her feet to the tips of her fingers. She had beautiful, arched hands with long fingers, and almost tentacular arms, and a slim, sinuously wavering torso that Derek dutifully filmed.

'What's going on in these opening pages?' said Philip, after she had played for a couple of minutes.

She looked puzzled. She had not expected to be tested in this way. She was not even sure she understood the question.

'Page one after the grave,' he said. 'It's breathless, jumpy, all very urgent and nervous. But look, see here, five chords and you're into this hymn-like song, which becomes so ardent and flowing.'

She nodded. This was a fair description.

'What d'you make of this contrast?'

She frowned again. Language was not really her medium.

'Panic, turmoil, terror,' he continued, 'next to passionate vitality?'

She looked at him with deep brown eyes. 'No time to waste.'

He smiled triumphantly. 'Exactly! This sonata movement has no time for transitions. Extremes are pressed together, suggesting the adjacency of opposites, minor and major, fear and abandon, panic and exaltation. Already in a couple of pages Chopin has set life against death. Without being too fanciful I think we can discern breathlessness in the first subject material. In the development this progresses to, shall we say, consumptive coughing. The crisis of the development is a sequence of spasms. Even if you resist the link to Chopin's health, the net effect is absolutely sick and desperate. And yet it abates, the dark night of the soul, and the second subject returns. "Let me live, let me live," it seems to say. It's interesting that Chopin's most passionate stretch of melody stands toe to toe with music of such morbidity. Fear of death, you might say, has squeezed out an amorous desperation. In the coda, passion and terror are welded together, bringing us to the end of present-tense life in this sonata. From now on there's no hope. The scherzo is a *Totentanz* in mazurka rhythm, the funeral march is exactly that, and in the finale Chopin takes us beyond the grave.'

He looked at her keenly.

'How do you address a work like this?'

She sat there waiting.

'For the pianist,' she said, 'is very hard.'

'You can't fake it.'

'You have to be quite brave.'

'This music stares death in the eye. It thrusts us at panic, grief, resignation, and terror.' He paused for a moment. 'Chopin rounds off with a smashed-shut door. After that, we can move on. To acceptance. Or rebirth. But not in this sonata.'

She nodded, taking it all in, hands resting on her lap, fingers entwined.

Derek's camera ran discreetly a few yards off, following the silent exchange of looks between teacher and pupil. She was getting what she had come for and was deeply thoughtful.

Philip gazed at the keyboard in ongoing concern. What he had said to her could be known. How to assimilate it pianistically was another matter and for the time being it was better to let the words sink in.

She was in no great hurry to touch the keys.

Chapter Twenty

PHILIP WAS MORE EXCITED by the prospect of having tea with Ursula than the idea of playing for her. His cleaning lady had spruced up the piano room, perfected the kitchen surfaces, cleaned the loo and bathroom; and Philip had purchased the creamiest gateau from the local patisserie and dug out his best bone china. Wine glasses were buffed to a sparkle, should they prove necessary, and Chablis was chilling in the fridge.

He wanted the house to be bright and cheerful and welcoming. Freshly cut flowers stood before the overmantel mirror. The furniture was arranged just so, covers twitched, cushions plumped, and all of a sudden the place looked rather grown up.

She was due at half four, and now everything was ready, and he found himself passing from room to room like a temperamental set designer, beadily aware of the precise impression his living quarters might make on a female guest. This was a date of sorts. Having a beautiful woman to the house required special measures. She must be welcomed lavishly, made a fuss of, made to feel at home. He was so grateful to her. After tea and gateau he would play something or other, and this too would be a gesture of thanks for her kindness and support. He wanted, quite innocently, to show off. Ursula had paid him the great compliment of believing in him and that kind of faith required a gift in return. The whole set-up was, indeed, rather heady. He would play for her alone. She would listen, transported, her loveliness serenaded by trills and flourishes and the gorgeous sound of his Steinway: a sexy scene in the right hands, and he had certainly indulged a few fantasies as he set out the tea things and found plates for the cake. The sheer impossibility of anything romantic happening made it easier to fantasise.

His anticipation peaked at exactly four-thirty and remained on a high for around ten minutes. He was primed for the door bell to ring, ready and expectant, his sociability raised and on call as though he knew how easily conversation would flow between them, an effortless duet just like the first effects of champagne. By a quarter to five he was glancing at his watch and worrying about the traffic. By five he was a little let down, his excitement diffusing. He supposed she had forgotten or written down the wrong day, or got stuck at the office with something more urgent. He tried to call her mobile, switched off; checked his own for messages. It was a little inconsiderate of Ursula to be running this late, to keep him waiting – though what did she know of his light heart and the spring in his step? He wandered around like a visitor in his own home, still tidying things, keeping up the vigil, but with a sinking feeling. His earlier eagerness seemed foolish now. He was setting store by things that could not come to much. He even wondered whether Ursula had taken fright. The rendezvous was a little staged and self-conscious, perhaps. Philip sat down in the armchair, his big hands locked together. The room had grown dull in the overcast afternoon light. A few minutes later he stood in the kitchen waiting for the kettle to boil. He watched the squirrels on the fence outside and the thrushes darting from twig to birdbath.

It was so much harder, these days, to brush off disappointment.

She arrived on the dot of five-thirty. He found himself greeting her with an almost theatrical aplomb, raising her knuckles to his lips and guiding her shawl as she revolved. She wore silk and devoré, a gold necklace. Her hair was lively, brushed up, a chaotic halo of corkscrew; her lips and eyes were subtly intensified by make-up. She came through the hallway in a great surge of feminine arrival, glancing through doorways and up staircases as he led her to the kitchen.

'Nice kitchen!'

'Wine?'

Ursula seemed to think she was dead on time.

'Can I drink while you play? Surely not.'

'You've come all this way. Your every need must be answered. Wine, gateau, cup of tea?'

'Gateau!'

'Take a look.' He cracked open the fridge.

She was aghast.

The gateau sat in buxom resplendency on the lower shelf.

'Oh, wow!'

She was looking her absolute best.

Philip wore a black cotton suit, a black shirt underneath: casual, relaxed, elegant – or so he hoped. He was quick with the wine bottle, adept with the corkscrew.

'How's the office?'

'You don't want to know. Pressure, chaos, computer mayhem. We'll cope. We always do. You're looking smart!'

He smiled.

'I really do like this kitchen.'

'Sit down and enjoy it.'

'Are these Amtico tiles?'

'Something like that.'

She sat down, leggily arranging herself around the chair, propping an elbow on the table top.

He joined her with bottle and glasses and they talked about where she lived, life at the agency, a recent trip to Barcelona, and he was reminded of how familiar she seemed. Ursula's type of beauty was so benign, based around laughter and smiles, lively, quite unselfconscious. Here was a woman ready to do business with the world. A long future lay before her, and its recipe was new and different to what women of his generation had known: the sense of entitlement, of emotional self-determination, of certain pleasures being recruited as part of a necessary mastery over good fortune. She had the centred look of someone with an accrued inner life, which she valued and held to herself as an asset to be shared – eventually – with the right man. They talked about her job a little. She loved music and was devoted to the cause and appreciated the concerts deeply, but she belonged to other parts of life as well. It was the social exposure to men and women of passionate interest she found most rewarding.

'Um, we've forgotten the cake,' he said.

'What about some music?'

'Oh yes.'

'What are you going to play me?'

He was happy here in the kitchen, sitting and talking.

'Are you ready?'

'You bet. Might just pop to your bathroom.'

He rose, taking a bottle of wine in hand. 'Upstairs.'

He wandered through to the piano room. It seemed almost a shame to break the flow of conversation and become the performer again. He sat on the stool and pressed his hands together and considered what to play. If he was going to play, he had better get on with it. He could serenade her in the loo. He gazed at the keys, waiting for a prompt, and then it came, perfect, the G major Prelude by Rachmaninov, pure and spring-like, left hand first, evenly undulating, a liquid current, bright, clear, sweet, ringing, and then the right-hand melody, calm, upwardly arching with birdlike trills and flutters, extending the radiance of the key across the whole soundboard and filling the room with a fresh lustre that greeted her as she came through the door and made her way to the back of an armchair.

She stood there motionlessly. He could barely detect her in the corner of his eye, but her attention was keen, and it felt good to have a listener attached to every phrase and every shift of pedal and the sound washes his playing manipulated; and when he ended the prelude he waited barely a second before securing her attention with the first note of another piece, Chopin's Aeolian Harp Étude, the swells and hues of which filled the room more copiously than the Prelude, as though he were bringing the Steinway's declaratory beauty of tone to life in levels of growing intensity; and when the last surge of arpeggios had risen and fallen like the foamy wake of a water nymph, dispersing into an aqueous shimmer, an afterhaze of tone, his head fell to one side, almost out of modesty.

'Beautiful, Philip. Please, more!'

It came to him as a swelling, a physical knowledge. He needed to know, of course he needed to know, and now was the moment, and so he said 'Ursula' as he rose, fastening her interest with what sounded like a question, and making his way towards her casually, an easy stroll, which somehow enabled him to glide into her arms before she realised what had happened, and kiss her.

She looked back in amazement, and he kissed her again. For a moment she was frozen and held his eye, before he kissed her a third time.

'Philip!'

He kissed her yet again, and this time she had to go through with it. She yielded a bit, lips breaking their seal, softening, head moving in some sort of response, hand opening against his jacket.

He followed the kiss with an embrace, gently supporting the small of her back. His heart was hammering with excitement.

They turned a little, away from the armchair, and she saw the edge of the recamier coming up, and looked at him again in confusion as the two of them subsided on to the long seat, Philip placing her against the deep cushions, she settling under him in a twisted position, which she corrected rather awkwardly with a heave of her backside. Her eyes caught the window-light as she stared back at him and for a moment they both adjusted to the unscheduled amorousness of this new position, and the new relation he had forced on her. She looked a bit strange now. She was recovering from an unopposable physical declaration.

When, in this new arrangement, he leant forward to kiss her, she was more nourishing, and he could sort of tell from the way she regarded him that she was able to commit to the experiment, for the moment at least.

He placed a hand on the side of her face, fingertips immersed in her hair. The face that gazed at him could not know how beautiful it was, how haunting. And now she shifted, getting more comfortable. Perhaps in her imagination, she had prepared for this scene.

He had no voice, no words. Speaking was unmanageable. He held her face and wondered if her silence was an obstacle or an invitation. She was resolved perhaps that he should get on with it, tunnel through the strangeness.

His breath, did it smell?

Her youth was what he was stealing, he thought, as he ran fingers inside her blouse. She lay tensely waiting, almost daring him to get on with it. He had been far too sudden to expect help from her. The pleasurable present hovered on the moment as his long fingers slowly found the fastener between her shoulder blades, a tricky twist, requiring a moment of real effort before the bra came loose. She followed his eyes as he gazed at her. Her stare was brave.

He hesitated. Ursula seemed to exhibit a kind of defiant beauty. She knew very well the value of the spectacle before him, her eyes enormous, her areolae an echo of those eyes, two of everything. Would Philip now strip off or was there more fondling in store?

Was she going to lie there getting all cool and goosebumpy as he stared at her? Perhaps he needed something more from her: permission, reassurance, touch? Her look seemed to ask all these questions whilst trapping amazement. This was a decorum buster.

John, for one, would not be amused.

He put his hand on her breast experimentally, contact in that place, to which she responded by compressing his hand slightly with her own – a sensuous granting.

He was so uncertain. He could see the worn, grey back of his hand on white bosom, and feel the furrows in his brow, and as he drew off his spectacles and put them on the table, the moisture around his eyes; and it daunted him, the unbattered fairness of her neck and shoulders, the intrepid clarity of her eyes; because one never knew, these days, what kind of lover you were, what sort of figure one cut, and whether his vintage of concupiscence would be edifying or not – which made this trance of gentle contact the more important, for what it implied, for what it tacitly conceded.

She stared at him, her breathing even, her head easily settled on the cushion as he dusted her cheek with his knuckles. A human being was a continent of accessible life and history when one got into this position.

'Come on top of me,' she said.

She seemed so familiar, even sexually familiar. All that pleasing line and contour, the rise and fall, the darkness of hair found an exact reception within him. They were part and parcel of each other. In which case his desire to touch mapped her need to be touched.

There was more kissing suddenly and it came about quickly that her blouse and bra were on the floor and Philip was deliciously engrossed in the festival of her breasts and mouth.

He felt his cock snagging on his Y-fronts.

'Come on.'

'Just a minute.'

'What's . . .'

'Hang on.'

He supported his weight on an elbow and shucked off his trousers. She allowed him to ease her skirt, knickers and tights down. The recamier creaked alarmingly. Soon there was an equality of nudity, a meeting of the old and the new. Ursula was unbashful and he found he didn't care, was eager to press on with what they had started and was relieved at how easily he got inside her, and how right it felt to be in possession of this tensile creature with her arched back and twirling hair. She was thriving under him, as if coupling a man twice her age was the easiest thing in the world.

There was a certain stop and start to proceedings, the awkward preliminaries of concerted copulation. They both had to struggle with the hard base of the recamier and the plethora of cushions in the way, sliding off, burying Ursula's face, and yet there was a corner of compromise between her lithe length and this rigid piece of furniture, and when they found it, he was alarmed by the sudden anguish of her pleasure. Her shoulder blades rose as she moved into the animal position. This effortful connection was part of what the body did well. It fuelled him: the line of her ducking back, the wobbly tense thigh of a leg braced against the floor, the hair cloud crashed into cushions and upholstery, the sheen of skin, making it so crucial to climax.

His orgasm rose up forcefully and was almost painful, a wake-up call to the parts, a cobweb-clearer, leaving him with gritted teeth and a toppling wooziness; and gradually they subsided on to the recamier, Ursula crumpling under a wounded man, her cheek smudging against the edge of a cushion, arm arcing up balletically.

They lay still and naked, the familiar returning gradually. He was slowly aware of cold semen between his belly and her back, and the near end of the piano, and the roofline of houses across the street.

He adjusted his weight so she could turn and look at the ceiling mouldings or into his eyes if she wanted. Her hair was in disarray, her chest rosy. She gazed at him flatly. Ursula was somewhere else for the moment, in the middle of her own version of what they had just been through. Absently, she reached up to his face and rasped the silky ball of her thumb against his stubble.

He had made himself known to her of course, biblically, and in other respects.

'I thought you were going to play the piano,' she said softly.

He smiled. 'That was the plan.'

'Gateau, white wine, a little Chopin.'

'The offer of cake stands.'

Ursula seemed less familiar now.

'Drop of Chablis?'

She bit her finger.

'Yes, please.'

She sat up a little as he poured the wine.

'Philip!' She almost laughed. This was nervousness, self-consciousness.

'I surprised you?'

Ursula looked to one side.

He took her hand, clasping it as he kissed it.

She regarded him with wary admiration. 'I think you were inspired.'

'I was!'

'It's quite interesting to be . . . surprised.'

'You weren't . . .'

She put her hand on his knee, gave him an even glance. 'Not really. I mean, it was maybe in the air.'

He smiled at her.

She pulled him towards her and kissed him on the mouth.

Her eyes were about two inches away. The pupils seemed enormous. Bits of light were reflected in the irises.

He was pulling in his stomach a little, but generally he felt comfortable with his nakedness. What Ursula saw in him was never any kind of physical beauty, he knew that, but the calibre of an older man's appreciation. She had wanted him to be stirred, to be forced into the open from behind the shield of his experience, where she could manage him as an equal. Now, as he looked at her, he felt her maturity and innocence so oddly mixed and entwined. She was young, all right, the far side of that mid-life hilltop that he had rolled over, but her poise was incredible. He had absolutely surprised her. She still was at the dress-rehearsal stage of ideas about him when he struck; and here she was, regarding him half humorously, half in shock, because Ursula had no idea what to expect from this pianist character.

'I fancy some of that gateau,' he remarked.

'Cake and Chablis. Do I just lie here?'

'You're on odalisque duty.'

'The Sultan has spoken.'

'Here.' He cast his shirt over her.

'Perhaps I should get dressed.'

'Don't do that! Madness!'

'Really?'

'I'll flick on the central heating.'

Ursula laughed. 'Romantic.'

He stood tall and naked. 'I'm doing my best.'

'You're doing wonderfully.'

'I could light a fire. There are candles somewhere.'

'Get the cake first.'

In the kitchen he was merry and fleet of foot. Out came the gateau, plates and spoons, a tray. Doubtless the neighbours could see him through the conservatory glass, bollock-naked. Bully for them. All in all, a very smart kitchen. Good old Laura, he thought. She had given him a bloody hard time, and a first-class kitchen. He was longing to be back in the living room at the scene of a miracle. He zoomed back, tray on high, like a Grand Hotel waiter in the buff.

'What's so funny?'

She was laughing.

'No half measures.'

'I don't believe this is happening.' She covered her face with her hand. Her smile was lovely.

Philip got the cake on the coffee table and was soon sectioning it and serving it up on side plates.

Ursula munched and licked fingers, making a mouthy meal of the creamy treat. 'Hmmm. Heavenly.'

She put a plate down and sipped at her Chablis and basked in luxury.

Rich creamy foods were not recommended at the moment. Nor was wine. He ate with a reckless sense of triumph.

'Tea at Philip's,' she declared.

'Only for very special people.'

'The gateau, or the sex?'

He cleared his throat. 'Well, I know I'm not really supposed to have sex with my agent.'

'Oh don't!' She frowned. 'God, what would . . .'

What would John think, but this begged too many questions. She was silent for a moment, calculating something, consequences, how things would look.

Philip was concerned. The setting had plenty of charm, but

Ursula was at the beginning of complications if this went any further, and as he came across and sat next to her he was determined that it should go further.

'Ay-yi-yi! Talk about unprofessional!'

'You are hardly to blame,' he said.

'It's all your fault, Philip.'

'Tell John I ravished you.'

She was nearly pained by this, then horribly amused.

'Don't think so.'

'Listen, I . . .'

'It will be a mess.'

'Don't . . .' He wanted to give her a way out, just as a matter of chivalry. He touched her to dispel John, the office. 'Don't let it be a mess. This is all a bit crazy.'

'It is crazy.'

'I'm ancient.'

'Yes, I know.'

He smiled at her emphatic tone. 'You're so ridiculously young.'

'It's a scandal, all right!'

'It *is* a scandal.'

'Oh, shut up!'

'You don't mind?'

'Have I shown much sign of minding?'

'I wouldn't blame you if you did.'

'I don't care about all that.'

He stared at her seriously.

'Honestly, Philip.' She was half-teasing. 'I like mature men.'

'Who said anything about mature?'

She laughed.

'I'm just a child prodigy with grey hair and wrinkles.'

'This wasn't exactly an accident.'

'You think we're a pair?'

'Who knows! I like you.'

'Well, I like you.'

'Of course.'

He felt himself glowing with unfamiliar happiness. 'Well, in that case I'm going to fall in love with you right away.'

She liked the way he just tossed it out.

'Which would hardly be convenient.'

She touched his face very sympathetically. 'We can put up with some inconvenience.'

'You're indescribably beautiful, Ursula.'

She drew deep breath as he passed his hand across her shoulder. He was cherishing her skin, the soft side of her bosom.

'The great pianist,' she exhaled.

The great pianist's hands were otherwise engaged.

'By now we should have been in your bed.'

'This is all so flattering,' he said.

'I'm flattered.'

'You're flattered?'

'Well, of course!'

He smiled at her.

'Of course,' she said again.

In some respects and at certain times life could be so felicitous. He gazed at her in marvel. He would certainly fall in love with her if things went on like this. There was something in the air: the old romantic feeling, an unfamiliar excitement. None of it was quite deserved or earned or very sensible, and Ursula was both easy and mysterious. Whatever duty of care he owed her, they were launched now, on some basis or other, and it was impossible not to abandon oneself. Intimacy was a forgotten bliss. She flowed into all the empty spaces in a bachelor's heart. Before that shag he was only half human. Sex stood for so much more than he had remembered.

He felt the shadow of anguish pass over him.

'Operation next week,' he said abruptly.

She leaned forward, caught his eye.

'National Health have come up with the goods.' He nodded. 'Surgeon called me this morning.'

She seemed to absorb this.

'I have to go in on the Thursday. The knives come out on Friday.'

He relaxed back into the cushions.

'If there's one thing more nerve-racking than going on stage it must be opening up some poor bastard's insides and messing with his vital organs. How do these people do it?'

She reached over to stroke the back of his hand. 'Good to get the job done.'

'Yeah, good to get the job done.'

'Is it hurting?'

He shrugged. 'There are sensations.'

Her silence was supportive. This was territory they had to cover somehow or other.

He stared at the fireplace. He felt at ease with her, which made it easier to be candid.

'About the concert.'

She stirred, getting herself into a position of readiness. She had not expected this subject.

'Obviously mission impossible.'

'Well . . .'

'It was the expression of a desire. I'm sorry if you and John have been phoning around, wasting time.'

This pained her.

'It's all too late in the day. Nothing'll be free.'

'There are private venues,' she said.

'Oh sure.'

'People would come.'

'I want my audience.' He looked at her directly.

'It would be your audience.'

'My public.'

'But Philip . . .'

'It's for them I want to play. I owe it to them. They've already bought tickets.'

'Yes, but . . .'

'So there can only be one solution.'

She was fraught. This had come from nowhere.

'Don't you guys do anything. Leave it to me. I'll talk to Vadim. He'll understand.'

'Understand what?'

'That I've got to play and that we can share the concert next Wednesday. There's no need for him to stand down. He can take the first half, I'll take the second. We can dedicate the concert to Konstantine Serebriakov. The public will get the pianist they paid to see and his bloody protégé!' He looked at her firmly.

She smiled uneasily. 'Sounds fine. But Vadim would have to agree.'

'To be blunt, he can hardly say no.'

She was a little desperate now.

'You look worried.'

'He *has* said no.'

Philip bit his lip. He could feel the tension rising. He could not bear to be obstructed in this matter.

'What?'

'We asked him and he said no.'

'You asked him?'

'Philip, it was always the only option!'

He stared at her blankly.

'That was exactly the suggestion we made. Half and half.'

He was thunderstruck. 'He said no!'

'Well, John isn't going to put that much pressure on him because of all the changes.'

He shook his head and clasped his hands. It never occurred to him that Vadim would deny him his own concert.

'Did you explain about my . . . condition?'

She shook her head. 'Have you two had some kind of falling-out?'

'Well, yes, but even so. Christ!'

'I don't know what's been going on.'

'I'll have to deal with it. We'll have to talk. He's got to see sense. I'll just have to bite the bullet. Oh, Vadim!'

She shook her head and blinked. 'Actually . . .'

Philip glanced up.

'We did tell him.'

'You did!'

'Sorry, Philip.'

'Ursula!' He felt a limitless chagrin. 'I didn't want you to do that.'

'I know, and I understand why, and I respect that, but he was completely intransigent and it was our only hope.'

He looked up, horribly pained. He could not bear this news about his health to be in the wrong hands. Once people knew, he would cease to count in some way. Vadim would tell everyone, consigning him to the departure lounge in people's minds.

'I can't believe it.'

She was crestfallen. There was nothing she could say.

He covered his face in his hands and sagged on the sofa. He had so little strength for these upsets, for the vast reserves of emotional opposition they required. Vadim's cruel reaction called out for patience, understanding, tactical presence of mind. He was inflicting revenge, of course, and refusing to be drawn into Philip's drama, and was doubtless waiting for some sort of apology or retraction or backing down before he was prepared to consider Philip a human being; and this was so tiresome and stressful because he could not bear the idea of losing the concert. His last concert. This notion was too bleak to be real, but he was prey now to washes of melodramatic despair.

He clenched his brow, secretly mopping away flecks of moisture from the corner of his eye.

She sat there on the edge of the recamier, watching him anxiously.

Philip was ruined inside, the wine and cake doing him no favours. He was almost fluey with emotional exhaustion. She held him by the wrist and ran her fingers over his forearm.

'God, what a shambles. Ursula, I'm a wreck.'

She saw his eyes were red.

'Philip.'

He was finished off, bereft with this news. He had pinned so much hope on the concert.

'Let it go,' she said.

He gasped, head hanging.

'Wait till later. After the operation sometime.'

His eyes were streaming, an unexpected release. How funny to be crying in front of her like this. It was copious, drenching. His cheeks were slick. The back of his throat stung, catarrh everywhere.

'Sorry about this.'

'To hell with Vadim. To hell with the bloody concert.'

'I'm beginning to agree.'

'It's too close to your op. You need to wind down. Give yourself a break. You can play to me. I'll be your audience.'

He grasped her hand.

'You have nothing to prove.'

'It's not about proof,' he said.

'I know.'

'It's not about me, or my playing, or my reputation, or my career, or anything like that.'

'Philip, you're going to get better.'

'It's not about that, even.'

He wiped his nose with the back of his hand. He stared at the gateau. The day was losing light outside, a bank of cloud overhead. They sat in the frail light, their skin cooling. He drew a cushion over his lap. The ache was bad now, an acid heat that flared up and then diffused, and then flared up again. Disease in progress.

Taking on Vadim was going to require more wit and courage than he could summon. He would track him down, nonetheless. He had to prevail.

'I went to the cottage,' he said at last.

She shook her head.

'Those friends of mine. I told you about them.'

'The ones that died?'

'I went back to the house.'

'When?'

'The other day.'

She was listening now. 'Why did you go?'

He gazed at her for a long time.

'They crossed over and I felt that I was about to follow them.'

She stared at him.

'Didn't look nice.' He shook his head. It was hard to know where to start. 'A fire does its business. I suppose you could say the house, what was left of it, bore the scars of their fate like a memorial. Odd. I was trying to see where they'd gone, and getting as close as I could to the exit point. They took a part of me with them, you see. That little heaven of theirs – I was a shareholder. I knew what it was all about. Very rarely in life you find these glades and pastures, miniature Arcadias, where everything special comes together, as well as it can. A fleeting perfection of earthly happiness that makes you very uneasy. Because as soon as one sees and feels it, you know how precious and vulnerable it is. Those idylls can't last. But we were all inside this very happy world thinking, dammit, life can be this good, and when it is you bloody well deserve it.'

He ran his fingers around the stem of the wine glass.

'After the fire, I knew I'd never reconstruct that type of happiness again. They weren't my family literally, but they were the nearest I'd come. Actually, I adopted them quite tenaciously. When Katie was born I remember holding her, aged one hour, thinking: Right, she's mine. Bachelor appropriation. I'm going to love this little girl.' He smiled sadly. 'Loving is not an easy business for some people. I was very grateful for being let in on a family and allowed to nurture my own affection for them, within limits, my way, safely, without being chastised for inadequacy or selfishness, or emotional incompetence.'

He let out a long breath. He was covered in goosebumps. Ursula was curled against the cushions, quite still.

'Because they all died, it seemed easier to think of it as a mad singularity, something to blank out. How on earth do you cope with these shit-eating disasters? Do you fight, or submit? One has to hack on and the mind has strategies for hauling through pain. But every plan has a loophole. Every good day implies a bad day. Things will never be the same and what you can't see through the smoke and debris is that meaning has been sucked out of your life and no amount of brave determination not to be shafted by this fucking awful accident makes a shred of difference to the underlying reality – that life is tragic, and to develop the sinew and scar tissue and hide to cope with that fact takes years.'

He waved it off, smiling suddenly, as if trying to counteract his own vehemence. These declarations were actually quite good for the spirit.

'I had a good look around. Eventually enough was enough. I went up the hill for a walk. I had forgotten how beautiful it was round there. Wonderful views and colours. All just the same, identical. The birds and the trees and the flowers, just carrying on, year after year. I made it to the top of the hill and took in the view, the breeze in my hair, aware of so many familiar details – all those constants in the scenery looking good this time of year, and it came to me.'

She looked at him.

His eyes were suddenly bright.

'I'd say it was a high-pitched note, like tinnitus, but pleasant. Light breaking through cloud almost. Right up high. An angelic highness. Like the pinnacle of the most massive chord. I even thought the key was C major, and it came all the way down to the ground. A sonic pyramid, but clear, like glass. There are chords in Bruckner and Sibelius like this, composed of extremes, sky–earth chords, but this was new. Made up of high pitches, violin harmonics, and deep vibrations. An aural hallucination, or maybe I just put it there, like a composer sites a chord in his head. It followed me back across the field.'

He raised his eyebrows. 'All this music, you see, it comes from somewhere else.'

It was warming to think she would understand and he smiled faintly to be able to put it so simply.

'After that, you see . . .'

She nodded slowly.

He looked at her carefully.

'After that?'

'I have to play again.'

Chapter Twenty-one

THE WALLS OF THE lobby were ribbed with red panels. Two girls stood behind a spotlit desk smiling as he approached. They wore sequinned evening dresses cut high on the collar and slitted at the bust. The chesty welcome was tempered by the presence of shaven-headed bouncers, a pair, big as eunuchs.

'Good evening to you.'

It was long past his bedtime. He was not feeling lively.

Behind the girls were framed erotic cartoons penned by some nightlifer beloved of the management.

'I'm joining Mr Vadim Kuryagin.'

He wore jacket and tie. Why was it necessary to dress up for a strip joint?

The girls looked at him strangely.

He heard voices from the end of the lobby: a fat man in a suit and two streaky blondes.

'May I see if he's inside?'

'Firty-five pound.'

'I might not stay.'

One of the bouncers moved.

Philip reached for his wallet.

He followed the red carpet and came to a pair of swing doors. A diminutive bunny girl took his ticket.

As he crossed the portal, space opened out and sound welcomed him. He was looking across a room with patches of brilliant light and zones of darkness. There were heads and figures in shady recesses, circles of disco flooring, bright bodies on dance platforms. The faces of punters sitting round tables were doused in rose light.

He went forward and a pillar slid away to expose a group of men on stools encircling a dais on which a naked girl gyrated, hand-over-handing the dance pole as though it were the audience's representative member. Her legs stretched long and tense on stiletto heels. She charitably bent over, smiling upside down. Someone reached up to park a tenner between her teeth, sponsoring further flurries of booty duty and hip flicking.

The spotlights were penetrating. He could smell perfume, disinfectant, cigar smoke, the hint of vomit.

Trays of drinks sailed by, champagne buckets were parked by cluttered tables, and now he was escorted by an Italian-style maître d' in a well-cut suit, spreading looks of genial welcome over all and sundry, as if this were a family restaurant in suburban Naples.

He looked through the glow of low-hanging lanterns, trying to see the others. There were enclaves of 'businessmen', tinselly lady consorts, female limbs in cubicles beyond. Around one table a stag-night group sprawled, fairly blotto and dishevelled, team spirit flagging under the onslaught of drink and music and the writhings of two entwined stroboscopic females, pole-wrapped like a pair of flickering anacondas on a nearby dais. He passed a Middle Eastern roué and his face lifted lady friend, who confronted the goings on with wide-eyed ornamental amazement.

He'd been told on a tip-off.

First he phoned Marguerite, then her brother-in-law, whose flat in Piccadilly Vadim was supposed to be using, but somebody else sent him on a trail via two more telephone numbers. Eventually he got through to Nigel Winterbottom (of all people) – a Royal Academy pianist with good manners and a jolly-hockey-sticks delivery seemingly at odds with his preference for Bartok. A few years ago Philip had given him a lesson.

'Yah. I'm seeing him this evening. Will you be there?'

'Don't think so. Where are you going?'

'Peaches and Banana.'

'Peaches and Bananas?'

'Banana, singular. Somebody called Fouad is taking us.'

'Fouad?'

'Oh, one of Vadim's new chums.'

My replacement, thought Philip. 'Not a restaurant?'

213

'Not a restaurant, no.' Nigel laughed brightly.

'Are you meeting beforehand?'

'I'm rehearsing till ten. Vadim's coming back from Liverpool, and the general plan was to go to Fouad's about eleven o'clock.'

'Take a pack of condoms.'

'Well . . . I . . . you know, usual thing with Vadim. You want to see the guy, you have to join the roller-coaster. Will you come and rescue me?'

'I might. But don't tell him. It'll be a surprise.'

'Right you are.'

He had no idea what to expect tonight. Vadim's behaviour was off the rails these days. He was curious to see the limits of his protégé's intransigence. How much direct human appeal could he resist? At what point would some vestige of fellow-feeling break surface? His great hope was that Vadim wanted nothing more than to humiliate him in reprisal for his criticisms.

Suddenly, he saw them, right at the end. They were sitting in a semicircle around a table, Nigel, Fouad, four girls – dappled light falling on hands and faces. Vadim looked at him twice, double-taking as he approached. His face was a picture of red-handed surprise, masked quickly.

'Hello, Vadim,' said Philip, taking his place on a stool without further ado.

Fouad reached over to shake hands on the basis that any friend of Vadim's was a friend of his and welcome at the table. Nigel maintained the pretence of surprise with honourable conviction, offering a half-frozen smile that did full justice to the situation in which they now found themselves. He was wearing blazer and tie, slacks and loafers, and was at a grinning loss to be discovered in this den next to a dancer in schoolgirl uniform with blotched lipstick, hair slides, and a power-mounted Wonderbra.

'Very good to see you,' he said sincerely.

Fouad introduced Kasia and Mandy, their distinguished lady guests, Kasia wearing a nurse's outfit, Mandy in bunny garb. Vadim was talking to a cockney girl called Shiva, not Asian, who had the benefit of his full attention.

Philip rather felt he had gained the upper hand by materialising out of the strobe-flicker and smoke haze like a spectral Commendatore. He was dry-mouthed and headachy. The lights were confusing, the music draining. He was not well, but he was focused.

The maître d' approached to cement this new grouping and to exchange words with Fouad, who leant towards him in quiet conferral on the price of more champagne. Fouad was wreathed in smiles. His lined skin was nicely tanned, his eyelashes still long for a man of his age: mid-fifties. He seemed to be relishing the fulfilment of certain exchange rates between wealth and pleasure, which included the joy of hospitality (because he was obviously paying for everybody), and a certain sense of radiant amusement that his favoured-patron status at the club could make things not too fast, not too rushed, as though lap-dancing clubs were like Michelin restaurants where it was better if you could afford to pace yourself and fondle the details.

Nigel's Adam's apple worked hard as Mandy placed a hand on his thigh.

Philip felt quickly intoxicated by the first sip of champagne. He looked from one face to the next.

'Talk to our lady friends,' explained Fouad. 'A little later they dance. That way more personal. Philip, please sit here. By Vadim.'

Philip complied, shifting from his stool on to the semicircular banquette, whilst Fouad stood, hoiking his trousers and looking around the club. Vadim showed no intention of speaking to him. Philip inhaled deeply, fending off the background din of the club. He took another sip from his glass. He glanced at Kasia in her nurse outfit, and then thought of his operation.

'Shiva, this is love, not business,' Vadim was saying. 'You're so beautiful a million pounds would not be enough.'

Shiva's hair was drawn tightly back. She had catty eyes, rouged cheeks, good shoulders. She swayed to the beat of imagined music. 'I'll take a billion.'

'A billion lire is possible.'

She waved at Nigel across the table. 'You look nice.'

Vadim frowned.

Nigel nodded and tipped his spectacles. 'Hello, there.'

'What's your fantasy, then?'

His colour brightened. 'Ha ha.' He glanced at the others. 'I've gone all shy.'

'Can I dance for you?'

Vadim shook his head.

'Gosh . . . What d'you charge?'

Fouad stayed Nigel with a hand. 'You pay nothing.'

Nigel perked up. 'That's frightfully kind.'

'Go and sit in that chair,' said Shiva.

'Golly!'

Nigel moved over to one of a pair of chairs set apart from the table, next to a partition where he could enjoy the coming spectacle in relative privacy.

Shiva stood by the table wriggling off her leopardskin top. She was suddenly bare except for a strapless bra and a thong.

'God!' said Vadim, bathing his face in his hands.

Shiva walked over to Nigel, and bent forward like a crane hinged at the tops of the thighs, placing her palms on the arms of his chair, and rolling her shoulders before springing through a twirl that gave him a first view of her rippling caramel column of a body.

'Talk amongst yourselves,' he said, screening the side of his face with a hand.

They watched for a few moments until Fouad drew closer to Philip, leaning confidentially forward as though about to impart something of profound importance that it was essential for Philip to grasp, because in a sense they were all in this together, and certain fundamentals had to be shared between men of the world.

'Shiva,' he said, emotion in his eyes, 'has the most beautiful bottom in the history of . . .'

His host was momentarily lost for words.

Philip stared at him. 'You're from Saudi, Fouad?'

'From Lebanon. But I am English. I have British passport. But Philip, listen. I have been to many clubs. New York, Sidney, Bangkok. The best brothels in the world. Honestly. Listen. I have spent' – he rubbed his fingers together – 'thousands and thousands of dollars all over the world, but I have never seen anything like this Shiva. She is goddess. The bottom is' – he shrugged – 'from Allah. Divine. Can I have a Coca-Cola?' he said to a passing waitress. 'If I were a rich man I would pay for all the women in England to have a bottom like this, because I love this country, but you know sometimes I think people don't know how to enjoy themselves. Here they know. Listen, this is a good club! But still' – he spread his palms, pouted wisely – 'Shiva could change the whole country. Don't smile. It's serious. People watch too much television. Eat too much bad food. You need to come this place to wake up.'

'Nigel looks alert.'

'Vadim!' said Fouad. 'You have nice friend. Distinguished English gentlemen.'

Vadim drew himself closer to Philip and Fouad. He made no eye contact but sat solidly, arms on the table, eyes on the club floor.

'*Oh là là!*' Fouad's expensive dentistry was on offer as he smiled at Shiva, now sinking on her haunches, now revolving, hands on the floor, jackknifing back, scissor-splitting down. Her bra was wrapped around Nigel's neck.

Vadim looked across. 'This is where suicide bombers come when they die.'

'I hear you stole my concert,' said Philip.

Shiva finished off with a breast-shaking flurry a few inches from Nigel's face, then she cuffed him gently on the cheek and swayed back to the table, where she collected her garments and pulled them on. Vadim glanced at Philip before flourishing a bank note at Shiva, who was getting her breath back. 'For my friend,' he said.

'Hang about! Can't a girl have a drink?'

'That was super,' said Nigel, rather flushed.

'Maybe Mandy and Brit would like to . . .' Fouad smiled hospitably at Philip.

Vadim drew close, twiddling the note in his fingers. His breath was hot in Philip's ear. 'Money is good.'

'Fouad's money, I expect.'

'It is good money. Nice money.' He kissed the note, sniffed it, kissed it again.

Nigel leaned forward. There was a perspiration on his forehead but he had not loosened his tie. 'By the way, Philip. I loved your new Chopin disc.'

The girls were giggling. Nigel smiled diffidently. He knew he was a young fogey; but tonight he was a happy young fogey.

'You stole my concert,' repeated Philip.

'You're indisposed,' said Vadim, looking away.

'No. I'm ready to play.'

'I speak to my agent. He tells me Philip Morahan is having nervous breakdown.'

'Did he, indeed?'

Vadim raised the note, beckoning to Shiva. 'Promoters are crazy, insurance problems, you're not returning calls . . .'

'You never called to check.'

'You tell me not to cancel. Then you cancel. Then I offer to help for John's sake and now you are being hypocrite. Shiva!'

'What's that then?'

'Twenty.'

'I want fifty.'

'Fifty.'

'For two.'

'That's forty.'

'I'll make it a good one.'

Fouad nodded indulgently. 'I promise you, Philip, money has never been this valuable.'

'Let's go,' said Vadim, pushing Philip on.

'No.'

'Please come.'

'No.'

'You come, we talk.'

Shiva swigged back a half-glass of Perrier water, came off her stool and slinked around towards Philip, taking him by the hands. 'What's your name?'

Philip averted his eyes.

'Come on. I'm not going to bite you.'

'No thanks.'

'Please,' she said.

'When in Rome . . .' said Nigel with a kindly smile.

He felt dizzy as he crossed the floor to the chairs. As he sat he could see other dancers entertaining men across the room. The men watched with unnatural stillness, as though it required an extra level of concentration to get abreast of this snaking flesh with only one's eyeballs.

Vadim sat down beside him, patting his hand as he did so. Shiva stood her ground, one leg before the other to emphasise her hips, summoning their attention with overture poise.

Philip touched his spectacles and avoided her gaze. Vadim sat, hands together on his lap, smiling serenely.

'I hear you've been practising a lot,' said Philip.

'I practise all my life.'

'That's good.'

'Not good. Not bad. I sleep. I breathe. I practise.'

Suddenly she was smooching towards them, hands on the front clip of her bra, shoulders gyrating, knees bending.

'Vadim, my breakdown is over. I need to play. I must play.'

'Good.'

'On Wednesday.'

'Are you crazy?'

'Let's share the concert. Take one half each.'

'I cannot share concert.'

'Why not?'

'Because we don't believe in the same thing.'

'That's nonsense.'

'Look . . . she is . . . so wonderful.'

Shiva's hands were travelling her body in a self-embrace. Her pelvis swivelled in graceful arcs. Her eyes were shut tight.

'She is an artist. She gives everything.'

Philip was at a loss. He lacked the concentration to reply effectively. The lights seemed to be attacking him, getting under the lids of his eyes. He saw Shiva as an intermittent silhouette until suddenly she was close, bending towards him, her breath in his ear.

'For Serebriakov,' he said.

'Every concert in the world will be dedicated to that man.'

Her bottom was bucking in front of him now. He saw the two indentations at the base of her back.

'Look, I'm sorry about what I said to you.'

'I have a life, Philip. You have to understand.'

'Yes, I do.'

'You attack me because your old girlfriend had an abortion and you afraid suddenly – look at this – that all your good behaviour was a waste. You take out on me. What you said was not good, but why you say it was terrible.'

'Maybe. I'm sorry. I don't deny it. But, Vadim –' He had pain now, like bad indigestion. 'You know what I've been through. Have you no pity for your old friend?'

'You sound like Jewish mother.'

'Hey, guys.' Shiva was anxious to break up the back chat. 'Watch this!'

She was super-committed suddenly, running fingers through straps, and then facing away from them to flip out languid, teasy bendovers, and then straightening up, rear at the ready, hand on a side rail, bracing herself to send something through her body, some ripple or pulse that produced great spurts of gibbering arse-quiver.

'More, more.'

Her buttocks shivered to a stir-crazy climax of speed, a spasm of cross-ripple and shudder and paroxysmal deep tremor, the melons of her arse speed-blurring and bunching, trembling and tensing, shuddering and clenching.

'Have you no pity for me?' Vadim seized his wrist.

Philip turned. 'I'm your friend, for God's sake.'

'You insult my work because it suits you. Because you're unhappy. Because your star is not rising.'

Her palms were flat on the floor. A white line of tension ran up the backs of her thighs.

'Is everything I say envy?'

'There is no right way. To live your life. To play the piano. There is only improvisation. I'm not interested in this cult of purity or self-denial or self-sacrifice to reach the highest, the most beautiful perfection in art. This is vanity.'

'I agree.'

'What d'you hate most? My piano-playing or my life?'

Shiva was venturing towards the obstetric.

'I . . .'

'You cannot play this volcanic repertoire and live like a petit bourgeois. We don't belong with nappies in our hand. We do what we have to do. Anything else is a lie. Philip, you have no understanding. I made a mistake. I married someone who likes me to be famous but understands nothing. I'm not going to live inside a mistake. But this is irrelevant. Because music has nothing to do with this. Music exists outside all this problems.'

'Vadim, let me . . .'

Shiva was reversing towards Vadim's lap, the bulb of her backside looming.

'You cannot judge.'

Philip watched her bottom hover and bounce off Vadim's knees, then stir the air a bit, then bounce again.

He was feeling dazed and peculiar. So this was it: illness. He was truly sick. He looked into the glittering light and blinked.

The next thing he knew Vadim had got up and gone and Shiva was grinding his lap, earning every penny, and he was detached, which he remembered later with complete disbelief, as if something so disgraceful could not really have happened. He felt a pain below his ribs and tried to lever himself up. 'Excuse me,' he said, and she pirouetted off, slowing down and eventually halting on the spot as he made his escape, walking quickly to the loo where a few moments later he stood at a urinal, peeing and trying to get a grip, the pain seeming dimmer. He gazed at the tired face in the washbasin mirror, rubbed away dew from his eyes. He was so terribly weary.

He trailed back to the table, and here again it was infinite déjà vu as Fouad smiled his welcome, tipping the handkerchief in his breast pocket, and Nigel chatted amiably to Brit the schoolgirl as she rose, taking him in hand, and Fouad watched the two of them clamber off for a dance.

He sat next to Vadim. 'I have no wife or children. No parents. For me, you're like family. That's why I spoke out. One's allowed to be honest with family.'

'Honest is wrong. Honest is not true. Honest is for me crap.'

Philip sipped at his champagne. He had the beginnings of a migraine. The music had got louder all of a sudden.

'I'm not a crutch for you,' said Vadim.

Philip wiped his eye. He seemed to have a watery tear duct. 'Can't you accept an apology?'

'No, because you only apologise because you want this concert. You're selfish. Worse than me.'

The others were talking amongst themselves, Fouad sharing his ideas with Kasia.

Philip was grey-faced. 'Why are you so angry?'

'You insult my work, then you want to be on stage with me.'

'I was speaking from the heart.'

'Englishman's heart is a stone.' Vadim shook his head. 'Philip, you have no idea where I come from, why I'm like this, my parents, this Russian mayhem, how you cope with this history without going

221

mad. Why I am like this, why I do this, how I play? You don't understand anything of this. Because I cannot be any other way. You cannot play the piano like this and obey what other people who are having easy lives think is right.'

He struggled to see sense. He was suddenly weak with tiredness.

Vadim got up and went to the toilet.

Philip realised with a sinking heart that he had impugned Vadim's dignity as well as his vanity in the one area of his life where he had dignity, plenty of it, because like any pianist he lived for music, lived it every day of his life on his own terms, according to his talent, his temperament, and Philip had not acknowledged the imperative purity of energy that goes into all that. He had tried to force an equation between the artist and the life, mixing the two up, because he was probably disappointed with his own example, at his failure to find an absolute, which he had somehow projected on to Vadim, as if it were Vadim's task to live up to Philip's aspirations for himself, according to ideas that Philip had generated in order to hold on to something beyond the permutations of music itself, a reason for being. Temperament had enabled Vadim to exist without such props, to be free, protean, recreative, to chase frenzy when the mood took him, or play without style for better or worse, seeking combinations that would someday release secrets.

Minutes seemed to pass in a blink.

Vadim was talking to Mandy. Shiva had disappeared. Suddenly Fouad rose, guiding Kasia like a bride to a cubicled recess behind the partition. Philip saw a complex of suspenders beneath her nurse skirt. For an odd moment he pictured Marguerite in Vadim's Pimlico apartment, flicking through a magazine and crying.

He knew he was sinking, though whether into sleep or some tranced state he could not tell, but allowed the sharpness of his observation to fail, a general dimming and shutting-down. Flickers of female form dissolved and blanked out, or broke up in Cubist fragmentation as he struggled with the lights. He saw the black backs of punters standing up to look at something, the tireless maître d' threading about, girls picking their way around tables and chairs. He was sitting in Peaches and Banana and he had played his last concert. This was the tail end. It could just slide over you without your knowing.

He must have dropped asleep, because suddenly he awoke with a lurch and saw Vadim at a neighbouring table. A big man stood up. Shiva jiggled back. Vadim's arm was raised, pointing at Fouad.

It happened quickly: bouncers moving in fast, broad backs converging too late, because a rabbit punch went in and Vadim buckled. Shiva screamed. People at tables turned. There was sudden agitation, Vadim bucking up, hitting the man on the face. The bouncers surged bulkily, blocking off, separating. Vadim was in an armlock, grimacing with discomfort. The other man was holding his chin and glowering with pain. Philip rose suddenly. The bouncers were coming his way, forcing Vadim to the exit door. 'Release him, for God's sake.' Vadim tried to wrestle free and the bouncers crunched in harder. Philip tried to restrain them, but then somebody grabbed him and he was enclosed in frilly shirts and cummerbunds. 'Let go!' He was in an armlock being rolled towards the exit. He lost his footing. He was yanked back, buffeted through swing doors into a corridor, followed by a barrage of bodies. The two men were frog-marched down a flight of steps under an archway and on to the street where they were thrown free and fell on the ground. The maître d' was suddenly outside with his walkie-talkie. 'Sorry, gents. Strict rules. Thanks for your custom and goodnight.'

The fire door slammed shut.

Vadim's face was creased with a mixture of anger and pain. He flexed his fingers, worked his arm around in a circle.

Philip had felt a sharp pain below the shoulder. He had landed awkwardly and bashed his knee. He began to pick himself up. The pain in his arm was throbbing.

Vadim waited for a moment longer, as if taking stock. He was drunk, sitting on the pavement, and there was something the matter with his elbow joint.

They walked silently down the street. It took a while for a cab to come by. When it did they bundled in and sat either side of the back seat staring out of the window. Vadim's thick breathing was still audible.

The cabby dropped Vadim off first at Derby Square. He tossed a ten-pound note on to the seat and let the door crunch shut without another word.

Philip lay in his bed without sleeping all night. It was one of those nights you just had to get through and when in the morning he sat in the bath, testing the pain in his upper arm, he allowed himself a laugh because things couldn't get much worse than this.

Chapter Twenty-two

URSULA WALKED AHEAD OF him. The wind was settling, birds were singing. Clouds separated in the blue above.

He trod slowly on the grass, taking it in. The morning light brought all to the fore, the staples of the English countryside: oaks covered in green mist, baby thistles in the grass, spots of yellow underfoot – daisies, buttercups – which one noticed as scattered harbingers of the super-burst of yellow across the valley, a field of oilseed rape. It came up like fresh paint: the umpteenth impression of a type of landscape loved since childhood and encountered over the years time and again, which you could rediscover but never possess, and which seemed to exist as much in the imagination as on this particular morning in May.

Ursula had helped him pack. She selected somewhere at random, in the lee of the South Downs, a Georgian farmhouse with ensuite rooms (seaweed shampoo, thundering breakfast, crippling mattress). It was oddly familiar, this neck of the woods. Driving to the pub he had recognised certain landmarks not seen for decades and assumed that he had come here as a child with his father. The family had spent summers at an aunt's house near Fernhurst and the elderly schoolteacher had transposed his hiking activities from the Peak District to the South Downs. Gordon was a master of solitude. A Germanist, he had interrogated spies for MI6 in the fifties. He knew reams of poetry by heart and combined a romantic love of the countryside with Spartan self-discipline. His best friends were a dog and pipe. In later life Philip liked to think of him trekking across the Peaks towards a remote pub and a heartening pint. A tall man with a jovial laugh and a toothy smile, he was beadily appreciative of a person's character, thanks to a lifetime in the classroom. It was strange to think he might have walked here all those years ago. The same oaks would have seen him pass, lending a wisp of shade as he climbed the hill.

Ursula was ahead of him now. They had drifted apart, reveries diverging. She looked adventurous from behind, like someone who especially belonged in this scene of rolling hills. She pressed on as if drawn by the need to explore, to see round corners. She cut a fine figure against the rising meadow. It was easier to sense who she was from afar: a romantic woman who believed in destiny and who needed her own space. He admired her initiative. She had known what to do with him. He had allowed himself to be given an outing in the last days before his operation, which she had taken as leave. After this she wanted to go on to the seaside and meet her childhood self on the beach – inhaling the saline breeze, watching the seagulls come and go.

The entrance of the wood seemed familiar. He passed under the canopy and was sure he had come here before. The neglected woodland seethed with death and decay. Spindly saplings had given up the ghost at thirty feet and died on the spot. Full-grown sweet chestnuts toppled by the gale still lay on the ground, roots exploded, new limbs rising from horizontal trunks. Epic beeches had been tipped by the winds and caught, half slain, by struggling neighbours. Here and there a sprawling oak, dominating its patch, had elected to die, leaves retracting to a ruff from which forked, dead branches extended. The earth was soft and spongy, a mattress of bracken and powdered decay. Gliding through the wood was like returning to a primitive past and a primitive sense of the earth's fertility: a chaotic, prolific, sheltering richness generating awesome trees and flourishing bracken, an original beauty.

The soil became sandier, matted with clumps of needle and dead twigs bearing cones. Between the broad-leaf trees pine trunks rose like temple columns to unseen heights. A spruce plantation darkened the wood beyond, its martial ranks splicing vistas into nowhere.

Despite the lines of barbed wire and the sprouts of coppice, long since ready for the saw, all plans for the wood seemed abandoned. Rotting faggots stood in neglected heaps and would crumble at a kick: the pathway was strewn with fallen branches. Dead trees, sixty feet high, had been left to crash down in the next high wind.

The scene was like a battleground of stricken figures, everything abandoned to the struggle for light, with so much hopeless endeavour, as if the wood's primary use was not to grow trees but to enrich the soil with leaf mould and wood rot, to feed insects, fungi and moss.

He caught sight of a tree and remembered it instantly: a birch with a broad crown unusual for its candelabra elegance. The stalwart trunk was like a pillar in a Gothic cathedral, grooved and blackened with age. The upper limbs were witchily twisted.

'That's me,' he said, pointing at the tree.

Ursula came over to admire the birch.

'Serebriakov over there.' He indicated a massive oak tree. 'And Vadim.' A soaring pine had gone straight to the top.

'Yes, but look at all the other poor mortals.'

'I'm sure I've been here before.' He seemed pleased.

She was expectant.

'Somewhere near there's a glade of bluebells.'

He was having the memory for the first time: a lovely surprise. 'Over there.'

She gazed uncertainly through the trees.

Somewhere near, he was sure of it, the ground began to slope down. He remembered the footpath, the bluebell mist that went on for acres, softly lit under sparse trees, so endless that you lost all sense of perspective in the hovering blue.

'There are bluebells everywhere,' she said.

He left the footpath and cut across the ferns and brambles, ducking between low branches. He had his bearings now. He was following the light, the sense of the sun splintering through the roof of the wood. The soil was crumbly, ankle-twisting. He inhaled the tang of mould and pine resin. Ursula followed dreamily, picking her way through the undergrowth.

He came to an opening. He was pleased to see a vaunting beech tree with great cruising branches that took advantage of the open light, because this he remembered for sure. Was he ten years old then, or twenty?

He frowned at the fluke, and then was suddenly overjoyed to be standing on the same spot all those years later, standing where his father had stood. He gazed at the bright grass, at the break of blue sky. It seemed Gordon was here but a second ago, was here now in a sense, no less present for being in an earlier version of the present. His father had been so distant and yet he was knowable again through what he loved, would have loved on these walks, these long walks that allowed him to bear out the terms of his contract with life.

They crossed the track and followed a fox-run into the wood. After a while they came to a meadow with a pond and fruit trees scattered about. The grass was shiny. He heard the drone of a bumble bee. Ursula drifted into the space with a smile on her face, the effect of the sun.

'Great place for a bottle of wine,' she said.

Philip stood, hands on hips, smiling and nodding.

'Look.' He had seen a stile through a gap in the trees. 'We go up there.'

This time they moved through a firebreak along a smothered path pushing through the vegetation. She led the way, hair looming large over her wavering figure. It was hard to believe, looking at her now, that she had any connection to jobs and offices. She seemed naturally to sidestep the mundane. One day she would write, perhaps. Her behaviour was probably governed by the unconscious need of rich material.

The coppice was dense and limitless on both sides of the path, the fanning branches multiplying endlessly. He looked anxiously to the right and left. The bluebells were a kind of proof – if he could find them.

She had come to a stile, and when he looked up she was gracefully traversing it. Suddenly it was bright and open again and when he caught up with her he saw in a glance that a section of the wood had been cleared and all that remained was a wasteland of stumps and chewed-up earth, and what Ursula was staring at so intently was the wide view the clearing had opened. Without realising it they had been on high ground on the edge of a ridge, and the wood had been razed from the top of an escarpment of several hundred feet down to the valley floor, hectares of woodland sectioned and airlifted, so that one could see out over an aerial panorama of the South Downs across an undisturbed valley – miles wide – of field and forest. A high ridge ran across the view to the east and then plunged into the valley. Looking down one could make out the crowns of a thousand trees, viridian fields, ochre hedges following the wiggle of invisible lanes.

They paused, gazing in amazement at the distant scene, so far-reaching and tranquil.

'Eternal England,' she said.

He drew closer to her. 'Grander than a painting.'

'Amazing to think it's our country.'

'A far cry from what you read about in the papers.'

'How do we get there?'

He smiled.

'I want to get in and lock the gate behind me,' she said.

'Oh, you can never get back in. It's enough to know it's there.'

They gazed for several minutes in silence. He put his arm around her. She relaxed into his side.

The wind was light, gently ruffling the trees at the bottom of the incline. He could feel the heat of the sun in her hair. Birds hovered and flitted across the expanse of sky.

He felt the sensation gathering, an unfamiliar bliss. Everything one could have wanted from that view was still there, a landscape of promise, with its fertile woodland and thick fields and high pacific hills sheltering the valley, and beyond that, the bluey line of the Downs trailing to the distance.

He kissed her on the side of the face and she looked up at him softly. She was soothed by the pressure of his embrace.

He could let it go after all. Standing here was as nice as anything else, more than sufficient. So much of his life he had spent living in his head. If you chose to look around and live in the moment then this was the best that could happen, a relaxed fulfilment of sensation and feeling, doubly serendipitous, thanks to Ursula, who was more than enough in herself but always brought something else.

'I wish I were a painter,' she said.

'Yes.'

'Poussin would have loved this.'

'An English Arcady.'

'Arcady here and now in Tony Blair's Britain.'

'In some ways more compelling than a painting.'

'It forces you to look and look and look. And even then,' she said, 'I can never get enough.'

'Yes, but you'll feel better for it.'

'I want to live there, somehow. Be a bird or doe.'

'A faun!'

229

'You be a faun. I'll be a nymph.' She laughed.

He entwined his hand in hers, clenched tight.

After a while, she made to move on.

'Don't.' He halted her gently.

She came back to him, leaned into his side.

'Don't go.' His arm drew her tight. 'This is the best bit.'

She looked at him with a kind of tenderness, that could have been yearning, a welling of emotion to the surface, or pity for what was ahead of them both, which she shared from the depths of her heart, as though her predicament were a reflection of his, and it were better to let this be felt than spoken of, because there was nothing either of them could do except live through it to the best of their ability.

He kissed her almost confidentially on the forehead.

'There'll be lots of best bits,' she said, taking his hand, drawing him on.

'D'you know, I don't care about the concert any more,' he said.

She turned to look at him curiously, and then smiled.

On the return walk they divided again. He trod down the path, thinking about hospital and what it would be like to arrive with his pyjamas and wash things and a magazine or two. Once checked in he could be properly stoical. It would be easier to submit to the prospect of an operation from under the covers of a hospital bed. He would succumb to all that, letting them do what they needed to do, find what they needed to find. Afterwards they would gather at the end of his bed and report on the surgery, how successful, what grade of cancer, the next phase of treatment. He might enjoy being the centre of attention. It would be the first crisis, lowering by a notch or two his right to be alive. Thereafter he would be an invalid with carte blanche to feel sorry for himself, receiving phone calls from the people who cared. Unless he pegged it on the slab, of course. Always a risk nowadays.

He came out of the wood into a meadow blanched by the midday sun and saw her trailing through the grass. He followed at a distance, gazing at a tree that all those years ago his father might have stopped to admire.

Chapter Twenty-three

THEY WERE HAVING BREAKFAST in the hotel bedroom when the call came. It was a bright room with a round table in the bay window and a view of the pier. Vadim had phoned John Sampson that morning. John tried Ursula's mobile, left a message, and Ursula was now calling back while Philip ate his toast and read a newspaper.

'That's a bad idea,' she said.

Seconds later Philip was talking to his agent.

'Great news,' said John.

Vadim had changed his mind. He was ready to share the concert.

'Why?'

John claimed credit: artful persuasion, tact, persistence, but Vadim, it turned out, had called that morning out of the blue.

'Two days' notice. That's nice of him.'

'I'll have to run it by the South Bank people.'

'What did he say?'

'He didn't . . . well, I think he's had a change of heart.'

'Is it possible?'

'No time to print new programmes so it's Xerox handouts. There'll be a notice in the foyer. Sometimes box office likes to apprise punters of a substitution. A few migraines, but we aim to please.'

Philip felt sick. He promised to call back in half an hour.

Ursula was calm. She came across to where he was sitting, put a hand on his shoulder. After a while she sat down next to him. She was wearing a pale-green silk shirt and blue jeans. Her hair was still wet from the shower.

She waited, hands pressed together between her thighs.

Philip sat before his toast and marmalade in a daze. He had got

231

out of bed feeling poorly, enervated by the sea air. He found it impossible to line up his thoughts and was aware of a swarming sensation in his belly.

Ursula reasoned with him carefully. She said he was in the wrong frame of mind, nicely relaxed by the break; she thought it inadvisable two days before a major operation to put his system through the stress of a concert and anyway, his shoulder was sprained, thanks to Vadim, and he might not play his best. Things had moved on. Far better to stay a couple more days at the hotel, really winding down and sticking to the plan. 'It won't be easy to have sex after your operation. We should pack it in now.'

'They're not removing my parts.'

'You'll have stitches. You'll need to take it easy.'

He smiled at her.

She kept talking, and he kept thinking it through. He wanted to know why Vadim had changed his mind. Was it pity, largesse, repentance, cowardice, sinister rivalry?

'Two injured pianists celebrating a dead pianist. Great.'

He kissed her on the mouth and called John to say he would play. She watched him expressionlessly as he spoke to his agent. He wanted to do the first half, before the interval, and would need to programme Bach's A minor Prelude and Fugue, transcribed by Liszt, Schubert's A major Sonata, and the Chopin B minor Sonata. Vadim could play the second half as advertised: Liszt and Rachmaninov, with a duet for an encore. John relayed this to Vadim but was told that he had prepared the first half better and had to go first with the Waldstein and Funeral March Sonatas, which meant that Philip could not follow with the Bach, wrong in that position, and Philip anyway could not play the Rachmaninov. He approved of the idea of playing Chopin's third sonata after Vadim had played the second so agreed to perform after the interval. He would start with the G major and B minor Rachmaninov Preludes Opus 32, insert Schubert's G flat major Impromptu, and finish off with the Chopin. The key sequence worked well and the shorter pieces were manageable on short notice. The sonata was sort of 'ready'. He had forty-eight hours to clean it up, and two nights to sleep on it.

After the call was over, she ran her hand across his forearm.

He regarded her appreciatively.

She leaned forward to enclose him in her arms. This was the man she had fallen in love with. She would now have to go through an agony of nerves and worry.

She smiled uneasily.

'I just hope his arm injury is worse than mine,' he said.

*　　*　　*

She watched him get ready in the dressing room, shirt off, trousers off, a stripping-down and dressing-up, a practised transformation.

She sat on a chair talking about the news, another suicide bomber in Jerusalem, the weather, anything. He seemed to be listening and managed replies that were quite thoughtful, though all the time she could tell he was somewhere else. She wanted to be released, allowed to suffer her nerves in private out in the foyer with the milling people, or on the concourse in front of the Festival Hall, anywhere but here. But he seemed to need her, wanted her around and didn't mind if she talked nonsense, or just sat there, raising her eyebrows, smiling, looking at the clock, stomach churning, sipping at a glass of white wine that John Sampson had sweetly brought backstage. John was gleaming with excitement and pride. 'Full house. I saw Gerry Mandelson, Vladek Notar, Cosima Whatserarse.' He snapped a finger. 'Fat soprano features . . .'

Ursula laughed.

'She'll need two seats. Mikhael Aronowitz. Oodles of young lovelies. Are you all right?'

'Vadim's cutting it fine.'

'Oh, sorry.' John touched his forehead. 'Called this morning to say out of sorts. Could you do the whole concert?'

'What!' Ursula was aghast.

John's face collapsed with amusement.

'John,' she swiped at him. 'You devil!'

Philip turned away, adjusting his bow tie.

'The word's got round about Philip.' He was serious now. 'There's a head of steam out there. Pip, you'll be brill. I'll get out of your hair.' He glanced at Ursula. 'Before he does a Bruno Gillespie on the new suit.'

'Bruno Gillespie?' she enquired.

'He puked on me before an Albert Hall gig. Trashed a brand-new Turnbull & Asser shirt. That's got to be worth twenty per cent.'

Philip smiled. He was working his hands, massaging the muscles and joints. The plan had changed so that he and Vadim would start

233

the recital together, a duet, after Benno Alexandrovich had given an introductory speech commemorating Serebriakov, explaining the change of programme and introducing the artists. They had yet to rehearse and the plan was to run through it on the upright in Philip's room when Vadim arrived. They could probably wing it.

'If he's late, drop the duet,' said Ursula.

Philip breathed in and out deeply.

She had spent the last two days at his place, acting maidservant and helpmeet, shopping, cooking, running errands, taking messages, talking when he needed to talk, being out of sight and behind scenes when he needed to practise, which he did single-mindedly right through Monday afternoon and evening till 10 p.m., and then off again the next morning. He said it was much easier doing half a concert, but he was cutting it fine on the Chopin, certain passages in the scherzo bothering him, and couldn't get what he wanted in the opening movement, which was more a question of flow and integration. He played the work in slow motion, repeated sections a dozen times, broke off to play scales, thirds, octaves. She was amazed by the energy that poured through the piano and by how much sound was unleashed into the house. His coruscating scales and arpeggios were generated by huge reserves of focused physical energy, a current held in control, but almost frightening to behold when he played. His Rachmaninov B minor Prelude was there right off, immense, gigantically sonorous in the middle section, knocked off first time at the height of declamation. She could see he was enjoying getting his fingers into the keys.

Off the keyboard he seemed quiet, mildly preoccupied, as though husbanding resources. He lay down twice during the day and slept for an hour. In the afternoon on Tuesday they walked in the park and he seemed to enjoy the rose garden and waterfall, pointing things out, recalling stories. He was not quite the same as the man she had walked with in Sussex. He seemed alive with secret purpose, and occasionally his attention wandered when she spoke, but he always came back to her, was attentive, aware of her importance to him.

Over dinner the day before the concert he spoke about Chopin's music, explaining how Chopin's melodic line was fraught with accidentals, notes that are not part of the scale of a given key, but which fall between those notes and must push up or lean down in order to resolve. So many melodies or decorative fioriture were threaded with these accidentals it was as if Chopin craved the subtle pain and exquisite resolution they gave. Feeling had to be wrung out in some way, made to hurt. 'He inscribed suffering in his music. It was what he had become after all. But no self-pity, no sentimentality. He had the courage and the stoicism to depict the utterly tragic. Take the end of the Fourth Ballade, for example. After everything that work contains he ends it with such definitive and utter despair that is even more tragic in implication than effect.'

He released her at twenty-five-past seven. Vadim was still getting changed, and it looked as though they would scrap the duet as an opener.

The Russian came into the dressing room, hugged Philip, kissed Ursula, begged to be forgiven, made a great business of his injured arm, but glowed with excitement and energy.

'I have Nurofen,' he said. 'Improve neuro-transmission. Guaranteed no mistakes.'

'Vadim!' She smiled. She found him very charismatic. His eyes were full of mischief. He could do a kind of bravura chivalry when in the mood.

'Philip, sorry about the other night.' He whistled and raised his eyebrows.

'I heard about that,' she said. 'Very laddish.'

'Sociologically interesting,' said the Russian.

'I'll bet!'

'You don't like sociology?'

'It was full of sociology students, was it?'

Vadim shrugged innocently. 'Philip says I should widen my horizon.'

'Get dressed!'

He touched his half-buttoned shirt. 'Good idea.'

Philip gave her a flat look when Vadim had gone.

'Are you going to stay in here or watch him play?'

'I might listen from the stage door.'

She kissed him, squeezed his hands. 'OK.'

*　　*　　*

She felt hardly less nervous slipping through the auditorium, already half full, into the foyer. The gong was going. People were drifting to the doors. The bar was deserted. There were all kinds of faces, civilised faces, elderly Mittel European-type faces, eccentric, distinguished faces, young men with spectacles, girls in long dresses, the ranged middle classes, scented, measured, discriminating, now filtering into the expectant space of the auditorium. It was not the world, just a cross-section of music lovers who had come out that night with informed interest, knowledgeable listeners ready to concentrate hard for a couple of hours, because this was a part of their culture – a moment of musical history that could never be repeated.

She could sense the anticipation. She experienced more intensely than ever the burden of expectation focused on the empty stage, on the lone piano, on the evening's performers hidden backstage. With what confidence this crowd expected to be served by Vadim and Philip, who were only humans like the rest of them but would soon be tested by hundreds of ears, and whose playing would be completely exposed down there. With what confidence they must face the challenge, even while their hands shook and their hearts beat hard.

Friends called out to her as she moved down the aisle. Very few people knew about her and Philip, but she sensed from somewhere an awareness that she was specially connected to the hero of the evening, or to one of them. She sat down with a weird feeling almost of bridal pride, as if she in her way were part of this effort, this extraordinary production. She felt momentarily self-conscious as John, sitting across the aisle, pointed her out to a neighbour. What did it mean to be associated with a man everybody had come to see, to be the maestro's girlfriend, that special person?

Her heart beat fast. She felt for Philip, backstage, going through it for the entire first half, and then suffering the inevitable comparison with Vadim. She was full of curiosity for how Vadim would play. It was almost unbearable waiting for him to appear. She wanted the concert to start. She wanted it to be over. How could they endure such tension, poor lambs? What courage you needed to get through this hell?

When the lights dimmed, her heartbeat accelerated as if this marked the point of no return. She drew back her hair, pursed her lips, felt as though she were dissolving; and then Benno came on and the sense of occasion mounted, and he stood at the front of the stage, short, dignified, waiting for the audience's full attention, the stage lights warm behind him ready for the soloists; and when he spoke his voice was soft but carrying, almost confidential, grave. He must have been nervous, seeking the right words, talking of a legend, a figure of such global stature, and connecting the importance of that man, so loved and mourned, to the special task of the pianists tonight: to commemorate his art and to carry the torch. He craved indulgence for changes to the programme and to the scheduled concert and thanked the artists in advance for gearing their preparations to this special occasion. He concluded by saying that Serebriakov did not see classical music as a privilege but as a necessity, 'and hence my deep and personal gratitude to the great performers we are going to hear tonight'.

Ursula brushed a tear from her eye and watched in dumb suspense as Benno left the stage and the lights came down a notch, and the wait for Vadim began. She heard the applause before she saw him, and suddenly he was there, crossing the stage quickly, a large figure, masterful, energetic, coming authoritatively forward into the blaze of applause, bowing, deadpan, but hugely focused, getting on with it, and then he turned and the clapping subsided, and her heart was in her mouth as she saw him ready himself on the stool, handkerchief tossed inside the piano, cuffs touched, and suddenly he was off, straight in, hands into the keys, wrists low, minimal movement, vibrating out the soft rapid C major chords of the Waldstein Sonata, his energy released into the auditorium instantly; and as her nervousness converted to spellbound involvement, and Vadim seemed possessed by the spirit of music, its bristling vitality and headlong impetus, recreating the adventure of the piece in his own terms, discovering bar by bar its turns and flourishes, so that Beethoven as they listened was coming up as if for the first time: as she listened to all this on the edge of her seat already, watching him transformed by concentration, a different person, she was excited and humbled and almost ashamed by the accident of her meagre acquaintance with such a consummate talent; and as the movement progressed and he continued to heighten his grip on everything that passed in the stream of sound, she looked at his focused profile, so alien to her now, with the admiration of a stranger, as though she could never know personally the real being who played like this, could know him only in this state of enthralment, sharing his possession, submitting to it, feeling the full marvellous force of his intelligence as it drove his fingers forward. This then was Vadim, living life a million times faster than all of them – wondrous, awesome, utterly enslaving.

She wondered, after the Waldstein, how Philip could possibly follow on from this, and felt almost guilty at the thought and distressed about not dissuading him. He was a great pianist, too, different to Vadim. He would find his way, she hoped. He was not strong; mentally he was not strong; he was living on the edge of a precipice, and throughout the Funeral March Sonata, which Vadim played with such command and electricity and dark colouring, she was unable to take her mind off the prospect of Philip's playing, the awful vulnerability of his arrival on the platform, the agony of self-possession required, the whole hazard of finding concentration equal to his talent, and the occasion, and what had gone before. It turned her stomach. The moment was drawing closer, and every second Vadim was growing stronger. When the Funeral March came, she found tears in her eyes again; how gravely Vadim participated in all the music could mean; how profoundly it struck her now, the reality of this music; and then in the finale she became torpid, almost drained, so utterly exhausted by tension and emotion that when the applause started she could hardly bring herself to clap, but just listened instead to the wild frenzy of release around her, the hard clapping, as if the audience were determined to refract and discharge the energy Vadim had transmitted, to pay him back for as long as it would take to recover from the shock of his brilliance.

She gathered herself slowly, people pushing past her. She was dreading the task ahead.

She must go to see him. She must get him through the interval.

*   *   *

The applause hit him hard, deafening, people rising, already standing, and he had not played a note, the encouragement was startling, a barrage of welcome. He bowed slowly, taking it in, looking to the back, aware of friendly faces with smiles and raised hands, cheering him on; and he nodded and acknowledged, hands gripped tight, feeling rather weird, even light-headed, hoping it would settle, or sharpen up when he was facing the keyboard, that long-awaited moment.

He flicked his tails back over the stool. He felt good doing that, in charge, and prepared himself, audience hushing down, the last moments before commitment was irreversible, important not to rush, to try and get an image, the sound and flow of the piece in his head already. He remembered telling himself that he had everything to offer and nothing to fear, that he was unique in his way and must now just relax, be himself, as though alone. He felt a tremor in his hands as he raised them, but they did what he wanted with that first phrase, and now he was locked in the moment-to-moment of it, the hot burning awareness of the sound he was making, the dotted phrase, so melancholy, travelling out now. The keys were easier than he remembered. They depressed as he wished and his fingers seemed at last comfortable, even though he was constantly adjusting to the acoustic, his intimate relation to sounds travelling hundreds of feet and heard at a distance, qualified here and there by a cough or a rustle. He had to loosen up a little. The phrase-making was becoming tight, and yet this tightness was his arm's way of staying in control. There would come a point when he would feel as he played, but he had to be careful, modest, because not everything seemed ready yet; perhaps reflexes were slower now. He must find his way.

The fortissimo section was secure, well graded, and it was good to leap at those chords, to embed one's fingers deeply, allowing the muscles of his hand to tense at full strength, recovering command, but as the piece moved to its second summit he felt that he had lost his sensitivity to something, and that the pulse was false and the sound did not carry properly. And, as he played the climax of semiquavers that spilled from the top of the piano, like a million leaves falling through the air and being tricked with by the wind, stirred into flurries before dispersing, the audience seemed remote, like the painting of a crowd in the corner of his eye, and he sensed he had lost their energy: suddenly they were not helping him. He strived to listen harder, to envelop himself in the acoustic – although now the sense of disembodied sound, sound travelling out beyond his control, was distracting, as though his perspective and the audience's were at odds.

The applause after the second Rachmaninov Prelude was warm, still committed, so something was going on. He bowed quickly and thought distractedly of Vadim, whom he had hugged after the first half, tears in his eyes. One of them at least would have been great tonight. He had to take strength from that shattering performance of the Funeral March Sonata. There was a current of something that he could still latch on to.

He felt even more frustrated with the Schubert, as though the Impromptu did not allow something he could do and required something he could not do. His dynamics were too familiar to him, the colour changes a rehash, and now that the piece was launched, going smoothly and uninterestingly along, it was too late to stop and come back in the right groove: and as he played, concentrating for all he was worth, the awful feeling came over him that time was slipping away, concert time, during which nothing much was happening to him or anyone, and that he had to abandon something in order not to be bored with this relationship.

He went off stage this time, to allow the audience a break. He took a sip of water from a plastic beaker, felt them waiting for him but not tensely enough, as if they were still recovering from the impact of Vadim's playing and having trouble concentrating; and he suffered a stab of anguish at the thought that this was his great moment, possibly his last concert, and that his desperate desire to do something special had been an impossible dream, and he now had the sense of having to fight through the feeling, on top of everything else, that the whole opportunity was sliding away. He tried to focus – the B minor Sonata ahead of him, the Funeral March Sonata behind him. He tried to remember his sense of the two pieces, Serebriakov's words, his own ideas, but the thread of all that was irretrievable, a million miles away now, and when he went back out, he stepped on to the stage with a sinking heart, thinking that this performance was bound to be mediocre; even his nerves were insufficient, and a horrible lassitude broke over him as he went across the platform to renewed applause, this time less ecstatic, and took his seat again, gazing at the keyboard with forlorn uncertainty. He could tell already. It wasn't there. The atmosphere was slack. He sat waiting, a long wait. Waiting for quiet, and beyond quiet for absolute silence, pin-drop tension mounting all the time, intensifying suddenly to a pitch he could no longer bear. Now he had them. Now the current was live.

Later, in bed, in the small hours, going through every inch of the recital in his head, he recalled the clarity of that moment, becoming fully awake in sharpened light, a way to attack the phrase, fingers curled, a falling arpeggio, then driving chords, martial, propulsive, getting stuck in and meaning business with the instrument – something came over him or into him. At the time, it felt like rage.

He was going at it much harder and faster than planned, and this was disconcerting because adrenalin had to do it now, lift agility and reflexes through the awkwardnesses of the opening page: semiquaver fourths, contrary-motion arpeggios, he saw them coming and going within his compass, playing of bite and energy and dispatch, the geography of the keyboard, spaces and intervals, coming into muscular focus, every note struck in the centre, the tone penetrating, yes, a plangent intensity that was his hallmark sound reaching out, grabbing the audience; and then the tender flow of the second-subject aria, a slight relaxation, but a long way to go yet, and now the half-tones and inner melodies and liquid accompaniment, the sense of provisional homecoming, Chopin at his most fulfilled and expressive.

In the development section he was alert again, hearing new things, an onsurge of latent drama, the first subject transformatively propelled, but inconclusively so, as if this were a search for the material's true destiny and Philip was driving that hunt, then sidestepping into a parallel reverie, the wandering dream that interrupted Chopin's quest for order.

Something had clicked, he was certain, by the end of the first movement. He had an ingrained sense of command, and as he dusted his forehead with a hanky, he wondered how long this renewed mastery had been incubating, because it seemed now so assured, so deeply founded, so new. He felt the tension of his own desire for expression as a fabulous power over sound.

But he had to pay attention before the scherzo, which started molto vivace, in a gossamer rush of quavers, leggierissimo, and had to be whirring along before it began, like a butterfly, already airborne, flickering on a current of air that whooshed to the height of the keyboard and down again; and as always with this movement you had to think your hand into a shimmering lightness of touch before contact with the keys, so everything was immediately on course.

In the third movement he began to feel something drawing on him, an undertow. The first two movements had roused all his powers, all aspects of touch and dexterity exercised to fullest life; all reflexes, all impulses, everything he could be aware of was drawn to the tips of his fingers, and now the music simply drew him into its mood of stoic tranquillity; and he felt as he played the full value of every note, the rise and fall of long lines, the essence of the work flowing through his arms. And as the movement closed he felt in his whole being how the final bars arrested everything that had gone before, all the momentum behind the first two movements, everything that had contended to have a place in the sonata was laid to rest by the last cadence; and yet, as his fingers compressed the low B major chord, softly resonating, almost humming; as his fingers depressed that last B major chord, a lovely chord, a chord that leaves a dying glow of sound before its release, a chord that collects and gathers everything into a carrying softness, even in that peerless moment of resolution infinite energy was stored. And as he held fast to that last chord and heard its balm travel deep into the auditorium, enthralling his listeners until the last sounds had long since died away, so he felt an upsurge of tempestuous energy.

The implacability of those initial octaves, great bars of sound, bottom, middle, top and round again, that set the instrument ringing, rousing the audience – like winching a crossbow to the point of maximum tension before releasing the bolt – even as he hit the keys with a steel touch, he felt the teetering precariousness of the energy they released. All his strength and nervous energy was evoked, set tingling in his neck and shoulders.

The audience were moving, getting on to the edge of their seats.

He had it, that ominous rhythm in his body, and as he watched his left hand stretch and creep on its belly, he was suffused by the eeriness of music that started soft and low in the keyboard, rocking and loping, its innate violence in tether, and then cranked up an octave, flecked with desperation, like a stalking beast barely in control of its own ferocity.

The B major chord was like cannon shot, and now as the rhythms reconfigured and energy exploded, and as he played with full attack, detonating chords, which released teeming right-hand semi-quavers over a stentorian tenor motif, he felt he was playing for his life in every sense, in the midst of furious battle, in the grip of relentless drama and constant technical danger that he had to outwit and surpass. Bass octaves thundered. His semiquavers were super-articulate. He was hearing everything, desperation billowing from the instrument, because the situation was desperate, abso-lutely desperate, and as his hands converged and the main theme came back but with more to do in the left hand, complicating the rhythm, now at the limit of urgency, he sensed in a flash that he was fighting for Poland, a sidelight that vanished as the first subject cranked up an octave and once again he was riding for his life, caught in the current, with its shifts of voicing and harmonic slinks like a churning of tonal mud under cavalry hooves.

There had come a point, as there often would, when he saw himself playing – a moment of astral detachment – saw himself caught up in the mayhem, as if from a front-row seat, looking on at this concentration and hyperactivity as though he could see for a moment what it was like from outside to witness this furious catharsis, and just for a moment he was oddly self-conscious, suddenly detached, his immersion lost, so that it took a whole page of dreamlike playing to catch up with himself, to get back on the bus, and several seconds longer to embed himself in the onward rush and catch up with his fingers. And then the fast scales came back, brilliant runs from the top of the keyboard at spinning speed, twirling into the bass like missiles, and these you could not play without total togetherness and whiplash commitment; and when the main theme returned for the last time, the left hand spinning out cartwheels of semiquavers, which gave the impression of stabilised velocity, a fusion of effort and urgency, of absolute inexorable determination to force this theme over the brink, to get beyond this time, to convert this desperate headlong figure for better or worse; when he came to this point, goosebumps went up the back of his neck, both in terror at the coming crisis and at the glory in sight. He fastened on and pushed, driving himself beyond strict control into untethered expression, feeling and playing with unbridled intensity, and felt his heart race, so nearly there; and this was the bit they would love, had been waiting for, up, up and over, and now the notes came down, razor sharp, brilliant, a spangling arpeggio in the home key, followed by an eruption, scintillating, right up and around, pure tension, the climax of Chopin almost; throttling back for the final climb, the right hand travelling chromatically up, the left hand beating out that ominous figure for the last time, and then a spilling-over of glitter and sparkle; the final chords ratcheting, bass octaves thundering, straining to the ultimate cadence, deep B, grand, growling, right hand teeming from on high, the triumph, the summation, the last crash of octaves dispatched, skewered to victory, instrument ringing. Arms back. Wild release. Victory.

ACKNOWLEDGEMENTS

Grateful thanks to Mike Jones, Liz Calder, Mary Tomlinson, and all at Bloomsbury, to Felicity Rubinstein, my agent, and to the following readers and friends for their helpful comments and/or assistance: Margaret, Roderick and Rowland Williams, Pip Torrens, Claire Wrathal, Mark Roberts, Isobel Dixon, David Sherwin, Lucy Parham, Christina Lawrie, Katrine Mac-Gibbon, Tony Mulholland, Mark McCrum, Sue Spence and Clive Kaye. Thanks also to Carole Blake and Julian Friedmann for their kind support. I am eternally grateful to Fiona Williams.

The following books were also helpful: *Lipatti* by Dragos Tanasescu & Grigore Bargauanu, Kahn and Averil (1988); *Sviatoslav Richter Notebooks and Conversations* by Bruno Monsaingeon, Faber and Faber (2001); *Arthur Rubinstein, A Life* by Howard Sachs, Phoenix (1997); *Solo*, by Bryan Crimp, Appian Publications and Recordings (1994); *Remembering Horowitz*, edited by David Dubal, Schirmer Books (1993); *Conversations with Arrau* by Joseph Horowitz, Limelight (1984); *The Lives of the Great Composers* by Harold C. Schonberg, Abacus (1998); *A Winter in Majorca* by George Sand, Palma de Majorca (1992); *Chopin's Funeral* by Benita Eisler, Knopf (2003); *Chopin* by A. Boucourechliev, Thames and Hudson (1963); *Chopin* by Arthur Hedley, Dent (1966); *Piano Notes, The Hidden World of the Pianist* by Charles Rosen, Allen Lane (2003); *Great Pianists of Our Time* by Joachim Kaiser, Allen & Unwin (1971).

A NOTE ON THE AUTHOR

Conrad Williams was born in Winnipeg and lives in Willesden. He read English and Law at Cambridge, qualified as a barrister and now works as a film agent. His first novel, *Sex & Genius*, was published by Bloomsbury in 2002. He is married with two children.

A NOTE ON THE TYPE

The text of this book is set in Linotype Sabon, named after the type founder, Jacques Sabon. It was designed by Jan Tschichold and jointly developed by Linotype, Monotype and Stempel, in response to a need for a typeface to be available in identical form for mechanical hot metal composition and hand composition using foundry type.

Tschichold based his design for Sabon roman on a fount engraved by Garamond, and Sabon italic on a fount by Granjon. It was first used in 1966 and has proved an enduring modern classic.